To Brother Johnny:

It is a privilege to know you as Judge, Brother and best of all as a real friend. If I were to be asked to give a definition as to what a Mason is, I could answer with two words, Johnny Gorman. You have led our lodge to an outstanding year. We have experienced un-equaled growth and once again our lodge is beginning to achieve honored status in our community.

I hope you enjoy the book for it is about mountain living and volumes that have been passed down from generation to generation. Thanks again for being my brother.

Charles E Hill

BLOOD
MOUNTAIN
COVENANT

BLOOD MOUNTAIN COVENANT

A Son's Revenge

Charles E. Hill

www.ivyhousebooks.com

PUBLISHED BY IVY HOUSE PUBLISHING GROUP
5122 Bur Oak Circle, Raleigh, North Carolina 27612
United States of America
919-782-0281
www.ivyhousebooks.com

ISBN 1-57197-378-8
Library of Congress Control Number: 2003103966

Printed in the United States of America

This book is fondly dedicated to my family: my wife, Jacquelyn Lance Hill; my children, Gina Collins, Elliott Hill, and Stacy Hill; and my grandchildren, Matthew Collins, Cory Collins, Charles E. Hill III, Lance Hill, and Andelin Hill. It was because of their encouragement and lasting persistence that I finished the story.

Foreword

The mountains of Georgia have always been special to me for many reasons, not the least of which is simply their grandeur and beauty. One cannot view their splendor without acknowledging the presence of God and His Omnipotence.

Growing up and living in those mountains caused my Dad once to write, "The one thought you had every day was a sense of wonder and curiosity as to what lay on the other side of the mountains."

Choestoe was and is a special place in the Georgia Mountains. The Indian name was "Where the Rabbits Dance." The mountains surrounding Choestoe bear familiar names such as Brasstown Bald, Double Knobs, Blood, Slaughter.

The people of Choestoe were as unique as were the mountains surrounding them. Out of that small place in the mountains came leaders and leadership qualities that still exist today. Great preachers, justices of the Georgia Supreme Court, college presidents, authors, journalists—all of whom left their mark on our society in positive fashion; and today we still have one of the greatest, if not the greatest, of political leaders in Georgia, in Senator and former Governor Zell Mill, whose family lived in Choestoe and instilled in him the core values of mountain people.

So this book is about my family—my great grandfather, who died in violent fashion never yielding his great belief in the rightness of his position. It is about my grandfather and the impact the death of his father had on him the rest of his life. It is about my grandfather's family, including my father and the values that life in the mountains instilled in them.

My first cousin, Charles Hill, by marriage, has done a magnificent job in the writing of this book. He shows great talent and skill in describing the events and the places where they occur.

He gives to us a living history of a unique place as well as a most unique family and people. He shows us that the mountains create uniqueness and that in turn creates, nurtures, and builds the uniqueness of the mountain people.

Again, from the writings of my Dad:

The rugged mountains themselves had a wonderful effect on the youth. Our parents had but one rule and that was live the simple life—eat simple food, wear simple clothes, work very hard, and become rugged like the mountains.

The mountains become part of us. Blood Mountain, Slaughter Gap, Enotah (Brasstown Bald), Tesnatee Gap, Frogtown Gap, Wolfpen Gap—we knew them in every season of the year. We ran over them by day and night. We hunted raccoon, possum, wild turkey, deer, and pheasant. We learned astronomy at night from their high summits. We listened to the fox hounds as they chased the nimble fox through one mountain to the other. We loved the mountains as our parents loved them. That love has never deserted us. We thrill at the approach now. Many of us are many years from childhood, but the first appearance of the mountains in the distance with their blue tops sends a thrill through and through. The beautiful sunsets, the rainbows, the stars—nature is never more powerful than in these lovely mountains. Whether it rains, snows, hails, sleets or thunders or there are spring flowers and birds, what a wonderful land it is. And how all the mountain people love it. These people become like the mountains in which they have lived.

Hopefully, this book will bring to the reader a vivid realization of how the mountains in our lives shape and mold them.

Bert Lance

I would like to gratefully acknowledge the following individuals who assisted me in many different ways in the writing of this book: Dale Elliott, Lillie Casey, Gwen Connally, Melissa Hood, Jack Lance, Bert Lance, Jerry Lance, Bobby Lance, Cecil Lance Jr., Bob Short, Senator Zell Miller, former Representative Ed Jenkins, Chris Fox, Louise McTaggert, Robert Butt, Tom Gilliland, Patti Kay, Betty Sellers and John and Kay Yandell.

James "Jim" Washington Lance
(1/31/1861–9/2/1940)

The Harvest

Spring was the perilous season,
And sowers that entered the gate
Were plowing the earth with treason
And scattering seeds of hate.

And now the harvest is ready,
And I with foreclosured breath
Must rise from my dreams unsteady
And reap with a sickle of death.

—Byron Herbert Reece (1)

Chapter I

THE REECE FIELDS

"Jim, Jim, wake up; Jim, do you hear me?"

From a small, dark, musty cave lying nigh the apex of Blood Mountain and being created by some unrecorded, violent upheaval of nature, a female black panther lazily arose, scattered two nursing, protesting kittens, stretched, and slowly crept outside her well-camouflaged den. A large chestnut, blown over by the strong winds that constantly buffet the towering mountain, partially covered the entrance. In addition, the thick overgrown profusion of rhododendron, mountain laurel, and ivy aided Mother Nature, completely obliterating even the hint of an opening. A bloodcurdling scream arose deep within the panther and was emitted with pent-up fury, echoing from Blood Mountain to Slaughter, to Coosa Bald, to Bald Mountain, glancing down into the quiet, peaceful valleys, finally rolling into the small hidden coves where its eerie sound was finally muffled by the roaring angry surge of Wolf Creek as it started its lonely trip to the gulf. The scream of a hunting panther sounds like the scream of a woman in much travail and is to serve as a warning to others that there is the hunted and the hunted, and she surely is the fiercest hunter of all. The other animals hear this scream and heed its unveiled message. The beaver slaps its tail in sudden alarm and dives frantically, seeking the comforting protection of his well-built dam. The otter and muskrat slither into their holes and burrow faster, deeper, hoping that this time the panther will have distaste for digging. The rabbits hop further back into the bracken and remain still, depending upon camouflage and good luck for survival. The lonely secretive screech owl, the harbinger of death, calls out his mournful call, for he recognizes that the executioner will find his way into these quiet valleys, penetrating with a quick thrust, awakening the Death Angel, shattering forever our mountains' cloak of innocence.

The creatures of the forest aren't the only ones to hear, recognize, and respect this eerie warning as it reverberates from high up on Blood Mountain. We are the John Lance family. We live in a small cabin along-side Lance Creek at the foot of Lance Mountain, situated so that we are well protected from the north wind that howls its cold, lonesome song from ridge top to ridge top. This little cove is our home, and we contentedly farm the small fertile patches, tend to our own needs, fend for ourselves, and ask no one for anything. We are at peace with the world, living here in harmony with Mother Nature. Mountain people are independent, and we are no different from the rest. My dad, John, the patriarch of our family, is an ordained Methodist minister of the old school. He believes and preaches in "an eye for an eye and a tooth for a tooth," teaches us the same, and puts his trust only in God. Dad believes that God gave man sense to look after his own and expects man to do so. Anyway, God might just be tied up with something more important, such as trying to heal the rift among the citizens of our county because of the Civil War. This is the year of our Lord 1875, and the bloody, divisive war has only been over a scant ten years and is still being fought and refought in our area. Why? Because some of our young men, even some of the boys I know and used to respect, turned out to be traitors. To what I don't know, but a body ought to be proud of where he lives, who he is, what he stands for; be ready to defend those principles; even be willing to "lay his life on the line," says Dad. So, when Dad says, "Jim and Joe, put our mule in the barn and go fetch in our cow. I think I heard the faint tinker of her bell up toward the Reece fields, and take the gun just in case," it isn't out of fear, but out of respect—respect for nature and respect for God, for creating such a noble, perfect hunter as the black panther, who is somewhat like us, who lives in harmony with nature, who kills not for pleasure but for sustenance for her and hers, filling one more link in the continuing saga of life.

My name is Jim. I am fourteen, the second oldest male child, Lafayette (Fate) being the oldest at fifteen; and because of my aggressive temperament, I have already been thrust into a role of leadership, a role certainly not wished for, but one that would have likely come sooner or later because of my God-given physical attributes. Even at this early age, I stand five-feet-eleven and weigh one hundred and seventy-five pounds, every bit of it rock solid, honed to a hardness of steel by a life of outdoor living. We siblings are constantly overseen by two caring parents who also believe that the way to keep a lad out of trouble is to work off his excess energy by having him struggle from sunup to sundown with a dumb, cantankerous mule whose wishes are forever diametrically opposed to his. Dad always says, "Tilling the good earth, now that's God's work." Now I don't want to sound sacrilegious, for I am a God-fearing boy, but for the life of me, I never have been able to find in the Bible where the Lord did any plowing with a mule. Wished for or not, I am molded by my dad to take over and tend to my mother Caroline; my sisters Mary, Lou, and Emma; and my younger brothers, Joe and John Jr., in his absence.

Well, Joe, my ten-year-old brother, and I pick up the gun, call our dog Nick (what mountain family could exist without a dog?), and start toward the Reece fields. Now the Reece fields aren't all that far away, being only about three-quarters of a mile from home, but three-quarters of a mile seems a mighty long way when you are fourteen and have in your care your younger brother, especially when you recall sitting around the hearth in the winter listening to adults tell scary tales of big, black panthers that would secretly hide, just waiting for a chance to pounce and devour the unfortunate. I had to contend with all of this and more because night was fast approaching.

We dare not tarry, as we sometimes did, with darkness coming on, so we start out alone at a fast pace. My gun is held at ready alert, my finger gently resting on the trigger. I can get off a quick shot, if one should be called for. Before long, we hear the faint tinker of a familiar cowbell, and our steps become faster. Thank goodness; it looks like we are going to find her this time without tromping over half of the Reece fields. The tinker of the cowbell becomes much louder. It seems that she has heard the terrifying scream of the wily panther also and is as anxious to see us as we are to see her, and she is rushing to meet us. Our cow, Joe, and I, just we three, have a glad reunion there on the dark, scary, tree-lined trail, and we quickly hightail it for home. Shortly we are in sight of home, just we three. The relieved trio soon splashes across the cool waters of Lance Creek, turns up the small dusty road, throws open the yard gate, and heads for the comforting safety of the barn. When we step back outside, night is beginning to shroud the little valley with its tentacles of darkness that will soon envelop our small homestead. There stand Mom and Dad holding hands, grinning in love and self-satisfaction. They tell us how brave we are and how proud they are of us, that we are true Lances, and no panther could or would dare tackle two Lances. Years later, Mom told me that it wasn't just we three, that Dad had traveled behind us at a safe distance and returned in front of us, always keeping us in sight, making sure that nothing or no one would harm us, teaching us to have confidence in ourselves, enabling us to face any foe or adversary without fear. Is it any wonder then that I feel the way I do about Dad, that I want to follow in his footsteps, that I want to be like him in every way?

I know that if anyone ever harms Dad, my soul will not rest until I have satisfaction, and I have already vowed to walk through Hell backwards and barefooted if it takes it to avenge anyone who dares touch in harm one silver hair on this Saint of God's head. I never thought that my vow would have to be carried out; little did I know what lay ahead.

Now, our seeing Mom and Dad holding hands might seem strange to others; it certainly is not the accepted mode of conduct among mountain folks, but it is to us, for we are a close-knit family, and the holding of hands is nothing more than an outward sign of an inward love and affection. This care, concern, and love for each other started when Dad was twenty-three and Mom was fifteen. They, along with all of the neighbors for miles around, were attending a revival at Old Salem Methodist Church. It isn't that mountain people are all that holy; there just isn't much of anything else to do. As is the custom, the ladies and young girls enter the church through a separate door and sit on one side of the church while the men and young boys enter through another door and fill the pews on the opposite side. The church is built as a Tabernacle to God, a place for worship, not as a place for young people to court and touch; such is the reasoning for the separation of the sexes.

Dad told us that he would forever remember the sermon topic that day, "Where can you find a virtuous woman; her price is far above rubies," but not necessarily the sermon. Dad recounted with a smug grin how he sat on the third row, chanced to glance across the aisle, and there on the second row was the prettiest girl he had ever seen. She had on a red dress, with auburn hair and a complexion as fresh as spring itself. He felt funny inside; they exchanged quick glances and both shyly looked away, hoping that the stern elders hadn't noticed. Dad admits that he couldn't recall anything about the rest of the sermon, though the reverend was quite pompous and pounded the pulpit, stomped the floor, preached on hellfire and damnation, got louder and louder, and waxed on and on. Dad's thoughts were on Mom. He had seen "The Lily of the Valley," "The Rose of Sharon," and "The Jewel of the Nile" all in one night, and he didn't have to leave Choestoe to do it! When the sermon was over, he nervously inquired of one of his buddies, "Who is that pretty girl on the second row? I'd mightily like to meet her."

"That's Caroline Turner, my first cousin. Do you want me to introduce you?" That was kinda like asking a bear if he likes honey.

"I sure do," Dad replied.

The proper introductions were made, and it might not have been love at first sight, but it certainly was at second. Dad became a regular caller at Jarrett Turner's house, and a year later, they were married. You know, Mom and Dad think it's kinda strange for mountain people to hide their affections the way they do. Dad says it's no sin to hold hands in public, that sin is letting evil thoughts enter your head. Dad is probably right; he usually is.

Chapter II

OUR TRAITS

You might be wondering about us Lances—how we got here, where we came from, what we believe in, and general family traits. Well, family tradition has it, passed down one to the other, that there were four Lentz brothers who came to America from Germany. Lentz, so I've been told, means "springtime" in German, but as English and English-speaking people were much more prevalent in our settlements, for the sake of convenience the name was changed to Lance. Legend has it that our forefather was Peter Lentz, and when he arrived on these fair shores for a new beginning, he almost at once sent back to Germany for his sweetheart. When Peter met her at the boat, she was making her wedding dress; however, when the first baby came, the dress, so carefully made, was traded without hesitation for a cow so that the baby could have milk.

My grandfather, Samuel Lance, was born in Buncombe County, North Carolina, and he is the one responsible for us being here in Union County. A friend of his, whose name has long since been forgotten, vaporizing as the dew in the face of a warming sun, was to have a duel with a fellow from Union County, and as fate would have it he became sick, not being able to fill the appointed date. Dueling custom has it that if you are sick, you have the right to name a replacement, so my grandfather, Samuel Lance, being noted as a fighting man, was chosen to fight in his stead. He came to Union County by request, to uphold the honor of a friend, fought the duel and won, leaving his adversary, against whom he had no malice, lying motionless upon the cold ground.

My grandfather came here in the spring of 1839. The mountains that we now call home were alive with the promise of new life: the early blooming sarvis; the dogwoods shining white with millions of blooms; the virgin timber that hadn't felt the edge of an ax, standing regally, reaching, stretching toward the blue sky, their canopy so lush that the sun was blotted out; the sparkling streams, brimming with native speckled trout. All of Mother Nature seemed to be saying, "Come; enter in. My resources will be yours; let me clothe, feed, wrap your body with warmth. Come let us live together in peace and harmony."

Sam Riley Lance returned to Buncombe County, told his brothers of this land of promise, and started making arrangements to return. This he did, and one year later, he came back to Union County with his family. Grandfather lived in Union County most of his life, except in his later years when he moved to Hayesville, North Carolina. Dad's brother James H., for whom I was named, married Mom's sister Phoebe. They moved to Hayesville, North Carolina, so I have double first cousins over around Hayesville. From reports we get, they run true to form, being people you can count on in a fight or in need. As Dad says, when the flag is run up the pole, you can bet the Lances will be there to salute 'er.

My grandfather wasn't the only Lance to get itchy feet and want to be part of something new. Within the year, Grandfather's two brothers and their families also moved to Georgia. Martin and his crew settled over in Lumpkin County, and W. H.'s clan settled in Dooley, the lower end of the county. They were now situated about twenty-five miles from each of the others, if you imagine a wagon wheel with three spokes and Union County as the hub. We aren't as close now as they were in Buncombe County, but they all admit living here is much better.

The terrain of Choestoe is somewhat similar to Buncombe County, with the mountains being almost as big but not nearly as steep, and the land is much better suited for farming, with plenty of small rolling hills, which make excellent pastures. The rich, loamy, fertile bottomland lying alongside the branches, creeks, and rivers makes for excellent crops; for after all, we are primarily farmers.

We Lances tend to be a bit clannish, and it's sort of like if anyone hurts one Lance the others feel the pain, so it sure does make a body feel better to have kin nearby. Well, being clannish isn't anything that you need apologize for; rather it's something to be proud of. It's nothing but right to look after one another. Why, I've seen small birds band together to run off a hawk that they thought was fixin' to harm their young. Surely we aren't expected to be any different from the fowls of the air. Why, that's just nature, the way things are.

I don't want to mislead you by making you think that we Lances are small and a bunch of scared people having to band together for protection, not liking to fight. On the contrary! We tend to be big, much bigger in fact than most of our neighbors, most standing around six-foot-one, weighing upwards to two hundred pounds. And shun a fight? Why, there's little else in life as much fun to us as a good knock-down-drag-out. Take Dad for instance. He's six-one and weighs one hundred and eighty-five pounds, but looks a little thin, especially now that his hair is starting to turn a slight silver, and him with that long beard. But don't be fooled. To render him out, one would not get one drop of fat; he's all muscle. It's best to not be fooled by Dad's quiet way of getting around, now that he's a preacher of the Word, 'cause still water runs deep. From what I've been told by kin, no one man could best Dad, and I know that to be a fact. He can throw those maul-like fists with the best, knows no fear, and will wade right in, never backing up an inch, especially when he is upholding a principle he believes in or protecting the honor of another Lance. Why, even now, I know Dad will fight if he has to, particularly against whiskey, 'cause in every sermon he preaches, he speaks out against it. I don't believe I've ever seen anybody against anything as much as Dad is against alcohol. It's like in the Bible, and he's the voice crying in the wilderness, 'cause people seem to tolerate—even enjoy—having whiskey around. Dad's not scared of anything; he'll continue to rail against this vice, but he'd never turn anybody into the revenuers. That's just not the Lance way of doing things; they don't snitch on others. One thing you can count on though: Dad's a lot like Sampson; he'll pick up the jawbone of an ass and wipe out an entire army if it takes it to stomp out this curse of mankind.

You may wonder why I'm so sure he wouldn't rat on somebody else, even if he were doing wrong. Dad told me so and related this true story about one of our neighbors, Thompson (Tomp) Collins. Two men pulled into the Collins' yard and asked him to take his team and help them pull a loaded wagon to the top of Tesnatee Gap. A deal was struck and Tomp started out, not inquiring as to what the cargo was. They didn't volunteer it, and as he was an independent sort of individual, and he reasoned that it was none of his business.

The pull was difficult, for Tesnatee was a steep mountain, and the so-called road was little more than a rock trail. Before the travelers gained the top of the Gap, federal agents stopped them. The two men fled into the dense underbrush, leaving behind the wagon loaded with moonshine. The agents told Tomp that he would be set free if he would only tell them who the two fleeing men were. He answered firmly, "Never." He was arrested for possession of untaxed whiskey and sent to a prison in New York, where he served several years.

Most people, including his family, reasoned that he was dead, but years later, he appeared in his front yard in Choestoe, having walked every step of the way from New York, the identity of the two fleeing men still secretly penned up in his head. Most people up here are certain that the two men were part of a family that lives yonder at the foot of Yellow Mountain. They'd do something like that, even let somebody else and his family suffer, while they got off scot-free. However, Dad says he woulda done the same thing if he had been Tomp, and he would have.

Another trait of Lances is the distaste that they have for somebody that won't tell the truth, a feller that wouldn't know the truth if he heard it. We have some neighbors that seem to think it's an honor to tell a lie, and if it is, then they are most honorable. Why, they'd climb a tree backwards to tell a lie, when they could just as easily stay on the ground and tell the truth. They live up underneath Yellow Mountain and only a short distance from home as the crow flies. Speculation has it that that crowd might be responsible for Tomp spending some of the better years of his life in the federal pen. Dad doesn't want us to have any truck with them on account of one sin leads to another worse one, and he says if they don't change their way of living, they're going to come to some bad end.

Anyway, Dad suspects they're still dealing in moonshine, and all know how he feels about that.

Now, I don't want to make a body think that we Lances are perfect, leading a life that others would do well to copy; we make no such claims. The blood coursing through our veins is the blood of fighting men passed down to us by our ancestors, and because of this we might sometimes be a little boisterous, enjoying fully the give-and-take of "fista cuffs," but tell a lie, never. We believe that your word should be your bond. If a Lance tells you something's a-goin' to happen, it is. If he tells you he's going to kill you, then you'd best start Jim Collins and John Souther to a-makin' your coffin; more than likely there's going to be a funeral in Choestoe.

I have had it impressed upon me since I was a youngin' to do exactly what I say, and if I tell you I'm going to meet you up on Slaughter Gap to hear the hounds run, then I'll be there come hell or high water. It is with us and should be like Cussin' Tom Henson says, "If you promise to meet a dog at a certain place, if anyone doesn't show up, let it be the dog."

We find stubbornness and independence to be firmly engrained in the constitution of most Lances; why, we're as independent as hogs on ice. Now, I don't claim stubbornness to be exactly an admirable quality in us, or anyone for that matter, but it's there just the same. We can be led, if you go about it in the right way, but you'd just as well save your breath when it comes to ordering us to do something. We'll just stub up on you, and we might be a whole lot like a mule in this respect; you can lead him to water, but you can't make him drink. Another neighbor, John Duckworth, says, "The Lances could teach a mule how to be stubborn." He may be right.

The Lances don't claim to have invented, or have a lock on, being independent. It's just there in practically all mountain people. I've often wondered, given some thought as to whether we were born independent or does living in these mountains make us independent? I don't profess to know the answer, but I have come to see that these mountains and the area herein are independent in themselves, not being a bit scared to shun the normal, buck the expected, and go their own way. What I mean is, the watershed from south of these mountains does the normal and flows into the Chattahoochee, eventually emptying into the Atlantic the easy way and as expected. But here in Union County we find something quite different. The watershed—Lance Creek, Helton Creek, Crump Creek, Wolf Creek, Stink Creek—and other tributaries in Choestoe flow into the Nottely River. It then begins its long, arduous run of destiny by flowing north, contrary to the way most rivers flow, picking up along the way the other tributaries and finally emptying into the Gulf of Mexico. The Nottely is independent, goes its own way, and was made by God this way. Isn't it likely then that since we live here and were created by God also, don't you imagine He means for us to be independent? I think so.

We believe in being neighborly and helping others in time of need. After all, this trait of helping others led us to be here in the first place. We are taught to live by the Golden Rule—do unto others as you would have them do unto you—but Dad cautions us not to get too thick with our neighbors, lest familiarity lead to contempt, which creates a climate for hard feelings.

We do live in an isolated area, being separated from the other part of Georgia by expansive, formidable mountains which make travel somewhat hard, leading us to depend upon ourselves, our wits, and our neighbors for survival. However, survival here isn't all that hard when you look around and see all that God has put here for us. These huge, hostile-appearing mountains are God's fruit basket, filled with chestnut trees that are loaded with chestnuts; chinquapin trees bent over with sweet chinquapins, manna from Heaven itself; and persimmon trees, laden with mouth-puckering fruit until the first frost, then turning into savory goodness that causes the lowly possum to grin in satisfied pleasure. The towering oaks, their girth being such that two, sometimes three men have difficulty reaching around, provide the acorns that furnish mast for deer, squirrel, bear, and the other fauna of the forest. And the pure, crystal-like sparkling streams and roaring rivers, their virginity running pure, never having been defiled by the silt of pollution, offer up to us their bounty of goodness. These gifts from God often grace our tables, providing us with feasts of such proportion that words can't describe them. If you haven't sometime or other slid your feet under a table laden with these delicacies and partaken of a meal of poke salad, venison, squirrel dumpling, bear steak, possum, and sweet potatoes or rabbit mull, and for dessert one of Mom's stack cakes that are light and fluffy—for she has never been known to make a sad cake—then you've just not lived life to its fullest.

We do have neighbors, and most of them you can hang your hat on. The Fradys live a piece over the ridge; just a little further down is the Campbells that run the mill; the Sosebees live 'cross the mountain in a cove; the Hensons further down Wolf Creek; the Millers on the road toward Bald Mountain; the Collins, Southers, Spiveys, Hoods, Sullivans, and Allisons up on the river; the Dyers and Hunters along Stink Creek, all good people. But our closest neighbors, the family living 'neath Yellow Mountain, now I don't know about them. We've tried to be neighborly, but they'll certainly take advantage of you, borrowing and never returning. I'm beginning to think like Dad, that they should just be left alone. In fact, my instinct says, "Do unto them before they do unto you." However, Mom says, "There's good in everyone—just be patient; right will win out in the end." Little did I realize what lay in store.

The traits that run through the very fiber of most of the Lances are certainly not unique just to us, and I don't intend to portray that we are the sole custodians of being independent, stubborn, truthful, and neighborly, much of which would be considered the heart and soul, the very necessary ingredients that go into the making of an individual into a good citizen. Some of these traits might be found to a greater degree in some of our neighbors. However, there are some characteristics that we probably possess more of than most other families, these not necessarily being admirable qualities: one being the short-fused, fiery, "don't tread on me" temper that constantly requires tempering by caring parents, much like the prime steel that goes into the making of a good knife, enabling it to hold a fine cutting edge. My parents both say, not in a bragging manner, because we are constantly doing mischievous deeds that bring disappointment to them, that all of us youngin's have the strength of character to amount to something, to be good citizens, to make them and the rest of the Lances proud, if they can but harness, put a rein on, guide, and nurture this compelling, fighting spirit and turn it into something useful for God and all of mankind. They pray constantly that no unforeseen incident will ever occur to harden our hearts, turn us from God

Almighty, thereby unleashing our fighting spirit to wreak havoc upon our enemies, real or imagined. God forbid that any family ever has to suffer the enraged wrath of an incensed Lance, for they would be far better off to try and hog-tie a hurricane or to catch lightning in a jug.

Dad is the patriarch of our bunch and is important for our well-being, but no less so than Mom, to whom we point with no little pride, and rightly so, as being the matriarch. She is one fine lady, and we are so proud of her. It is easy to see why Dad loves Mom, and it was mainly because of her influence that he accepted the call to the ministry. Through love, care, and devotion, she has been able to corral the fierce spirit of an independent man and channel his unbridled energy into a force for good. Now they both as loving parents are trying to do the same with us.

Mom's outward beauty has waned somewhat probably because of the pain associated with bearing ten babies and the untold work that goes into being the constant comforter and tender of the little ones. Mom not only looks after the tots but also finds the energy to cook three large, filling meals that satisfy the palate of a hungry man, wash, iron, quilt, can, and in her spare time help in the field. The fellow who penned "man works from sunup to sundown, while woman's work is never done" must have followed Mom around. The beauty she may have lost hasn't vanished; it's only been transferred to another place, from an outward temporary phase to an inward eternal phase, much like the changing of a pretty cocoon into an even more beautiful butterfly.

The inner strength, the tenacity for finding good where there is none, and the way Mom casts this peaceful glow to others is a source of comfort to everyone and us that knows her. She is like the huckleberry growing upon the forbidden face of Cow Rock. There is nothing there to support life, being mostly a barren, rocky, precipitous cliff, a haven for rattlesnakes, but this bush reaches, stretches, searches, sending out young tender tendrils until they find sparse soil. Then they catch hold, clutch with fierce determination until they can take root, and then bring forth fruit as a sign of its triumph in the face of difficult odds.

I remember the thunderheads boiling up, and then the violent summer storms that would often rock our community, where thunder and lightning would link arms and dance merrily back and forth in our little cove, shattering the quiet tranquility of the valley with an awesome display of God's might, confirming how puny we are in ourselves. I recall the fear that gripped us, causing us to run to Mom for comfort and the loving, secure way she gathered us around her, eased our anxiety with words of solace, "Now, now, don't fret; we're in God's care; everything is going to be fine," and she was always right.

Mom is a very religious person, a true saint of God, but she doesn't get to hear Dad preach much or to attend church that often on Sundays, and neither do most mountain women. It certainly isn't that they wouldn't have liked to—they surely aren't less religious—but this is just another fact of life in the everyday, most times worldly existence for mountain women. She and they are just too busy with the kids, and somebody has to fix dinner, for no telling who or how many guests might come home with Dad for dinner. The commonly perceived notion of smartly dressed, dainty, saintly ladies, sitting piously in church on Sunday, is a misconception.

Mom and Dad have a special love each for the other, an interwoven dependency upon one another, an understanding that surpasses mere words and is evident by the sly grins and secretive nods of agreement. Every evening when there are flowers blooming in the meadow, Dad will stop and lovingly pick a bouquet for Mom. He can be seen coming down the dusty lane with that long stride of his, leading his mule, carrying the small bouquet, singing a happy tune, for these are happy times in this peaceful cove. Dad will bound lightly up on the porch, step inside, buss mom on the cheek, hand her the bouquet so lovingly gathered and say, "For the woman I love." This is a love of passion in that they give of each other, a love of compassion, a love not ashamed to be confessed, and a love based upon Christian principles.

Their dependency one for the other is so great that should some unforeseen event separate them, I fear the one remaining would be helpless and live in abject misery, just praying and waiting for the Death Angel so they can once again hold hands and pass secretive grins in an eternal Heaven. If Mom should pass on to her eternal resting place before Dad, why, I can just see it now—Mom there in Heaven waiting on Dad

15

to join her, and when the glad day comes she will see him striding down the path of angels, stopping along the way to pluck flowers from their garden for her a bouquet. Dad will come stepping through the Pearly Gates, give Mom a quick tender kiss, hand her the bouquet and say, "For the woman I love." Mom will take the bouquet saying, "John, I love you too; what took you so long?" Such is their love.

The peaceful quietness of these mountains for the most part remains as God has intended, until the forces of nature decide it is time to remind the inhabitants that they are only the temporary custodians of a beautiful yet strong land. The earthquake of 1811 centered on New Madrid, Missouri shook this area with strong tremors, causing no little damage; fear was rampant. An occasional gale-like wind; a torrential downpour, coupled with awesome fireworks from the heavens; a paralyzing ice and snow storm with no visibility atall—all of these tend to point out that these mountains were here long, long before we were, that they will remain long, long after our temporal bodies have turned to dust and been scattered as the fallen leaves.

Chapter III

Sheriff Charles Hill

Sometimes a man takes it upon himself to shatter the peace by doing an act of cowardice that brings sorrow, regret, and disgust to an area, snuffing out forever the flickering flame that promises so much light, holds so much potential, and has only begun to burn brightly. My Uncle Debarris has told me of such an episode happening in May of 1867 to Union County Sheriff Charles Hill, who was only twenty-seven at the time.

Debarris became acquainted with the Hills through a quirk of fate, a happenstance where two men met and liked each other immediately because of the bitterly fought disagreement between the North and South. These two men fought for the Confederacy, Debarris with Co. A, 6th Regiment, Georgia State Troops, as a private; Napoleon Hill in Co. A, 29th Regiment, North Carolina Infantry, then later as a major in Ledford's cavalry regiment, Army of North Georgia.

It was court week in Union County, and practically all of the citizenry was in attendance. Through an introduction by D. W. (Dolph) Lance, a cousin of Debarris, he and Napoleon met, being introduced as Confederate veterans. This naturally brought about extended conversation as to which regiment they were in and the major actions in which they participated. They soon found that they both had been in many major battles, but had one thing in particular which helped them to bond and find common ground: a battlefield injury that continued to bother them for the duration of their lives. Neither one complained about his injuries, for each considered it a small price to pay in fighting for a cause they believed in. And though both had been heavily outnumbered, sparsely supplied, and facing impossible odds, they had been able to delay the Union's relentless march for months and in the process garnered much fame as some of the South's best fighting men.

God, the Omnipotent, the Answerer of all Prayers, heard the passionate pleas of these two war heroes and through His infinite mercy, saw fit to return them to their beloved mountain homes. Their service had not been without a price to themselves and their families. Debarris had lost so much weight from the poor rations that he was just a shell of his former self. Napoleon had fared little better. The food for officers was more palatable, but he had been wounded in the arm, making movement very difficult. However, they still could be numbered among the lucky, for they did return, and so many, many of their compatriots had not, spilling their blood without really knowing for what they were spilling it.

The families at home paid a price also, not faring as well as before because they had been asked to contribute to the war effort by tightening the belt and giving more. The belts had become tighter and tighter, and families kept on giving and giving as their brave young men, the future of the South, paraded off to war, many never to return.

Debarris and Napoleon did keep in touch, chancing to see each other on occasion and for certain on court week, held in Blairsville twice a year, in April and October. Now these terms of court were something special to behold, as the normally slumbering county seat became alive with a variety of activities, and most of the people in the county could be counted on to lay everything else aside and attend. On any day in a normal week, the dusty streets would be lucky to have five wagons travel over them, but on court days, the streets were jam-packed with wagons in all manner of repair, filled with screaming kids and loaded down with goods for bartering purposes. The courtroom would be a sea of sweating, curious onlookers, nervously fanning, hoping to dissipate the tepid, oven-like heat that bore down on them oppressively, and they were anxious to see the learned colonels display their aplomb, hoping for the stern judge to make some examples out of others. The courtyard would be abuzz with frenzied activity as people renewed friendships, visited friends, told tall tales, planned future political endeavors, swapped horses, and bought patent medicine that was double-back guaranteed to cure everything from the tight hide on your milk cow to sexual maladies. From the number of screaming, sometimes obnoxious children milling around the general vicinity of all this activity, it would seem that sexual maladies were few, but they bought just in case.

It was at one of these court weeks that Napoleon told Debarris that his young brother Charles was seriously thinking of running for sheriff on the Democratic ticket. And if Charles did, the Hills would appreciate Debarris's and all of the Lances' support. Debarris answered in that blunt, cut-to-the-chaff way of his, "Napoleon, I know and respect you, and I have met Charles, but only briefly. Will he stand?"

"I know he's young, but he's cut from the same bolt of cloth as we are. He's got grit, maybe too much; he doesn't know the meaning of the word fear. Yes, most definitely, he'll stand," said Napoleon.

"That's enough for me," replied Debarris. "You can count on me, and I'll see what the rest of the Lances think."

"If Charles does throw his hat in the ring, and it looks like he will, we'll come up to Choestoe soon and let you know."

Now there's only one thing in this world that I know of that is more certain than the sun rising in the east and setting in the west, and that is the Lances and Hills will vote a straight Democratic ticket in the fall.

Charles Leonidas Hill did choose to run; a trip to Choestoe was made, the Lances pledged their support, and in November of 1866, Charles Hill became the newly elected sheriff of Union County, sworn to carry out the duties thereof. Then six months later, just barely into his term, tragedy struck.

The first six months of Sheriff Hill's term was smooth sailing, as sheriffing goes. There was nothing much exciting to do, for by and large the mountain people are peace loving, most having moved here in the hope that they will find something better, and they have. Oh, he on occasion had to lock up an individual or two for disturbing the peace, after they had become overly fortified with "the floater of imaginary dreams" and decided they were more of a man than they actually were. Usually though, the next morning after having spent a sobering night in jail, their headaches subsided somewhat and their hat size shrunk several numbers. Then they were appreciative of the kind manner in which they were treated by this new sheriff, thankful that he hadn't or didn't let someone else prove how little of a man they really were after their egos had been strutted to abnormal size by Barley Corn.

Sheriff Hill and his deputies left Blairsville the morning of May 14 to arrest a William Campbell for robbing a poor widow woman of her earthly possessions. Her possessions, admittedly, were few, but still they were hers, hers to keep and all she had.

This William Campbell lived on the other side of Ivy Log Gap, which actually put his place of residence in Towns County. Sheriff Hill knew, though, that if he took time to send a warrant to Hiawassee and waited on its return, then had to travel twenty miles to arrest him, William Campbell would run; he was that type of fellow. Anyway, the sheriff reasoned, and rightly so, that Campbell didn't recognize county lines when he so cowardly came over into Union to rob this poor widow. Why should he be treated any differently? And this wasn't the first time this man had crossed over into Union County to steal and then sneaked back into Towns County, using this imaginary line as a haven for his thieving adventures.

The posse knew William Campbell, if not personally then certainly by reputation, for it was common knowledge that he was a petty thief; a robber of the helpless and a shrinking coward, he would stick a knife in your back but didn't have the guts to look you eyeball-to-eyeball. The scorn, the personal distaste that each member of the posse felt toward this man, was expressed by the sullen scowl that was firmly set upon their normally smiling faces. The good-natured give-and-take that is commonplace among a party of friends was sorely lacking on this day. The only distinct sounds disturbing this quiet May morning were the metallic ding of shod hooves hitting upon the rocks lying loosely on the mountain trail and the squeaking saddle leather of the laboring horses, for the trip from Blairsville to Ivy Log Gap was beset with sharp terrain.

Sheriff Hill was immersed in his own thoughts, about the arrest he was sworn to make and about the nature of things, for he was an intellectual, philosophical sort of fellow. His thoughts turned to God and the way he created the world to follow an orderly plan. Why couldn't man be as orderly? There was spring, summer, fall, and winter, four distinct seasons; and they eerily seemed to parallel the stages of growth in human development. Spring was a new beginning, strikingly like infancy. Summer was growing up, the teenage years. Fall was akin to the harvest, and in this stage, we should let the world benefit from our ready-to-harvest knowledge. Winter was sadly like old age and the inevitable death. If the uninformed knew of these thoughts, they might have questioned his mettle, as it is common to perceive that the more intelligent you are, the less courage you have. Nonsense—Sheriff Hill knew that it is not the lack of brain that makes you brave; some people are just born with more courage, a gift from our Creator, and he was thankful that he has been.

The winding mountain path was much steeper than the men remembered, and it had already taken the better part of the morning because of the necessity of resting the laboring horses. Sometime around noon, the determined posse reached the crest of Ivy Log Gap. They let the horses get a good long blow—and the tired riders a much-needed stretch. Sheriff Hill stepped away from the rest of the posse to a small opening, cleared by local hunters so they could better hear the merry notes of the chasing hounds, and gazed below. He bowed his head in reverence to Almighty God his maker, for he was surely in His cathedral as the sheriff beheld the pastoral scene below, cattle and sheep grazing peacefully together in the lush green valley. Smoke trailed from the chimneys, lazily rising toward the heavens, there to intermingle and be swallowed up by the clear blue sky. He turned slowly, his eyes beholding the majesty of these mountains about him and the way Mother Nature was gently dressing her own. This was spring, a new beginning, the sheriff's favorite time of year, and he was so thankful to be alive.

After this brief respite, the posse mounted, eager to continue their fateful journey, and they soon crossed the Union-Towns county line. Campbell's cabin, a poorly built log building, lay alongside a small creek and was situated close to the foot of a mountain. The cabin had a porch located so that no one could come down the trail unnoticed. It was built this way, not by accident but by design, because of the line of work that

Campbell chose to follow, allowing for a quick getaway, if one should be needed.

When the posse reached the top of the mountain, some quarter of a mile above the cabin, Sheriff Hill told his deputies to wait while he went alone to arrest the fugitive. The deputies were willing to go, wanted to do so, and put up no little argument, pointing out again that Campbell was not to be trusted, was a low-down backstabber. The sheriff responded in that considerate manner of his that they had come to respect so much: "I hired you all as deputies to help me, not do my job. I was elected to take this risk. If any blood be spilt, let it be mine. I've decided to go down unarmed and make the arrest. I'm confident even Campbell will be man enough not to shoot an unarmed man." The deputies stayed, filled with trepidation, and the sheriff started on his journey, unaware of the fate that lay in store. The brave sheriff knew that his approach wouldn't go unnoticed, so when he was about fifty yards away, he hollered, "Campbell, I've got a warrant for your arrest. Come on out peacefully. I'm unarmed."

Campbell grabbed his pistol and said, "Sheriff, if you'll go away, I'll promise to leave in the morning and never come back."

"You know I can't do that; I'm duty-sworn to take you in," answered the sheriff, and he stepped up on the porch. Campbell was inside the cabin with the door securely latched. Sheriff Hill failed to notice the door being slowly cracked, and from this crack, this buzzard of the night fired at point-blank range, striking the unarmed servant of man in the belly. This gutless serpent fled into the dense underbrush, leaving a mortally wounded good man behind.

The posse, hearing a single loud report from a revolver, sat momentarily in stunned silence, and then realized what had happened. They mounted hurriedly, spurred their horses into furious action, hoping for the best but fearing the worse, and quickly raced toward the small cabin. When they got there, they found Sheriff Hill lying on the dusty ground, writhing in convulsive agony, clutching his stomach with his hands as his lifeblood flowed from the gaping hole.

The deputies flew into swift action; from somewhere, a wagon was procured and filled with quilts. The badly wounded sheriff was gingerly loaded into the wagon for transportation back to his dad's house. The trip was a ride of torment as the carefully driven wagon bounced sharply upon the ruts made by the down-pouring winter rains, and with each bounce, the sheriff passed in and out of consciousness, pokers of fire shooting searing daggers of pain through his weakened body.

A courier had been sent on ahead to tell his family that he had been badly wounded. His mom and dad anxiously paced back and forth, waiting for the wagon carrying their beloved son to arrive. They rushed to him and embraced him tenderly, as only parents can, and he slowly opened his pain-filled eyes, nodded weakly in recognition, then passed back into blessed unconsciousness. He was carried with care and placed in his own bed, the bed of feathers that had so often cuddled his body providing warmth, rest, and sweet peace. The family and concerned friends gave as good a nursing care as is known, but Sheriff Hill knew that he had suffered a mortal wound, that the stomach acids would work on that filthy lead ball, releasing poison that would finish what that coward had unfurled, but he suffered in dignity—if there is such a thing—never complaining or screaming out in pain.

Tragic news travels fast, and the Hill house was already filled with sympathetic friends concerned about the sheriff, for he was genuinely liked.

One of the concerned friends who rushed to Ivy Log was Debarris. The minute he heard the tragic news, he laid everything else aside and headed out to be with his friends, to see how he could be of service, for it is with the Lances: once a friend, always a friend.

Debarris arrived at the Hills' house and sought out Napoleon, asking, "How's the sheriff?"

"His time is short; he's not going to make it, Debarris," Napoleon sadly replied.

"Napoleon, if only I had'a taken that deputy job when Charles offered it to me, then I would'a been there, and no way I'd let him go in there alone; I feel guilty myself."

"Debarris, it's not your fault; we're just going to have to play the cards we've been dealt."

"What, then, can I do? Has the scoundrel been caught?"

"No, I'm afraid he got too big a jump, but he's got kin living down Wolf Creek from John's place; he might just slip in there for rations."

"I'll get word back up to the Lances. If he comes there, and I hope he does, then I promise you, Napoleon, he's a caught man."

Debarris and the other Lances watched the homesite secretly for weeks; William Campbell never showed up.

Three days after the cold-blooded shooting, Sheriff Hill gave up the ghost. He is buried at Antioch Cemetery in Union County, and his epitaph says it all:

"God my redeemer, lives and ever from the skies,

looks down and watches my dust till he shall bid it rise."

Another misfortune of the Hill killing is that the thief of the night, who shot an unarmed, good man, made good his escape. William Campbell was never apprehended, evading man's justice temporarily, but he one day must stand before the judgment bar and face the Supreme Judge.

Chapter IV

THE WILD BOAR INSTITUTE

When I was growing up, education, "school larning," wasn't considered to be all that important. It was commonly thought that being a good farmer; being able to plow a straight furrow; being a good hunter; and being good with a froe, ax, maul, or other tool was much more beneficial to one's survival than being capable of reading fluently or adding a long column of figures. And who knows? That perception at that time, under the circumstances that we had to face each day, might have been the correct one . . . what right do we have to question the motives of these individuals who did survive, most quite well? However, times change, and if we are to contribute to society and better provide for those who depend upon us, then we must be capable of changing with them. This I so often have heard Dad say.

Dad didn't know how to read when he received the call to preach God's word, and as he says, was handicapped for a while by not being able to read from the Good Book and partake of the Bread of Life for himself. But Dad was a determined man, and in that dedicated way of his didn't let this handicap stand in his way for long. With the help of a friend, William "Bud" Miller, who was a mountain teacher and taught him the ABC's, Dad learned to read by his lonesome. Bud was a true friend to our family, and it was he who further reinforced upon me the importance of an education. In this regard, I am lucky to have had such a friend; and even though Bud was somewhat older than me, the age difference didn't matter.

Even in the summer, when we are the busiest, Dad finds time to read the Bible. But in the winter in particular, when the sun seems to make a hurried dash across the sky, bringing short days and long nights that cause you to shiver shamefully from the cold daggers hurled by a relentless north wind, he has more time to ponder the promises of God. Mom sits on one side of the warm, peaceful, glowing fire in a high-backed Reid rocking chair,[1] rocking slowly while she contentedly knits. On the other side, Dad smokes a pipe and has the big Bible of his spread out, reading to us kids, teaching us in that compassionate way of his about God and His infinite mercy.

Dad is different from some of our neighbors and insists that I go to school. Now, school isn't all that much, lasting only three months, from mid-July till October with two weeks out for fodder pulling, but this is the best time of the year. The cold, turbulent water of Wolf Creek has just begun to warm a tad, and here I will be in school, missing long days hanging out at the swimming hole with the other boys, whose dads are much fairer than mine, treating them like mature grown-ups, letting them decide for themselves, so I think.

Now, I have tried to point out to Dad that I don't need to go to school at all. Our mule won't move a bit faster if I tell her to "git up" using correct English. In fact, she doesn't move much faster when you give her a good country tongue-lashing, using all of the latest in cuss words, always of course out of earshot of my dad. I'm sure glad that dumb, long-eared ole mule can't talk. Dad is a Lance though, through and through. All this pointing out doesn't do a bit of good; it falls right off of him like water off of a duck's back, and he will just turn and walk away like he doesn't even hear me.

The schoolhouse—if one has a vivid imagination, for the structure dubbed as a house little resembles one—sits precariously perched upon six columns of uneven, haphazardly stacked rocks. It is a one-room building with no partitions, made of rough-hewn logs, and the air space

[1]Chairs made by the Reid family, who were North Georgia artisans famous locally for their straight-backed and rocking chairs.

between the poorly fitting logs is carelessly daubed with clay, befitting the unconcerned manner in which education is viewed. The schoolhouse perches unevenly upon these columns, causing it to be several feet off of the ground, leaving a crawl space underneath where boys and girls can trespass but are not supposed to. This center of education sits in a small clearing, hacked out of an unwilling, virgin forest that continually tries to reclaim it, evidently resenting the intrusion upon its privacy by a bunch of unruly, clamoring boys and girls.

The water supply for the students comes from a bubbling pure mountain spring located about three hundred yards from the school, and that spring has forever gushed forth, gladly quenching the thirst of whoever partakes. The water is carried to the other students in a wooden bucket by concerned volunteers who are willing to sacrifice some schooling for the good of others. When the teacher asks, "Who would like to go to the spring and fetch water?" and a multitude of hands go up, it isn't because they want to get out of school—no school kid has ever wanted to do that—but out of concern. We don't know anything about germs; there isn't a picture of one in the *Blue Back Speller*, and anyway nobody around here has ever reported seeing one, so we all drink out of the same dipper.

The name for this academy of learning is the Wild Boar Institute, named thusly by Cussin' Tom Henson because of the wild way the boys conduct themselves. This name, in actuality, is quite apt and further denotes the lenient, non-important attitude about educational matters. I imagine if you as a stranger in our fair land happen upon, by chance, the Wild Boar Institute, you will swear that you have found Mount Ararat, and there, sitting cockeyed, just as it landed high on one end, lower at the other, is Noah's Ark. Such is the way our school looks.

However, don't be deceived by the disheveled look of our school, because the young people who find time to attend are brilliantly smart, with minds having the mental capacity to unlock many of the mysteries that have befuddled mankind for centuries. So what if they don't excel in academics? Still it is this dilapidated-looking school that provides the indirect impetus. Now, I don't make unfounded claims about these students and their accomplishments. After all, what could possibly be accomplished by just going three months a year? Besides, we only have a slate to write on, kept clean by a goodly amount of spit wiped off on some part of our clothes, to the dismay of our moms, and no books atall to call our own. The only books belong to the stern teacher, who guards them with much zeal and is not at all hesitant to apply a sharp rap upon your knuckles if you dare approach these books, the keepers of secrets, without his permission. In addition, this teacher, as impossible as it might seem, teaches all grades from beginners to enders, their ages ranging from six to twenty-one. The reading classes seem like a lesson in futility as the teacher has all students reading at once, but out of this seemingly disorderly chaos of many voices comes understanding and order. Dad says, "Haste makes waste, with the greatest waste being a wasted mind." We waste our minds, some not intentionally, but through a combination of forces that really preclude us from fully plowing our fertile minds.

Maybe the students at the Wild Boar Institute don't accomplish deeds that the scholarly world talks about. If they or some other poor mountain person did, it would more than likely be stolen from them, they never getting the credit. However, in an indirect way they do, for we come to realize the importance of an education and are determined that when we are fathers, our children will be given every opportunity, and through them, talked-about accomplishments would be realized.

Of all the students, I probably least use my talents, letting them fall upon rocky ground, but I do learn to read, write, and count, certainly not fluently but enough to get by on. And I make lifelong friends, friends that you can depend on, friends that will stick with you in a pinch, one being the prettiest girl in school, who is so smart and can look at you with those big doe-like innocent eyes, making me dream dreams of me and her and eternal bliss.

Chapter V

THE FLYING MACHINE

I saw something yesterday that I know you're not going to believe. Dad didn't much believe it either when I told him about it . . . well, he didn't just come flat out and say he didn't, but by the puzzled, startled look he cast my way, you could tell he had his doubts. In fact, I didn't much believe it myself, and I saw it.

It is a lazy spring day in May 1876, when the sky is blue as a robin's egg, that I am asked by Tom Dyer, the son of Clark Dyer, to go home with him and spend the night. I want to for several reasons, one being that I can escape the humdrum nightly chores that are assigned to me, the least favorite and most dreaded one being milking. Our cow has an uncanny way of moving just enough to step on you, and this brings forth a pain of unbelievable sharpness as she slowly grinds your bare foot into the manure-filled dirt. She will look around innocently with those big eyes of hers as I shove her against the barn wall and curse a blue streak, not much caring if Dad does hear. I swear to myself that one day I'll break her of that foolish habit.

My parents allow me to go, as they believe close friendships should be carefully nurtured, like they do the tender young plants in the springtime. Another thing that Dad has so often said is, "Sooner or later you're going to need family and friends. Treat them in a manner so that when the need arises, they will react positively without you even asking."

They realize, with the exception of family, the most important thing that anyone can possess that will bring a semblance of contentment and security is the gift of friendship, one with whom your inner thoughts are as safe and secure as if they hadn't arisen. They believe a perfect friendship between two men is the most sacred morsel of thought that our minds can comprehend. Lucky indeed, then, is the man who is fortunate enough to be the recipient of such trust.

Tom's dad Clark lives in a cabin at the foot of Cedar Mountain. The cabin is situated on a little rise, affording an overlook of a smooth, lush meadow teeming with wildflowers that profusely bloom a rainbow of colors, thereby creating a natural display of dazzling beauty, a beauty that artists have often tried to capture, failing in a run of artificial colors. This quiet meadow lies alongside Rough Creek, named so because the course it chose to follow eons ago has worn down to a hard bed filled with rocks of assorted sizes and shapes. So the rushing water runs rough, flinging itself boldly into the air, then falling freely, occasionally catching sunbeams, which creates illusions of fantasy as it happily splashes on.

This little valley would have been a perfect setting for dreams, dreams of a life devoid of hardship, filled with riches, a life only of pleasant memories with happy endings, creating no need to ask, "What if?" But I'm not dreaming.

After a filling supper of good country food—for Tom's mother is a good cook like Mom and knows how to make liberal use of lard and other seasonings that give our food that special, unique taste, so distinctive of mountain cooking—Tom said, "Dad, show Jim your newest invention."

"Son, Jim won't be interested atall in that ole thing. You all go outside and play."

"Please, Dad, show 'em, please."

"Okay, son, only if Jim wants to see it. Do you, Jim?"

I am as curious as curious can be, a-busting a gut to, but out of feigned modesty, I don't want to overtly show my aroused interest, so I say quietly, "I guess it'd be all right."

"Well, then, come on with me."

We follow Mr. Dyer to a securely locked shed adjacent to the main house. It seems that Mr. Dyer is a bit suspicious of other people stealing his inventions, and he has a right to be because of the pilfering way of others, some of whom are low-down enough to steal the pennies off of a dead man's eyes. Mr. Dyer says, "Jim, this is my little workshop where I spend a lot of time, just piddling around, inventing things and working on ideas floating loose in my head." He opens the bolted door, and we step into the darkened room. The last rays of a lingering sun cast fading light through the open door, but the room and the objects within are still encased by a cloak of darkness, as our eyes haven't yet adjusted to the dimness.

"Dad, roll her out here in the light where Jim can get a good look."

I hear a groaning, a moaning, and a squeaking noise coming toward me, and the durndest-looking contraption I have ever seen is pushed through the door, out into the open air for me to gawk at. And gawk I do. My mouth falls open in bewilderment, and there I stand in stunned silence, looking dumbfounded at this . . . at this . . . "whatchamacallit." Mr. Dyer and Tom are having a good country laugh at my expense, and I'll admit I must look stupid as I walk around this "thing," giving it a thorough inspection, being too shocked at first to even utter a simple, "What is it?"

I'll describe it to you as best I can, but understand, this will just be a bumbling attempt, because it is extremely hard, practically impossible, to portray how the first of anything looks. The body of the "thing" remarkably resembles a coffin, except it has a seat in it, and no coffin will have use of a seat. Protruding from the body of the "thing," up toward where the lid would be on a real coffin, are two attachments sticking out similar to the wings on a bird; however, they are very rigid and can't be flapped. The front of the "thing" has a windmill affixed to it, and underneath, two wooden wheels are attached, enabling it to roll.

I still haven't figured out what the "thing" is, but a thought runs through my head. Maybe this is an improved version of a casket, so that when Gabriel blows his horn we can quicker gather to meet the Angelic Host in the air.

After a few minutes, I come out of my stupor long enough to say, "Mr. Dyer, what is that thing and what in the world does it do?"

"It's called a 'flying machine,' and it will fly through the air," replies Tom proudly. "Dad was sitting on the porch one day, noticed how gracefully the buzzards soared, and wondered why we couldn't, so he started working on this and invented it."

"Jim, I didn't solve the mystery of flight overnight, still haven't fully, but I built, tried, experimented, and finally, after many failures over several years, have a machine that will somewhat fly," says Mr. Dyer. "The body is built out of white pine because of its light weight, and the wings are white pine slats covered with cloth for the same reason. The apparatus in front is wound up like a clock and spins because of the gears' action, enabling the machine to stay up longer.

"Jim, I've told you how it works, but you haven't seen it work. If you and Tom will help me push it to the end of the meadow and help prepare it, then I'll fly it." We eagerly jump to the task at hand, and in no time, mostly because of my anxiousness, the machine is at the other end. The end of the meadow abuts up to a small mountain. Mr. Dyer has cut a wide swath from the top of the mountain to the bottom and upon this cleared section has built a wooden ramp. The ramp is approximately two hundred feet long, turns up at the bottom, and is built with a rail casings on the sides so the machine will not run off as it comes speeding down the mountain.

We push, pull, and tug, finally getting the flying machine to the top of the ramp. Mr. Dyer climbs into the machine, telling us to step back and watch. Now, there is no need to tell me to watch, as my eyes are unblinking, bigger than saucers, because I don't intend to miss one second of this flying spectacular. He turns it loose and it starts rolling noisily down the steep, wooden ramp; faster and faster it goes, gathering even more speed. By the time it reaches the turned-up portion of the ramp, it is only a blur, wood against wood, and then suddenly it is wood against air as the machine breaks its earthly bonds and soars majestically into the clear blue sky of Choestoe.

Well, now, I might be stretching it a bit; it certainly doesn't soar high like the buzzards, but it does get up in the air some fifty feet and stays there for a long time, so it seems to me. The flying machine gradually starts losing altitude, and by the time it reaches the far stretches of the meadow, about three hundred feet, it comes back down to kiss the good earth with a solid thud. The kiss is none too graceful, being more akin to a hurried kiss between two secret lovers, as the contraption ends up resting somewhat on its windmill with the tail stuck up in the air looking like a wounded bird of some sort. By the time Mr. Dyer works himself out of this tail high resting machine and walks around it, visually inspecting the contraption to see that nothing is amiss or broken, we are there shouting with unbridled enthusiasm.

And why shouldn't we be, me in particular, because this was old hat to Tom, but not to me, for Mr. Dyer has in all likelihood inventing flying! And here I am a young fellow from an isolated area, being one of the first to witness such a spectacle. I am lucky; few people even in Choestoe have gotten to see Mr. Dyer's machine, and certainly no one else in the whole wide world.

We are somewhat isolated here in these formidable mountains, but not totally, because we do get news of the outside world through periodicals and by word of mouth. It is here, as in most places, that the hushed, secret word is quickly spread, invading even the darkest cove with its "I promised not to tell but . . . " Mr. Dyer has been flying now for some ten years, and if anybody else had accomplished this same spectacular feat, word would have surely leaked out, because the civilized world would be calling his name, singing his song, heaping accolades of praise upon him.

We help Mr. Dyer put his strange invention back into the dark workshop from whence it came and securely fasten the lock, making it safe from prying eyes. The machine is out of sight but not out of mind, as I am consumed in fascination at this unusual contraption. I am determined to find out more about its working, so somehow or other before going to bed, the subject must once again turn to flying. And it does.

I have on lucky occasions been privileged, probably because of my size, to sit in on manly talks and at least in my own eyes have become proficient in initiating conversation with others. To broach the subject again, I say, "Mr. Dyer, how do you like flying?" Looking back, I can see that was a trite, shallow question to be asking of such a smart man, but so what? It worked!

Mr. Dyer is a reserved, reticent sort of fellow with a kind disposition, not given to boastful, distasteful bragging about his accomplishments, as are most true geniuses—and he truly is one. But after seeing that my interest is real, he opens up and explains to me as best he can, because some of the things he talks about fly right over my head. I have never heard of such ideas, and most are far more than I can comprehend.

"Jim," Mr. Dyer starts in, "the biggest problem to solve in flying is how to give the machine power enough to escape the pull of gravity. You do know about gravity, don't you?" I have to admit I don't. "Well, gravity is the force that holds us on the earth. If there wasn't gravity, chestnuts would float upward instead of falling to the ground. Did you notice at first how the machine went upward, leveled off, and then started coming back down? Well, that was gravity at work. If I can overcome that problem, then I can fly, just like the birds, go anywhere I want to. I'm working on this, have been for some time, and I about have it whipped. I've developed a perpetual motion machine, and with this I'm going to power the flying machine."

"A what kind of motion machine?" I ask.

"A perpetual motion machine," Mr. Dyer patiently explains, "is a machine that supplies its own energy, will run continually on its own, and doesn't require some outside force to fuel it. It's the exact opposite of a train that gets its energy from the converting of water to steam by the application of heat derived from the burning of wood or coal."

That night my sleep is fitful. I am so worked up with excitement that I toss and turn most of the night, like to never fall off to sleep, and when I do it isn't a very restful sleep. I dream of flying over Blood Mountain; dream I break the quiet peacefulness of our cove by swooping in low for a closer look, scattering the grazing livestock hither and yon, scaring the daylights out of the playing children and causing them to run to Mom for solace; dream of doing daring deeds in Clark Dyer's flying machine.

It would be many years later that Buck Candler, the father of former Supreme Court Justice Tom Candler, gave two young brothers named Wright directions to Clark Dyer's home. They said they had heard of a machine he had invented and wanted to see it and see how it worked. Mr. Dyer let them see it, but when they started asking a lot of questions, he, by nature being suspicious, became a bit leery and wouldn't fly it for them. They told him their names, claimed to be brothers, and they did look somewhat alike, but Mr. Dyer couldn't recall for the life of him what they said their first names were. After thinking more about it, he said he had an uneasy, peculiar feeling about those two and their business.

Upon hearing about Mr. Dyer's visitors, I went to him and said, "Why don't you get a patent on your invention? I've heard tell that would keep it safe."

He answered, "I know, but I just don't have the money to do it with. I would have to sell my mule, and my family would go hungry because no one can do without a mule."

I couldn't argue with Mr. Dyer's reasoning, because the owning of a mule at this time in the mountains was more important than the anticipated earnings from an invention that might never come to fruition.

Chapter VI

THE BOYS 'NEATH YELLOW MOUNTAIN

A year has passed and here it is, time to gear up for another term at the Wild Boar Institute. I've heard older people speak about how time flies, but I can't understand their reason for saying this, 'cause to me it sure drags on, just more of the same old everyday boresome stuff.

I, along with my brothers, have spent the past year helping Dad do the jobs that are necessary if we are to fare well, and we do. I would like to take credit for us faring so well, but in all honesty, I can't, because Dad is such a hard worker, never wants any credit, does what is expected of him, and always has the welfare of his family uppermost in mind, while I sometimes will let the hot sun get to me, being perfectly willing to lie down in the shade by the cool banks of Lance Creek and let nature take its course. If it weren't for Dad and his complete, trusting goodness and me not wanting to displease him, I'd more than likely be like an old grasshopper, eating, drinking, and making merry all summer long while the fields are lush with plenty and not having the foresight to store up bounties for the long, harsh winter that is sure to follow.

I'm not inferring that it is just Dad, my brothers, and me doing all the hard work. Mom and the younger children are doing their share also—drying fruit, cooking, canning, sweating over a red-hot wood stove, and doing other jobs that make the long winter seem shorter, sometimes enjoyable. A fact of life, a necessary chain of events in the life of mountain people, is that the male children, as soon as they are old enough, go to the fields while the girls and the younger boys stay at the house helping their moms. Probably if a tally were kept, Mom and her cadre of workers do more than Dad and his, but none is kept. It isn't necessary, because we are all family, love each other most of the time, and are in this thing together; that is the way things are. Oh, we have our rough spots, with there being frequent fights among us boys and plenty of arguing with our tattling sisters, just the typical, frivolous, growing-up happenings among a large family; but let someone pick on one of us, and then you have all of us to contend with, 'cause blood's thicker than water.

One of the never-ending jobs is the cutting of firewood. A ready supply of dry hickory is required for Mom to use in the cookstove, as it burns the hottest and gives off a constant, steady supply of even heat that can be easily regulated by the damper, allowing Mom to cook meals that are always mouthwatering with no bad surprises. Hickory is also the preferred wood to burn in the fireplace because of these same characteristics, and a good hot fire of hickory with its unbelievable feeling of warm comfort helps to stave off the frigid bite of the coldest winter night.

The fall woodcutting expeditions are really a fun time because of the comradeship, but I never let Dad know this because I growl constantly about the hot, hard work, feeling it is my born duty to uphold tradition and complain about how much I am having to do. Now, this cutting of the winter's wood is a job that takes cooperation, and because of it, I start learning the basic principles of teamwork. "Jim, stop riding the saw; I hardly can carry myself," Dad will have to say over and over, 'cause I haven't yet learned to push myself, so when I get the least bit tired I will let up, forcing more work on him. That is the most Dad will every say; he'll just shake his head and grin, because he remembers how it is to be a boy.

The woodcutting is good, clean, hard outdoor work, and I can feel my muscles rippling tightly under my taut skin, toning up, growing bigger and harder and stretching, demanding attention. And Dad notices, saying with pride, "Jim, if you keep on growing like you have been, you're going to be some man." My day has been made; I swell up with no little pride, looking like a puff adder, because I so want to make Dad proud and he has noticed. Needless to say, the rest of that day I do more work than the law allows. In fact, I carry Dad, and by day's end, we are both totally exhausted.

This time spent with Dad is a period of special fellowship, a time for him to teach me the things that he has been taught by his father and the things I will be expected to hand down to future generations: the intangibles that distinguish one family from another, the ideas and principles that go into making one proud to be who he is. It is a time to glean from him how to apply the common knowledge learned from everyday trial and error, the basic lore that makes mountain living somewhat easier. This knowledge means that you plant your beans on Good Friday, kill hogs when the signs are right, leave the leaves on the tree for a week or so after cutting to make the wood dry faster, that the wood from a hickory makes the hottest fire, and the danger of frost is over when the leaves on a white oak are the size of a squirrel's ears.

I haven't noticed that I have grown any the past year, but I have. I accompany Dad to Virge Waldroup's store, the in place to pick up some necessary supplies: salt, soda, a few nails, some freshly ground coffee, a little hard stick candy for the younger kids, and some cloth for Mom a new dress, a surprise from Dad. Dad is always full of surprises, not just for Mom but for all of us; this is just Dad, the kind, gentle caring person he is.

Mr. Waldroup says, "John, Jim sure has taken on a growing spell. He's bigger than you right now. Step up on these scales and let's see how much you weigh." I step up on them; they groan and moan, protesting the weight as they always do, then they balance there, standing smack dab on one hundred and ninety-three pounds. I have gained eighteen pounds in one year, none of it flab 'cause my body is work-honed to a hardness of steel. Mr. Waldroup asks, "How tall are you?"

I reply shyly, "I don't rightly know, but last year I was five-foot-eleven inches tall."

"Well, let me get the yardstick and give you a good country measuring. Six feet and one-half inch," Mr. Waldroup announces. "You not only gained eighteen pounds but grew one and a half inches taller. John, you've got a mighty big boy now. When he's fully grown, he's going to be a full load. I wouldn't want to tinker with him."

"Thanks Virge," Dad replies. "He's a mighty good boy, but nobody better rile him, 'cause he knows how to take care of himself."

Another chore that has been placed upon my, by now, broad shoulders is hunting and trapping. Well, it is called a chore but in all honesty isn't one to me. I thoroughly enjoy the clear, crisp air of a North Georgia night, following the hounds as they bay loudly at the fresh scent of a wily coon or chase the ambling, clumsy possum up a tree. And the thrill of sitting under a hickory nut tree as dawn begins to wipe away the cobwebs of the night before, hearing the squirrels as they bark, back and forth, cutting nuts so fast that the falling hulls sound like rain upon a tin roof. Or the peaceful feeling of being quiet, listening to Mother Nature reveal secrets, daring not move, watching alertly for the secretive buck to make a mistake and slip out of his camouflaged copse and show himself. The excitement that running hounds bring as they chase a circling rabbit back into the area from whence it has jumped. The anxiety of running a trap line, wondering what the thrown trap holds. If this be work then I love work; oh, the primitive thrill of a successful hunt, where the table is filled with meat because of your skill. Yes, we hunt not for sport, but for food to supplement our diets, for there is nothing sporting about hunger.

Most any mountain hunter can bring a squirrel out of the tallest tree with one shot from their reliable ole "Long Tom," but most aren't proficient enough to just shoot out his eyes, thereby not messing up the meat. I'm not yet, but I want to be, so I practice and practice until I can do this with some regularity, nothing like Debarris, though, for he never misses. One shot from him, and you can chalk up another squirrel for the pot, and it with no bruises.

When I inquire of Debarris why he is such a good shot, he replies, "Because of a lot of practice and the use of a Gillespie rifle."

"What's so special about a Gillespie?" I ask.

"The Gillespie just happens to be the finest muzzle loader ever made, and if I am going to trust my life to a gun, I want it to be the best. Daniel Boone carried a Gillespie rifle in the crook of his arm when he looked for a place where a man could have wing room and spit without hitting a neighbor, and I figure what's good enough for ole Daniel ought to be for me. Jim, notice how it is long of barrel, slender and graceful of stock, with a good deal of drop so that when it is aimed it fits snugly against your shoulder and naturally falls upon the target.

"Gunsmithing is a trade of the men of the Gillespie family, and sometime before 1850 we were lucky in that two of them, James and John, decided to move to this area and produce the famed rifle here. John lives in Towns County near the Union County line, and his distinguishing mark on the rifle is 'JG.' James lives here in Union County, and his identifying mark is 'JAG.' Mine just happens to be made by James. But each makes equally accurate and true rifles."

I become a good shot through practice and practice, not a great one, but when it comes to the use of a knife, now that is a horse of a different color. When I have some time, I am continually practicing with a knife, until having one in my hand is second nature, and it becomes just a further extension of my arm. From fifty feet I can throw my well-balanced country toothpick and stick it up to the hilt into a two-inch square target practically every time, plus I can skin and gut an animal as fast and neatly as any surgeon with a shiny scalpel. I love a knife, and there seems to be a natural bond of some kind between it and me. I don't want to brag, but I'm darn good with a knife; even Debarris says so, and he's been through a war and is hard to impress. However, I keep having this premonition about a knife; I don't know what it is, but I have an eerie feeling that my life might be changed because of one.

This foregone year hasn't been one completely devoid of fun. I splash and play many hours in the tingling coolness of Lance Creek, hunt spring lizards under the mossy rocks, and chase the elusive snake feeders hither and yon as they stealthy lace themselves through the bramble, thoroughly enjoying myself. And the evenings spent with friends, after a hot, dusty day in the field, at the swimming hole, swinging on a grape vine, finally diving, trying to touch the deep bottom of the frigid waters of Wolf Creek, will forever be stamped in my young memory.

It goes without saying that I attend all of the revivals, me being the son of a preacher, but so does everyone else. And from the size of the gathered crowds, a stranger might think there are no sinners in all of Choestoe; however, this isn't exactly true. There just aren't all that many social things to do, with everybody's time being tied up by the making of

41

a living, and these revivals give everyone a chance to mix and mingle—well not exactly. Mingling between teenage boys and girls is strictly a no-no, and suspicious mothers, probably because of a direct decree from God, hover over their precious young daughters who are just coming into bloom like a bantie hen in the presence of a circling hawk.

Sometimes at these revivals, funny things happen to break up the somberness of the occasion. Perry Hood is in attendance at one revival, even though he is a staunch nonbeliever, not being the least bit timid about castigating the Christian movement as a bunch of tomfoolery. At these revivals, when the invitations are given to join the church, the saved will go back into the congregation to try to get the unsaved to give up their worldly ways, to go to the mourner's bench for special prayer and correct guidance. All week Perry has been a favorite target of the good sisters, who vainly try to persuade him to give up his sinful habits and join them in the Heavenly Flock.

On the last night of the meeting, when the invitation is issued, they again descend on Perry and begin to talk to him in a frantic manner, they being fearful that this might be his last chance to escape the fiery pits of an eternal Hell. They tell him he is a good neighbor, well respected, that the only thing possibly wrong with him is his nonrepentance and unbelief. They say pleadingly, "Perry, the Lord knows everything."

Perry thinks they are harassing him just a bit for the entertainment of the others, so he says, "You say the Lord knows everything?"

"Yes, Perry, the Lord knows," reply the concerned sisters.

Perry rams his hand into his overall pocket and says, "Does the Lord know I'm a-goin' to take this chaw of bakker?"

"Yes, Perry, the Lord surely knows."

Perry quickly jerks his hand back out of his pocket and replies, "Well, then, I'll just fool Him; I'll not take it."

The pious elders and the saintly sisters swoon and faint at this sacrilegious outburst, this defiling of the Lord's word, knowing full well in their righteous hearts that there will soon be a funeral to attend in Choestoe, that poor ole Perry has crossed over the line and will most surely be struck down by a revenge-seeking God who is always sitting ready to mete out justice, to teach His people a lesson in how unforgiving He is. I laugh heartily at this outburst, thinking it is mighty funny, and am firmly rebuked by Dad, who certainly doesn't approve of Perry's conduct, but he reasons nothing will happen as there are no big sins or little sins, and the God he put his trust in is a God of mercy.

Dad is right again; nothing happens to Perry. So the self-righteous, unbending Christians who hastily washed and starched their very best, their "Sunday-go-to-meeting" clothes, getting ready to attend an "I-told-you-so" funeral, are left shaking their heads, being visibly disappointed. Here was a perfect time for God to make an example and He let this opportunity of a lifetime pass Him by. What in the world is this earth coming to?

Well, I've done about all of the gearing up I can, and the dreaded day at last has arrived, the day to once again enter into the curriculum at the Wild Boar Institute. It's not really that bad when you consider it, but if you even hint that you like school, you will be considered somewhat of a sissy and have to fight to prove your manliness, not that I dread fighting or anything like that, but boys by universal, unwritten tradition have eternally sworn that they hate school and I am not about to be the one to break tradition. After all, I can once again get to talk to the pretty girl that herself makes school worth attending. Oh, I have seen her on occasion at the revivals, but that is like Abraham (Ab) Duckworth, who was asked if he saw the moon one night and replied, "I did, but it was at a distance." Because you know how mothers are about their pretty young daughters, and she sure is that.

The first week of school goes pretty well, mainly because it takes the better part of the week for the teacher to get this milling multitude of inattentive students organized into some kind of working order. I do win the school arm wrestling contest, besting in the process some boys who are several years older than I am. This doesn't sit too well with them, 'cause the winner is somewhat of a celebrity, and here is a youngster, an upstart, muzzling in on their territory, getting appreciative smiles from the young girls that they want to impress. They don't say anything to me, even though their jealousy is poorly concealed. It is probably a good thing they don't, because I take to this newfound attention, really like it, will defend it till my last ounce of strength is drained, and they know it.

My friends, the younger boys and most of the young girls, hang around me, and this indirectly leads to a major confrontation in my life. I should have known by the hushed whispers that abruptly stopped when I came near that these older boys, the used-to-be strutting peacocks who have been reduced to paltry capons, will not take this besmirching without some type of retaliatory move, but I didn't. I might mention that I don't fare too well in the spelling bee contest, finishing next to last, but this doesn't seem to tarnish my newfound notoriety, and I have already decid-ed that my vocation lies not in scholarly pursuits but in something that is more manly, like courting.

The older boys, being afraid to tackle me themselves, go to four boys that live yonder underneath the Yellow Mountain whose ages range from seventeen to twenty-one. They tell them I have won the arm wrestling championship, the girls are wild after me, and I need taking down a notch or two. They report that I have made my brags that I can whip them and anybody in Choestoe and won't hesitate to do so, if they are ever found even speaking to one of the schoolgirls, which is a pack of lies. Now these four, or their parents either for that matter, have never seen the need of attending school; however, they have become quite interested in the young lasses, imagining that they are much coveted by doting girls who have to exhibit a great deal of moral restraint to keep from fawning all over them, as they are perfect material for husbands. And here is a youngster, still wet behind the ears, that needs to be taught a lasting lesson.

The students leave the school in small groups, according to the direc-tion they live in, with each student eventually separating from the main group and going his respective way as the group nears his home. In my group, going down toward the further reaches of Wolf Creek, are six stu-dents, with the distance from the Wild Boar Institute to home being about two miles. When I leave the other scholars and turn up Lance Creek, there will be three left who live on down the creek. I am lucky in that in my group is the pretty young girl (Virisa Jane) who is one of the ones remaining, and I intend to get to know her better.

After turning up Lance Creek, I still have a goodly distance to travel before reaching the safe confines of our small farm. The trail winds alongside of Lance Creek, more or less, following it as it meanders here and there, down from the higher mountains from whence it bursts forth, starting its journey originally as a cool, trickling spring. This trail has been hacked out of the wilderness years ago and maintained by our family as a passageway down to the more heavily populated area of Choestoe. After many years of uninterrupted growth, due in part to being located in a section blessed with fertile soil and ample rainfall, the rhododendron, mountain laurel, and honeysuckle have grown almost together, forming somewhat of a knitted, interwoven, dense canopy that tellingly blocks the drying rays of the sun. This cool semitunnel is shady, almost dark even in the brightest sun, and the sun itself doesn't dare penetrate into this haven until it shines directly overhead. The way the trail is situated, a soughing breeze will softly float down through its passageway, and the instant anyone enters this cubicle of nature, they notice the appreciable drop in temperature.

I stride boldly into this catacomb of nature, my feet only lightly touching the ground, for this has been a grand day; Jane has noticed my constitution, the way I have bested the others. I know she has 'cause she said in an offhanded way, "Jim, you're the biggest, strongest boy in school. I bet you could be one of the smartest, if you tried." My light steps are evidence of how I feel and are accompanied by me singing in a lusty, loud voice, a voice that breaks and cracks, 'cause I am at the in-between age, where my vocal cords are still debating as to whether I should be singing tenor or bass. To call this raspy, off-key rendition singing would be pure speculation, 'cause singing is not one of my gifts. However, I still belt out my feelings, giving it my best in a loud manner, eager for all to hear, for these are peaceful times in a beautiful valley.

I walk with no trepidation, but after going a little ways, I begin to have an uneasy feeling; the dense woods, usually alive with the sounds of nature, the chattering of squirrels, the singing of birds, have an eerie, unnatural quietness about them, as if the goodness of their domain has been strangely shattered by some evil force. I feel as if this evil thing is watching me. I can't see it, but my sixth sense tells me it is there, and it isn't good. However, I walk on with dogged determination, not wanting to meet whatever it is head-on, but Dad says, "Never flee in the face of danger; you are far better off to meet it face-to-face."

Then it happens! From behind a big boulder alongside the quiet trail, the stillness is shattered by a swinging hickory club, brought down with such force that the replaced air recoils suddenly, creating a swoosh as this implement crashes upon my shoulders with murderous intent. At the sound of the swoosh, I react instinctively and duck my head, bringing my arms up in a protective manner. It is a good thing I do, because this natural reflex saves my life, diverts the aimed blow just enough so that it glances off my arms onto my shoulders. I am knocked to my knees! I am defenseless, as the blow, intended for my head, has paralyzed the nerve endings of my muscular body. I lie there half-conscious, waiting for these perpetrators to have at me, and have at me they do. Even in this state, I recognize who they are: the boys from 'neath Yellow Mountain. My every fiber screams out: fight, fight, fight back! I try but I can't.

Then the slue of abuse really starts: blows rain down on my defenseless body, even more so than the rain during a raging storm, and the kicks delivered with fiendish delight lift my body upwards, and I fall in a comatose heap. This is only the beginning; they are a pack of red wolves, and I am their hapless prey. "Turn him over on his back. I'll castrate him with this dull knife; see if the girls will pay any attention to him then."

"Ain't no need in that; when we're done with him he'll be too scared to even look at a girl, 'cause if he does, he knows more of the same will be waiting for him. Let the girls wonder why he won't have nothing to do with them." Several more callous kicks are delivered to my groin to punctuate their sadistic decree. I am almost unconscious, but I can feel them as they claw at my eyes that are quickly beginning to swell. They are frantically trying to tear them from the sockets, intending to blind me. Salty tears mix with my free-flowing blood, and it pours down my ashen face to pond up beside the innocent trail. My clothes have been practically ripped off, so violent is the attack, and my bruised and bleeding chest lies bare.

"Let's brand him so he won't never forget." A cigarette is hastily rolled, lit, and ground into my bare chest. My burning, searing flesh has a putrid odor, and it defiles the pleasing fresh scent of the lush forest, but I smell it not as I lie unconscious.

I don't know how long this abuse lasts or how long they take liberties with my body, for I am senseless. When I rouse momentarily, the birds are singing, the squirrels are playing in the treetops again, and the forest has returned once again to normality, having blotted out the cruel, ruthless attack that has so violated its principle of quietness. This is how nature's creatures are. They have no lasting memory of such occurrences, and it is good they don't, for then the mood of nature would be one of dread, of death, instead of peace, hope, and life. However, I have a memory, and you can bet I won't forget—ever!

I know that if I am to survive, I have to turn on my stomach, because my mouth is filling with my own blood, and it is beginning to clot! I am choking. I try to push myself over, but my body recoils from the driving pain and I fail. I whimper slightly, for though death is hovering near, I am still a Lance, and no scream of pain will come from me. I feel around, touch a gnarled root of rhododendron that has been exposed through many washing rains, and grip as best I can. I pull myself partway up into a sitting position and vainly try to balance. I sway unevenly and pitch sideways, sliding down the embankment toward Lance Creek, landing on my stomach, where again I pass out. When I come to, I can hear the waters of Lance Creek gurgling, beckoning me, and I know that if I am to make it, it is necessary that I reach the creek. I start trying to crawl. It is a slow, toilsome process, and beads of sweat glisten upon my bloody forehead from the throbbing pain. One of man's strongest instincts is survival, and I'm not about to give in to the small quiet voice that says, "Jim, stop. Lie still, go to sleep, everything will be all right." So, unmindful of the surging hurt that is shooting through every fiber of my body, I crawl slowly on till my hand feels the water's edge. Inching on, I drop my head; it lies in the soothing coolness of Lance Creek, and its waters wash away the glistening sweat.

My next recollection is of a long, wet tongue licking my swollen, battered face, then a familiar frantic barking. Though my eyes are shut, and I can't see, I recognize my dog Nick instantly. In a weak voice, I plead,

"Go Nick go, get Dad," and then blessed unconsciousness cradles my hurting body, temporarily giving me respite from the throbbing pain.

Muffled voices coupled with the strong, penetrating, pungent odor of an onion poultice faintly tug at the orbs of unconsciousness that fill my aching head. I stir slightly, trying to bring some semblance of order, trying to halt the mad demons that continue to whirl wildly within me.

"Jim, Jim wake up," I hear Mom say as she gently shakes my violated body. The sudden movement, the shuffling of feet upon a complaining, squeaking floor, betrays the presence of others, then strong, calloused hands find mine.

Dad says, "Son, we love you." I try to open my eyes and gaze into the faces of the ones I love, for I know I will find comfort, but try as I might, I can't. My eyes are blood streaked, and the skin 'neath them is a sickly purple. They are almost swollen shut from the savage beating at the hands of the bunch that is genuinely evil.

I nod weakly and whisper, "I know you do, I love you all too; who else is here, what day is it?"

"Son, it's Friday. You've been unconscious three days now, and most of our Lance kin is here."

Debarris, always the warrior, speaks up, "Jim who did you in? We're prepared to ride, we'll hunt them down like 'yaller dawgs.' When we get through with them it'd been better they hadn't been born."

"Now, now, let Jim rest a while; we're just thankful that God is letting him get better," Mom says.

"That's right; vengeance will be ours, but not yet," Dad responds. The voices grow faint. I once again drift back into another world, but this time the demons have been conquered, chased away by watching, loving, supporting family. A contented smile graces my face. I feel secure and sleep.

My respite is comfortingly parted by the pleasing aroma of a hearty breakfast being appetizingly prepared by Mom for her family and the rest of the Lance clan, who have unselfishly laid aside personal business and rushed to the bedside of a battered, bruised son, one of their own. Their hackles have been raised; they have waited and waited for days, keenly anxious for Dad to give a consenting nod so that they can exact even more revenge than the Bible allows: "an eye for an eye and a tooth for a tooth."

The Cherokee and Creek Indians fought a war upon the mountains and ridges overlooking the valley of Choestoe, the intensity being such that the very foundations of this peaceful place shook with awe and fear. The Cherokees fought to protect this "Garden of Eden" from an invading barbarous horde envious of its beauty and lush bounty. Legend has it that the battle raged so fiercely that the innocent waters of Wolf Creek flowed red with blood for three days from the fallen warriors, and that the mountains upon which this pitched battle took place became forever named Blood and Slaughter Mountains. We still pray today that the waters of Wolf Creek will never be defiled again by the spilling of blood.

A further bonding is made between the Lances gathered in our home, a promise of loyalty that silently runs through our body, that has been secretly veiled but now more openly reinforced by a commitment of one Lance to another: "If a Lance is harmed now or forever more, neither his soul nor the soul of his ancestors will rest in peace until revenge has been duly claimed; only then will they be able to sleep the eternal peaceful sleep."

Therefore, they wait on, looking to Dad for the sign, hoping, even praying that it will be to ride, but the sign must come from him. I am his son; the decision will be his, and they will abide by it. This is the way it is, the way it ought to be.

Now, Dad is a good man, unquestionably so, a man of high scruples who loves his God, his family, his neighbors, and Choestoe. His gut reaction is to say yes! He has been deeply hurt by the action of a gang of worthless cur, heel-biting dogs too cowardly to fight honorably man-to-man; this is how he truly feels. But he realizes the consequences, the suffering others will have to bear; why, even innocent families might possibly be touched, for the havoc that will be unleashed will make the battle between the Cherokees and Creeks look like a friendly tug-of-war at a family gathering.

The pros and cons of an important decision weigh heavily upon Dad. The worried look, deeply etched brow, and the nervous pacing are further proof of a concerned parent wrestling with the forces of right against wrong. I know, because Dad told me so, what the decision would have been if the blood had been forever drained from my young body.

The smell of fried ham and the peculiar popping sound of eggs in a lard-laced frying pan, coupled with the odor of freshly made coffee, tantalizingly wafts into my bedroom and I stir. Though my eyes are still only partially open, and I can see only slivers of faint light, there is nothing atall wrong with my sense of smell, and my stomach churns feverishly, reminding me that I have been without food for what seems an eternity.

I sling my feet out of bed and rest on the edge of the warm feather mattress. Actually, I don't sling my feet out of anything, because my body is so sore and bruised, but anyway, I sit there, trying as best I can to move my still-protesting abused body, trying to garner enough strength to follow the beckoning aroma. I gingerly put a little weight on my feet and hesitatingly stand up into a half-crouch, I imagine looking for the world like an aged man filled with crippling rheumatism, and sway to and fro, trying to gain my balance, for my legs are anything but seaworthy. A small step is taken, and I feel faint and grab at the wall for support as the room spins around crazily, trying to pull me down, but I won't give in; I am a Lance. I must beat this thing, for there are fights to be fought, scores that must be settled! I lean against the wall, gather my strength, weave and stumble like a drunkard, and doggedly proceed on.

I call on what little reserve I have left, suck as much air into my lungs as possible, and gush forth, "Mom, I'm hungry."

"Son, you shouldn't have got out of bed by yourself," Mom says as she and what seems like a hundred others rush to my side, gather me in, and lead me to a seat at the table, not just any seat, but Dad's at the head of the table.

From my vantage point at the head of the table, I weakly but eagerly say, "Pass the eggs, ham-meat, gravy, and cornbread; I'm so hungry my belly must think my throat's been cut." A peculiarity, I imagine, of Dad's and of mine, and one that remains with me throughout life, is that we both prefer cornbread instead of biscuit bread at breakfast.

Mom says, "Son, I know how hungry you must be, but this fare will be too heavy on your stomach, 'cause you've been without anything to eat the better part of four days. I wrung a pullet's neck and made a big pot of chicken soup. I'll heat it up and give you the broth for your first meal. I know you don't think that's much to eat, but it's best; you've come too far to risk a back set." Of course, Mom and Dad know what is best; they always do, especially when it comes to the welfare and protection of their family. If I'd had my way I would've tried the heavy stuff, took a chance, but Mom sets that hot bowl of broth before me, and I dig in like a half-starved hound dog, forgetting what little manners I have. Why, I'll swear that is the best-tasting stuff!

The mood of somberness that has been hanging like a shroud over our mountain home begins to lift somewhat, as evidenced by the commencing of good natured give-and-take between people who genuinely care for each other, slowly at first, then faster. "Jim, pass the ham-meat. I'm real sorry you can't eat none of this; just smell it and pass it on down real quick-like. It would be a sin to waste any, so being a God-fearing man, forever shunning sin, I'll just eat yours," says Debarris with a sly grin.

"Debarris, give me a week or two and I'll eat you under the table."

Dad grins in that disarming shy way of his and says, "Debarris, Jim can really put away the grub, and he more than likely can back up his brag."

The dark cloud of despair caused by the evil actions of others is rent, lifted by the secret, moving power of a grin, signaling to the other gathered Lances that yes, the storm clouds have risen; Jim is going to be all right.

Once a storm gathers in the mountains it is a sight to behold, a force to be reckoned with. It sends out fingers of lightning that probe here and there seeking, searching, exposing supposedly hidden secrets. The thunder then rolls from mountaintop to mountaintop, finally rising in a deafening thunderclap. It becomes trapped in the small valleys, and it rages on and on until its energy is spent and transferred back to the soil.

A storm has come into this peaceful valley. Dark clouds have gathered. It rages for a while, temporarily abates, and blue skies once again bathe the valley, signaling goodness. The forces of evil believe the storm is over. However, its energy hasn't been fully spent, and it will gather once again; when it does, it will be crying out for vengeance and satisfaction, its life being sustained by the hands of the family wronged.

When breakfast is over, Dad says, "Jim, do you feel up to talking?"

Mom interrupts, "Now John, I want this as much as any of you, but this is too quick. Look how pale Jim is."

"I'm a bit tired," I admit. "Let me rest a few minutes, then I'll be ready to talk." I am led back to my feather bed and gingerly lie down. My sore, aching body once again seeks and finds the comfort of the bed's deep folds, and I quickly fall into blessed oblivion.

Now this statement of Mom's, that "she wants it as much as anyone," is entirely out of character for her, but by the steel glint in her normally peaceful eyes, you can sense that she means it, and she isn't just talking about who did this loathsome act either. Mom is like the rest of the Lances this time, because a part of her has been defiled, a part that emanated from deep within her very being, and now her soul cries out for satisfaction in the form of revenge.

The Indians believe, and I've always heard, that "if you kill a rattlesnake, its mate will hunt you down and strike out with its deadly fangs, delivering the poisonous venom deep, exacting revenge." Why should we do or be expected to do less for ours than a slimy creature that slithers and crawls on its belly?

The minutes turn into hours and still I rest, nestled into the snugness of my bed. I again hear muffled voices rousing me, reminding me that there are others, not just me and my immediate family, and they are concerned for me. There are questions to be asked, answers that need to be given, yes, answers that only I can give, that demand and cry out for explanations, and they are branded deep into my memory. The others, the ones that laid aside personal business to be at my side, are sharply anxious, and they deserve to hear from me who the perpetrators are. I wipe away the lingering cobwebs, rise from my bed, and head toward the muffled voices. I surprise myself with how much more energy I have gained through the mysterious healing powers of a bowl of broth, not just any broth, but one carefully prepared and steeped in love.

"Jim, you look much better," Mom says as I come shuffling toward my gathered kin.

"I feel much better. Can we sit at the table? I'll try to recount what happened to me as best I can," I reply. I am seated once more at the head of the table.

"Son, take your time, but tell us."

I commence speaking, softly at first: "Though I was half addled, I recognized who they were."

I recount every blow, all of the degrading details and every sordid act of the vile attack, reliving every horrid second. My voice rises and I shout out, "the boys 'neath Yellow Mountain!" I am not the only angry one. The clan of kin sits gripping their chairs with such force that their knuckles turn white. They mutter undistinguishable words under their breath, shuffle their feet in decided anger, and when I say, "the boys 'neath Yellow Mountain," chairs are kicked over as they jump up in unison, cursing out in total disgust, saying as one, "Let's ride. We'll teach that damnable bunch a lasting lesson." The pent-up fury is strong, being of a force much greater than the spring thunderstorms that frolic and play on our mountaintops and in our valleys. If a voice of dissent isn't heard, and soon, the valleys of Choestoe will surely reek of death, brought about because of my spilt blood at the hands of the boys 'neath Yellow Mountain.

Dad steps forward and starts speaking in the voice of his that commands attention, the voice of a mountain preacher that has waxed loud and strong, causing others to turn from their ways of sin. A voice not entirely of dissent, but one of reason, saying, "The blood that courses its way through Jim was once my blood, and this blood is the very blood that pulsated so strongly in our ancestors, for we are kin, blood kin. Now our blood has been defiled, and we will seek and get satisfaction, but not right yet. Let them revel in a false sense of security. Let them lie around the hearth, brag about their so-called brave deeds. Let them believe all is well. In due time Jim's body will heal, and since he was the one to suffer the most, though we suffered with him, he needs to be a party to the avenging of the spilling of our blood."

Debarris speaks up, saying, "John, I agree with you. You are a lot more levelheaded than I am. It will be a time before Jim is up and about. I know that if I were in his shoes, I would want to be in on the action, strike the first blow. Yes, we understand your wishes and will abide by them. We will go on back home and tend to things that we are way behind on, but we will be anxiously waiting for the word, ready to ride with our blood kin."

My kin ride away, going their respective ways, and I watch sadly as they go, for I will miss them; but my sadness is lessened because I am glad, glad to be a part of them, glad to be a Lance.

However, this healing process is a process that will not occur overnight. Mom and Dad realize this more than I do, for many times during my recuperation, I dejectedly remark, "I don't believe I will ever be free from the soreness that completely covers me." I find it is like the thick fog that often rolls in, engulfing our little valley in a gray blanket of mystery and wonder so deep you can't see. My ribs are especially bothersome, and they are the slowest to heal. Why, on occasion, when I am unfortunate enough to sneeze, it feels as if one of the Yellow Mountain boys has stuck a knife deep into my side and twisted, so sharp will be the pain. Mom and Dad continue to boost my morale by reminding me "Athens wasn't built in one day"; healing takes time. God is still and will always be on his throne overseeing his flock, making sure that his children are protected. Yet, sometimes I wonder, if God looks after his own, and I know he does because Dad says so, why would He allow me to suffer at the hands of those who aren't His own and have never claimed to be. Dad says that "everything works for the good for those that believe in the Lord," but still I sometimes wonder. It's a good thing Dad can't entirely read my mind, though he seems to know my every thought, for then I wouldn't have to wonder because he would take me behind the woodshed and show me the errors in my way of thinking.

Anyway, I did heal after six weeks of staying around the homeplace. Four weeks of this is spent in complete rest, doing nothing more taxing than eating Mom's good cooking or winding our mantel clock and checking its coal oil content, which we put in a can lid and place underneath the ever swinging pendulum.

The next two weeks I spend with Dad plowing and hoeing our patches. Surprisingly, by the end of the last week, the soreness is completely gone and I can once again feel my muscles tighten, my biceps bulging under my loose homespun shirt.

The regimen I am led through by Mom and Dad is one to speed the healing of my battered body, a regimen of love and yet of much more, one not unlike a Roman gladiator in preparation for battle, for we all realize that soon I will face the biggest battle of my young life and I must be ready.

I might mention here that though my body is completely healed and my stamina back to where it once was, I still can't do a full day's work. At about four o'clock every evening, there seems to be a strange tugging at my heart, a longing, something I can't quite put my finger on that urges me homeward, and I blurt out, "Dad, I'm mighty tired, can I go home now?"

Dad grins, for he knows and remembers, and says, "Sure son, go on home, it's been a long hot day." I hightail it home, my big feet barely touching the ground, spruce up a bit, and before long I hear someone coming up the path singing a lighthearted melody, in tune with the gurgling waters of Lance Creek. I wait anxiously for this someone to appear. I go to meet her, feigning indifference, trying not to show how I really feel. We link arms and walk back to my house, sit on the steps, and plan and dream, dream and plan. This special someone is Jane Henson, and she has come by my house every day since the ordeal, making my recovery faster. Jane's parents would have probably objected to this linking of arms, most in our area would, but Mom and Dad can see no wrong in it and neither can I. This is how it is with a loving family.

Chapter VII

DAD AND ME, THE WAY IT OUGHT TO BE

On Friday of the sixth week, Jane asks if I am going back to school and I reply, "Yes." "Jim, don't come back, please don't, because the word at school is if you do, the crazed bunch plans on killing you this time. The older boys who are jealous of you anyway are betting you don't have the gall to show up. I'm so scared for you," she says, her voice fully revealing the trepidation she feels.

"Jane, I must go back; if I don't, I will never be able to walk in these valleys with pride, and I don't intend to go through life being ashamed of who I am. Deep down, even though you think different now, you would lose some respect for me. If fate decrees it to be so, and we become more than just best friends, I want us to walk together side by side, being able to hold our heads high. We will do this, not in vanity, but in self-satisfaction, making our families proud, for we have much to uphold."

Jane responds in that sweet way that affects me so strongly, "Jim, you might be right, but I don't care if you are; you are so headstrong. What of our future? If you're killed, it will only vaporize like water boiling and be no more. I can't help but worry; I've got so much to lose."

I open my arms and Jane comes to me. We hug comfortingly, gathering strength from each other, knowing full well that danger lurks, that others will try to change the inevitable and this love that is meant to be. Then I gingerly kiss the one I love for the first time, and she weeps softly. Though I'm not familiar with how to comfort anyone, being a whole lot rough around the collar, I remember Dad saying, "Now, now, every-thing's going to be all right." Moreover, it always was. So I repeat, "Now, now, everything is going to be all right."

Jane looks up at me with tears slowly flowing from her brown, inno-cent eyes and sobs, "Jim, I do so love you; please, please be careful."

Jane must have had a premonition of the events that will soon tran-spire, because that very night as we are sitting around the kitchen table eating supper, Dad says, "Jim, I've been thinking it's about time for you to go back to school. What do you think?"

"Whatever you think is best. If I start Monday, we'll have time to pass the word on to our kin this weekend," I answer. My spirits soar, for I know with absolute certainty that I can count on my kin riding with and protecting me.

But my spirit, that only moments before soared like an eagle, crashes to rock bottom as Dad says, "Now son, that won't be feasible, for we don't know when the scum from 'neath Yellow Mountain will attack, if they do. Our kin will ride with us, no question about it, but it's not right to ask them to. We'll just have to travel this road by ourselves and play the cards as they are dealt to us." I am totally unprepared for this kind of an answer. What had happened? Had Dad lost his mind? Doesn't he remember how I had been abused the first time? Can I expect anything less this time? Many puzzling, unanswered questions keep shooting through my head, and I'll admit I am scared, really scared.

Suddenly these haunting doubts disappear as quickly as they have arisen, instead being replaced by the remembrance many years ago of my younger brother, a screaming panther, Dad, and me.

The weekend passes by much too fast. Monday morning rolls around and brings with it opportunities. There is the opportunity to renew friendships and the opportunity to spend more time with Jane, but over-riding all of the positive aspects is the nagging doubt and the uncertainty of a confrontation that is sure to take place, for the pack has gotten the scent of their prey. They have tasted my blood and are intending to bring me to the ground, for I am their prey, but I don't intend to go as a lamb because there is the promise of the future. The fight to survive is man's strongest instinct, and I will fight till every ounce of strength is sapped from my body, and then I will fight on.

The streaks of light haven't yet penetrated the total darkness of Lance Cove when I smell the overwhelming odor of a good breakfast being cooked. Mom's breakfasts are so good that I always find them hard to resist, seldom necessitating a get-up call from Dad. This morning is no exception, and I sleepily arise, clumsily feel my way to the front porch, find the basin filled with cold spring water, and wash my face. The invigorating slap of cold spring water shocks my system, instantly breaking the shackles of my night's repose, and I am alert, ready, and raring to go.

The sounds of a happy kitchen, the metallic clink of silverware being scraped on empty plates, the unmistakable blowing of coffee being cooled in a saucer, the good natured-clatter—all are lacking this morning. Even the younger members of our close-knit family pick up on the tension in the air and for once, they are quiet.

I am not terrified about the conflict that is sure to come, but cautiously apprehensive, for when you are scared, Mother Nature steps in to provide you with extra senses, giving you added awareness, sharpened reflexes, and a little edge. She has already provided me with one big advantage, my size, but I have already learned because of my childhood scrapes that this bit of an advantage often times is all that separates the victor from the victim, and I am fully intending to be the victor because of the promise of the future. With this in mind, I start asking Dad questions, learning from his past experiences as to what I might expect.

To those not enlightened, this might seem odd, for Dad is a preacher, a righteous man. What possibly could a holy man know about earthly conflicts when he is only concerned with heavenly matters? However, Dad hasn't been a Sower of the Holy Seed forever, and I vividly remember Debarris recounting some of the fighting episodes Dad was involved in as a young man. It is a stated fact sworn to by those who know him best, the ones Dad ran around with, that he has never felt the dirt upon his back. He can and will whip Cox's army if they are foolish enough to cross his path. "Dad, do you think they will be waiting for me on the way to school?"

"No son, they hunt at night in packs like red wolves,[2] then lay in bed until noon, and I'll bet you can count on your fingers the times they have seen 'Ole Sol' rise above Bald Mountain. No, I'm not worried about you getting to school, but getting back without them setting upon you is a different matter. They may not know you're back in school the first day, but we can't count on it. It always seems that bad news finds a way to fall on curious ears, while good news flies on overhead. We best assume that they will know and prepare accordingly."

"Dad, then you're going to meet me at school, aren't you? I know how they act; with you along they won't dare show their ugly faces."

"No Jim, I'm not, for it's like you think, they'll never fight man-to-man; they're too cowardly. If they think they have the advantage, they'll attack like the pack of wolves they are. But we'll be prepared."

"We'll be prepared." I have again become a "doubting Thomas," for the stakes are so high and I have so much to lose. A puzzled look forms upon my forehead, and my head sags dejectedly. How can we be prepared if Dad isn't with me? It is beginning to look like it is going to be just me instead of we.

I raise my head and stare into Dad's eyes, penetrating into his very soul, and there I find abounding love, care, and concern of such bounty, I feel ashamed for ever doubting his intentions when it comes to matters concerning his God and family. I shed a secret tear and thank God Almighty for my dad.

I trudge off to school carrying my slate in one hand and my country lunch box (lard can) in the other. Mom believes in feeding the body almost as much as Dad does in feeding the soul, and when we are away from home, she always prepares us something to eat. This is another characteristic of parents that care, forming the epitome of the perfect earthly family.

As I travel down Lance Creek, all of the creatures of Mother Nature are promoting a full life by serenading me with their songs of thankful-ness—thanks for peace, serenity, and tranquility, for life itself in this

[2]Wolf native to the mountains of North Georgia. Smaller than the gray wolf. Hunted to extinction here, the last one being trapped in the late 1800s. Wolf Creek and Wolf Pen Gap are named for this species of wolf.

Garden of Eden. In addition, I too am grateful for life. Though my normal inclinations tend to lean toward more primitive matters, I become philosophical. What if all conflicts are ended, nation against nation, man against man, and all of God's creation can be in harmony with one another? What a grand world this would be! But I know this is not to be, for a serpent will again, rise in this Garden of Eden, spewing forth his noxious venom, poisoning those it strikes, causing them to retaliate harshly in ways that are contrary to their beliefs, changing their very foundations. With these thoughts in mind, I proceed on my way to the Wild Boar Institute.

When I arrive, the teacher and most of the students greet me cordially. Some are genuinely glad to see me, in particular Jane, for she was fearful I would meet the assailants on the way to school, and the younger set who have adopted me as one of their own. They look up to me as some sort of hero because I have protected them on more than one occasion from the older boys and their bullying tactics. The bullies think it is great sport to run roughshod over them. In my mind, I have fancied that my image might have had some of its luster knocked off because of my beating, but to my surprise, it hasn't. They too realize how the bunch from Yellow Mountain works and understand I have been cheaply ambushed. Now the older boys speak, feigning they are glad to see me, but I know better. I can sense a coolness, a hesitancy that all too well reflects how they feel about me returning and how they secretly feel about my beating. Their feelings are poorly disguised and more than likely controlled by envy, for they are jealous, but they don't need to be because I have eyes only for Jane.

This day the teacher rebukes me several times for not paying attention. If he knows what is facing me, he doesn't let on, though I'm sure he does. Anyway, he is like most teachers who eternally seem to think that education is the most important thing in life, but I'll disagree; staying alive is the most important thing in life. It would have taken a fellow "dead serious" to concentrate at a time like this, and I'm not that fellow, never was, never intend to be, dead or educated, at least not now.

At recess and dinner, the girls congregate together, and I stay with the younger boys. The older boys meet in small groups and talk in

61

hushed voices about me. I know they do because Jane and the others hear them talking, placing bets about when I will meet my Waterloo. They are careful to stay out of earshot because I am a bit edgy anyway, and I have a sneaking feeling they are somehow or other responsible for my first beating.

My first day back at school ends as it has began, with the loud ringing of the school bell. I can't tell if this day drug by or flew by. In some ways, it seems to drag by, for there is the ever-present dread of "What if?" that fills the crevices of my mind. What if they do manage to kill me? What if they jump me before I turn up Lance Creek, and others are hurt in the ensuing melee, in particular Jane; though she is small of stature, I have no doubt but what she will come to my aid with the fury of a trapped wildcat. Time also drags by because I want the confrontation over. It has already consumed most of my family's every waking thoughts for these seven weeks now, and one way or the other it is time to put this chapter of my life behind me. I intend to turn the page and let this be it, but can I?

The groups gather as they customarily do and start home. In my group, the Wolf Creek group, there are seven students, and we seven commence homeward. This journey has been made countless times, and it is filled with many hours of cheerful play. However, the routine mirth, so common, is sorely missing today, for we all know what I will be soon facing. The other students all are concerned, but not enough to lay their lives on the line and walk the last mile with me, a mile they probably think will be my last, all except Jane.

When we reach Lance Creek the trail splits, making somewhat of an inverted Y. One prong of the Y turns up the creek, and the other leads down into the lower valley, following Wolf Creek as it flows northward. We pause shortly as we say our good-byes. I turn up Lance Creek, not intending to look back, for a lump has formed in my throat. However, before I have gone fifty paces, I hear a familiar sweet voice calling, "Jim, wait up. I'm going with you."

I stop and slowly turn around, and Jane is standing next to me. "Jane, you can't. I won't let you, for no one knows what I'm fixing to walk into,

62

not even me. It will be much too dangerous, and I love you too much. I want you with me all the time, but this last mile, I must travel alone."

"I understand Jim, for your mind must be affixed solely on the job at hand. I might get in the way, causing your senses to dull, causing you to suffer needlessly, even though I would be trying to help. Do what you must, but please be careful." Jane rises up on her tiptoes, busses me, then turns and slowly walks back down the path, turning around every now and then to wave, until she is out of sight. I stand still, my feet seemingly glued to the spot, and stare after her. I remain there for several minutes, wanting to follow her, wanting to flee from the evil, impending confrontation that is going to be thrust upon me. A confrontation not of my own violation but of others. I want the peaceful valley to be as it has been, but it is not to be. I am a Lance and will act like one, for it has been bred in me, passed on down by my ancestors, never to turn tail in the face of evil or danger. Now it is my time to do as my ancestors before have done, for today I most surely will face both evil and danger.

I turn quickly and start up the path that follows Lance Creek with a determined gait, wanting my enemies to see I am not scared, intending to raise some doubt about their undertaking. Dad tells me, and I have found out through personal experience, how hard you fight is largely in your head; a man that won't be whipped, can't be. I know the meeting will not be a social one; the odds, four against one, can at best be called "unfavorable," and I will need every advantage. As I walk onward, I listen to Mother Nature; if you abide by her rules, pay attention to her, she will signal when her principles of fairness have been violated. I am nearing the place of my near fatal beating, when suddenly a blue jay sounds out a call of alarm, alerting me and the fauna of the forest that not all is well in our peaceful domain. The forest and those that dwell therein become deathly quiet; the smell of death hangs heavily in the air!

Then, as if nothing out of the ordinary is going to happen, the four boys from 'neath Yellow Mountain come sidling out, carrying hickory clubs, passing them off as walking sticks. They act for the world like they routinely travel this path and this is purely happenstance them meeting me here. Could I have possibly been wrong? Can a tiger shed his stripes?

Can a camel pass through the eye of a needle? "Howdy Jim. Where you started?"

"Home," I reply.

"Where you been?"

"School."

"Have a good time? Did you flirt with any of the pretty girls?"

I am beginning to see through their plan. They want to get me riled, and it is working. "Where I go and what I do is none of your business," I answer sharply.

"Now Jim, don't git touchy; it ain't healthy. We're just trying to be neighborly." They start moving around me, and I turn as they move, trying to face them, daring not to turn my back to any of them for they are equally evil; but because of the numbers, somehow or other they are able to effectively encircle me. "Jim, we warned you the first time to not go back to that school, not to even look at a girl. You must be some sort of a stupid idiot. Don't never say we didn't give you a chance, that we don't play fair and square." They circle me, poking me with their sticks, continuing their smart remarks, having great fun at my expense. "We're going to castrate you for shore this time," says the one whose idea it was the first time as he runs his finger up and down the blade. He continues, "This knife is durn dull, but it'll not hurt you none, 'cause you're not a-going to know it," and the poking gets harder. Their breathing becomes labored, for they have worked themselves into a fighting pitch. I can tell that they are beginning to tire of this little game, and I can expect to feel the sickening thud from their clubs at any minute. However, they aren't the only ones tiring of this childish game and getting worked into a lather. I decide if I am going to die, I'll go out with honor by giving a good account of myself. I pick out the one with the smart-alecky mouth and am intending to unload on him, when I suddenly feel the swinging club upon the back of my knees, hamstringing me, knocking me to the ground. Blows start raining upon me, and I roll sideways, protecting my head, for I know a blow to the unprotected head will be fatal. I stagger to my feet, and they are all over me. I sling one off, and another takes his place. I am giving a good account of myself, considering the odds, but because of sheer numbers, I can tell I will lose the battle.

The quietness of our little cove is being shattered as we grunt and curse in a primitive battle, pitting the forces of evil against good. "Hold him still; I'll cut his damn throat." I see the sun glint off the knife blade, and I feel my arms being grabbed. I see my brief life flash by and wonder if this is the way it will end.

Then from up on the mountain, I hear a yell of such magnitude that the roar of Helton Creek Falls would sound like the quiet chirp of a small cricket. "Whoa, hold on a minute!" The startled protagonists stop their struggle and look up in fear toward this loud command. There comes Dad, sliding down to join me, and he is in a mad rush. He kicks rocks loose in his haste, and he looks like a man possessed. He is, possessed with love for me.

Right into the middle of this wild battle Dad hurls himself. The odds have dramatically changed. Now it is four curs against two purebreds, and knowing Dad, the way he is when his beliefs or his kin are threatened, I know those odds have swung in our favor. A sudden exhilaration comes over me; surges of excited energy fill every muscle of my body, and I sense no fear. I feel strangely good and think this is the way it ought to be, Dad and me fighting side by side against the forces of evil.

Here we stand, back to back, protecting each other, facing the jeering, cursing, and circling gang. "Son, we've a job to do. Let's get at it, 'cause Mom will be mad if we're late for supper," Dad says in derision, his voice showing the scorn and contempt with which he holds them. Dad swings a ponderous right, catching the one with the open knife flush on the nose. I hear a cracking sound, the distinct sound of bones crushing, see a stream of bright blood suddenly spurt upward, and it contrasts vividly against the cloudless blue sky. The knifeyielder flies backward as if he is jerked by some unseen force. He lands in a twisted, moaning, messy, blood-covered heap. Now there are three.

The one facing me swings his club in a big, loping arc, aiming it at my head, but I am too quick for him. I move like a cat, slip inside the wide swing, grab him in a bear hug, lift him up, and start into squeezing. He struggles mightily, clawing at my eyes with both hands, for he has quickly realized that his club is of no benefit and drops it, but I won't let go, squeezing tighter and tighter and tighter. I hear a gurgling, choking sound, and he suddenly goes limp. I stare coldly into his face. It has become a sickly purple color and has big, protruding, strange-looking eyes. I let go of him, and he collapses like a hog's bladder with the air let out of it. I turn to help Dad, but he doesn't need my help. I am beginning to see what Debarris meant, for Dad is a pure fighting-mad machine, being oblivious to pain, and he moves with no wasted motion, just fists being pumped like pistons on a train. He is poetry in motion. Now there are two.

The two remaining realize what they are up against. Dad is a mortal man, but because of his rage has taken on some sort of invincibility, and they are backing up in fear, swinging their hickory clubs mightily. However, since he is in such a frenzied state because of their vile, underhanded nature, the clubs to Dad are no more than matchsticks. He laughs in contempt, walking through their futile swings. Dad grabs the first one he can get to by the collar, holds him at arm's length, and starts slapping him sharply, saying, "This is for Jim (slap). This is for me (slap). This is for all of us," and he turns him loose, steps back a pace, and hits him with a left jab. He follows this up by unleashing a powerful right cross and says, "Rest in peace." Now there is one.

The one remaining, the one that cruelly ground a cigarette into my bare chest, stands there trembling in panic. He is now, as so many of his victims have been before, hapless, surrounded by two foes who have felt his stinging cruelty, one directly and the other indirectly. This lover of the night begins to beg, pleading for his life, probably remembering he never showed any mercy, his true colors showing through. "Please don't hurt me. Please, please let me be. Rev. Lance, I ain't never meant Jim no harm. Why, he's one of my best buddies, and there ain't nothing I won't do for him," he says as he falls upon his knees praying. Dad and I keep our silence, fully enjoying his pitiful plight. Evidently, he takes our silence to be a negative answer to his fervent prayer, for he curls up on the ground in a fetal position and cries hysterically, losing what little manhood he has left in a pitiable wash of tears.

"Dad, let me have a go at the slobbering milksop."

"No son, he is beaten worse than the others, for his mettle has been stripped, and he is no more than a capon." Then there are none.

We step back to survey the carnage lying about on the forest floor. The first, the one that Dad unloaded on with a ponderous right, is trying to sit up. He is vainly trying to hold his sagging body up by propping with one hand. He holds the other over his battered nose, and the blood flows freely through the cracks of his cup-formed hand. It forms a stinking pool of dried and fresh blood that stains the freshness of the leaf-covered ground.

The second, the one that felt the crushing power of my bear hug, lies on his back, appearing none the worse for his trouble, but the odd angle of the bones pushing up against the skin is a dead giveaway of broken ribs. In addition, he is still gasping for breath, and foamy spittle rolls from the corners of his mouth, giving the appearance of a crazed lunatic.

The third, the one that hit Dad's fist with his jaw, is lying in a crumpled heap, his jaw having taken on a bizarre shape, so brutal was the lick. Several teeth are scattered hither and yon in a haphazard manner around the body as further evidence, if any be needed, of the force of one of Dad's blows.

The fourth is still in a rolled-up fetal position, incoherently carrying on, gurgling strangely from the mouth like some wild thing that has been caught in a trapper's snare.

Here they lie, a-moaning, groaning, and a-crying in their own misery, experiencing just a little bit of the torment they have afflicted on others, but try as I might, I can feel no sympathy. I still have an uneasiness, a nagging uncertainty, a something that seems to be saying, "Jim, finish them off, for if you don't, you'll regret it." However, I know better than to even broach the idea to Dad, for he is entirely through and through a fair man.

"Son, are you all right?" Dad asks.

"Yes," I reply. "Just scratched up a little bit, but I would'a been a goner without you. What about you, Dad?"

"No, I'm okay; tomorrow may find me touchy and sore, but I can say none the worse for wear and tear. Son, I don't know of anybody I'd rather have backing me in a fight." This coming from a real fightin' man, now that is heady praise.

"The same back, Dad."

67

"Put 'er there Son; you'll do in a pinch, you're a man among men." Dad reaches out his big callused hand, the hand that has held a plow stock firm and true, and shakes mine, man-to-man. I have crossed over the threshold. I now am a man. I know I am, 'cause my dad said so!

"Son, let's go home. Mom will have supper ready, and I've worked up quite an appetite." We turn homeward. Though the trail is narrow in places, we walk side by side, my dad and me, as father and son, man-to-man. Today I prove myself to the person I had rather impress more than anyone in the whole wide world, my dad! On this day I silently reaffirm my commitment to my dad, to back him "to the ends of the earth" if it be necessary, and vow again if any harm ever comes to this "Saint of God," I will seek satisfaction over and over and over again. Little did I realize what the future held.

The atmosphere at the supper table is different from the pall of gloom that prevailed at breakfast. The laughter, the merriment, the good-natured joshing, the rehashing of the day's events—the ingredients that come together to form the heart of a happy table have returned. The spell of doom has been cast asunder, removed by mine and Dad's flailing fists. Mainly Dad's, but to hear him tell it, I am the hero. I know better; however, I don't protest all that much, offering up a feeble "Aw shucks," for praise of me by Dad is heady stuff. That is Dad the way he is, quiet, unassuming, always putting the feelings of others over his.

After we all eat a belly-filling meal, Dad says, "Let's go down to Virge Waldroup's store. Mom needs a few provisions, and I'll get a little liniment to put on the places that are bound to be sore. I'm sure it's no secret as to what the real intentions of the Yellow Mountain boys were, and it'll be good to let the neighbors know that you came out all right."

We walk into the store, and Virge greets us in a neighborly fashion, as is typical. "Howdy John and Jim. What can I do for you?"

"Virge, we need a few victuals and a dab of some good healing liniment," Dad answers.

"I've had a run on aid supplies the last little bit. You don't look like you need them that bad, but from the amount bought by my last customer, now he must'a been a-goin' to try and patch up a battered bunch," Virge says and winks knowingly.

"Yeah, I understand some local fellows got too big for their britches and was a-trying to 'sack wildcats,' but the sack came loose," Dad answers.

"From what I can gather, they musta had ahold of some mighty big ones," Virge says.

"Virge, you might be right, and the big one might just be here," replies Dad.

"I thought as much; sure does make you proud to be the father of such a stalwart young man, doesn't it John?"

"That's for sure Virge; he does me and the rest of the Lances proud." I pretend not to hear; however, my chest swells in satisfied appreciation just the same, looking, I'm certain, like the strutted bag of our cow before she freshens.

On the way back home, when we come to the trail leading to the Henson place, I say, "Dad, I think I'll go over and see Jane for a minute."

"Sure Son, go ahead. Jane is a mighty fine young lady, and I remember how it was with me and your ma." I can tell Mom and Dad have talked about Jane and me, and they approve. This means a lot to me, for though I think I love Jane, at this stage in our courting, if Mom and Dad didn't approve, it wouldn't be. Such is my love for my parents.

Though I am a man, and a big man at that, I leave Dad and step lightly, my size elevens barely touching the ground, my heart pounding, skipping beats, in eager anticipation of seeing Jane. There is some sort of premonition between people in love; they care, hurt, love, and sense things before they happen, and that is the way it is with Jane and me. I cover the distance in record time and find Jane at the gate waiting, and this reminds me of the many times I have seen Mom wait on Dad.

On many occasions, I've seen Dad open up his Bible and read I Corinthians 13:4-8, "Love suffereth long, and is kind; love envieth not; love vaunteth not itself, is not puffed up, Doth not behave itself unseemly, seeketh not her own, is not easily provoked, thinketh no evil; Rejoiceth not in iniquity, but rejoiceth in the truth; Beareth all things, believeth all things, hopeth all things, endureth all things. Love never faileth." This is true love, the love spoken of in God's Holy Book, the kind Dad has for Mom, the kind I want for Jane and me.

Jane opens the gate and flings herself into my arms. "Jim, you're all right! I was so scared for you. Tell me what happened?" We sit there in the yard, under the cooling branches of a big white oak. The gentle breezes waft down from Ben's Knob, and I tell her about the occurrings that transpired a few hours previously. I feel so at ease around Jane. She has a way about her that brings out the best in others that she touches, and now she has touched me in a special way.

After a few minutes of sweet solitude with Jane, for time passes so swiftly when I am with her, I say, "Jane, I must get on home; night will soon be getting here."

"Jim, I wish you didn't have to go. Will you be at school tomorrow?"

"Maybe," I answer, trying not to appear too anxious, but I wouldn't have missed it atall. "Good-bye Jane."

"Good-bye Jim. I'll see you tomorrow if you are at school."

I turn slowly and start home, looking back every now and then and whistling a happy tune, for these are again happy days in Choestoe.

Chapter VIII

THE CELEBRATION

Sometimes, when you walk alone, and I am a good walker because of years of practice, the pendulum in God's clock of eternity seems to swing slower and slower, making a walking trek a work of labor, but not this time, for the walk home passes quickly. I am preoccupied, daydreaming about an idyllic life spent with Jane. As I draw nearer home, my view being somewhat obscured by the shank of a steep ridge as it presses near, almost abutting the very edge of Lance Creek, I hear a loud commotion coming from what sounds like our front yard. My daydreaming abruptly stops. My heart pounds in nervous anticipation, and my pace quickens. Surely another catastrophe hasn't befallen our family, for we most assuredly have suffered enough the past months to last a lifetime. However, have we suffered as much as we are going to?

My home comes into view, and I see a gathered crowd. A haunting realization sweeps through my mind, bringing with it a dread and an apprehension, for I know that a gathered crowd usually signals one of two things. First, that a party is in progress, celebrating a happy event, an occasion of some sort, but I know of nothing that has happened lately worthy of such a gathering. I quickly pass this fleeting apparition by. Then a feeling of real despair descends upon me as I realize what the second could be, and my shoulders sag. Death, the by-product of the "Grim Reaper," will bring out a crowd like the one I see, some out of idle curiosity, others because of genuine concern for the bereaved family. Could death have visited the confines of Lance Cove while I was at Jane's and snatched Mom or one of my brothers or sisters? Surely not—Dad and I have only been gone a short time; however, I remember Dad reading from the Bible, "We know not the hour nor the place," and I rush on.

Drawing nigh, I begin to recognize who they are—our clan of kin. There is my granddad Samuel; Dad's brothers, James, Andy, and Debarris; and John Frady, who married Dad's sister Harriet. I am hailed loudly by my granddad, "Hurry up Jim, time's a-wasting. What took you so long, as if I didn't know?"

"Come on big Jim, the party's just beginning," says Debarris.

I slowly open the yard gate and ask, "What kind of party?"

"The party celebrating the way you and John tended to that Yellow Mountain bunch," says John Frady.

"Whew, you had me worried for a minute there; I thought somebody might'a died," I answer.

James, my uncle for whom I was named, adds, "From what I hear, that worthless bunch of curs are not apt to raise their ugly heads again any time soon. Jim, I'm proud you are named after me."

Andy chimes in, "I understand you and John made a hell of a fighting pair."

"Now, now Andy, let's not use profanity in front of the ladyfolks," Dad says.

"Well it's true, ain't it?" Andy replies, and Dad grins in amused satisfaction, for it is true.

Dad speaks up, and when he does, everyone listens, not because he is family or a preacher, but because everyone respects him, for he is a man, and a just man at that. There is always much substance in what he says. "We're all family. We're in this together because we are family. We'll cry together, for when you harm any one of us, you've harmed the rest us, for we are kin, blood kin."

The men of our clan, all except Dad and his boys, go down by the creek where a jug of moonshine is secretly stashed and have communion with this floater of imaginary dreams. Evidently the counsel it gives is to lighten up and live life to the fullest, for tomorrow may never come, because the party roars on, growing louder and louder.

Now you may think this is "two-faced," Dad letting the others drink and carry on like this at his house, especially with him being a "sower of the seed," but it's not when you know Dad and the kind of person he is.

It is not strange for every mountain family, including the most sanctimonious, saintly deacon, to have in his house or have ready access to whiskey, of course for medicinal purposes only. This is just a fact of life, a tradition of sorts passed on down to us by our forerunners, helping them to better cope with the hardships of mountain living.

Don't get me wrong; Dad doesn't approve of drinking by his family or neighbors, for he remembers how it is. He remembers the many times when he was younger and "feeling his oats," partaking freely of the readily-available, free-flowing moonshine, how the sparkling clear, innocent-looking potion freed his tongue and made him feel stronger, wiser, and more invincible than he really was. He remembers the countless times he was involved in knock-down-drag-outs, and the patches of skin uselessly scraped loose, the muscles needlessly abused, all because of the effects of a fickle, so-called friend. Oh, Dad won the fights, but is there ever a true winner in any fight?

When he was called to be a messenger of God, he eternally railed at this vice, pointing out its dangers in practically every sermon he preached, exposing it for what it really is—a polluting tool of the devil. However, Dad will never turn anyone in if they choose to bootleg or drink, for that is not the type of person he is. Yes, Dad wants to see changes in others, but not because of harsh, hell-threatening consequences, for he prefers a more permanent change brought about by example.

After several hours of celebrating a victory brought about because a wrong has occurred against one of our own, Debarris says, "Men, we've partied long enough; it's time we go home, but there's still one thing sticking in my craw. The rest of us didn't get in any licks. What say we swing by the Yellow Mountain boys' places on our way home, leave them our calling card, dare them to come out, let 'em fully realize that no matter what happens, we'll stick together."

Dad again speaks up, saying, "Go by if you want; you have a right to, for we all were wronged, but don't get into trouble by doing anything foolish."

In most gatherings, even in a mob—and if I were on the other side, this crowd could rightly be called a mob—there is a leader, a man that commands, yes, demands respect. Dad is such a man. He has a natural grasp of what needs to be done. The commonplace saying "cream rises to the top" can be used when it comes to Dad, for when he speaks, others listen. Just a few words from him defuses a situation that might have become touchy because a wrong has been done, magnified further by the steeping of this injustice in liberal portions of corn whiskey.

Granddad Samuel, the first Lance to come to these parts, who came to settle a wrong for a friend and still maintains a fiery, combative attitude, replies, "We'll behave Son, but we'll rub a little salt in the wound, lest they forget. They opened up this can of worms. We shore didn't, but now we're going to fish with them."

They go off into the night with Granddad in the lead, heading home, but not directly, for first a side trip is to be made.

About thirty minutes later, arising from behind a ridge that splits our cove from Fed Fields lying underneath Yellow Mountain, a barrage of shots, yells, and shouts can be faintly heard. The noise penetrates the stillness of the night, sounding like the hue and cry of a mighty battle, but it is one-sided, for there is no answering volley. It continues for several minutes and then abruptly subsides, being swallowed up by the serious quietness of our noble mountains.

If you assume that a liberal sprinkling of salt has been rubbed into the wound, you assume correctly, and the pent-up ferocity of a proud family has been somewhat eased.

I awake Tuesday morning to the persistent crowing of our rooster, Mother Nature's alarm clock, and stay in the bed for a while, reminiscing about yesterday's happenings and events that covered every range of my emotions. I have faced evil. I looked death square in the eye and spit in its face with the help of Dad. I've gone from a boy to a man. I've felt the love of a beautiful young lady and been shown unfathomable care by the Lance clan. As my world is, more or less, confined in scope to the Choestoe valley, and since it is able to provide aptly for my limited needs, what more can a young man ask for?

74

I jerk out of bed, despite no little protest from my sore body, and go to the kitchen. If we are the winners, and I know we are, for we were the ones left standing at the end of the fracas, why then am I so sore and feel achy all over? I think of the defeated malcontents and feel a brief tang of pity, for I know how they must be feeling. I felt the same way months before; however, the pang of guilt vanishes almost as quickly as it has arisen. A shortcoming of the Lances and mine, I suppose, is an inability ever to forget. I know I should be forgiving, but I can't, for it's just born and bred in me, and I will loathe their very names until the day I die.

Chapter IX

THE BOLD PLAN

"Son, we were going to let you sleep in today because you still aren't fully healed," Mom says. I reply, like the scholar I'm not, "Guess I had better go on back to school and get what little learning I can." Now, I am not in the least interested in school—Mom and Dad know that I'm not. I only attend to appease them, but today you couldn't have hog-tied me and kept me at home.

I cover the trip from home to the Wild Boar Institute in record time. I'll admit my keenness for attending today isn't brought about because of a sudden fondness of scholarly pursuits, but rather to test the reactions of the other students. Before, I was looked up to as some sort of a hero; I imagine I will be more so now. What red-blooded mountain boy doesn't secretly covet being looked up to, doesn't like to be the center of attention, especially around the young maidens. Why, that's what makes us do the silly things we do. I can find nothing at all unusual about this. It has occurred from time immemorial and will continue to do so as long as there is the ritual of boy winning girl.

I stride into the schoolyard, and the greetings I receive startle even me. I am hailed as a conquering hero, met with shouts of "Here he is! Good job, Jim!" Why, a crowd even gathers around me. I am getting plenty of attention and yes, I like it. Sir Lancelot in King Arthur's Knights of the Round Table wouldn't have been received any better, and why not? Hadn't Dad and I disposed of the dragons that live 'neath the

Yellow Mountain, who have been a curse upon our peaceful valley for years? The dragons aren't slain yet, but they would have been if it hadn't been for Dad and his total fairness. I wonder about the wisdom of Dad's decision, but he won't have it any other way, for he believes in live and let live.

At recess and dinner, the scenario repeats itself. Now, Jane seems to enjoy the laudation I am getting as much as I do, at least for a while, for it is commonly understood that we belong to each other. However, when the other young ladies begin to pay a lot of attention to me, Jane lets her jealousy show. Oh, I enjoy every minute of it, playing it to the fullest, for Jane reminds me of a mocking bird, shooing away predators.

Saying I disrupt school would be kinda like saying, "Bald Mountain is a big mountain." The schoolmaster doesn't seem to mind for a while, but he soon tires of the students' lack of attention. He reminds me and the other students what the real purpose of school is by asking me a question. I search every nook and cranny of my head for an answer and can't come up with one, so I get to stand in the corner for my trouble.

It is while I am in the stupid corner that I come to realize what the teacher has already picked up on. I am too old for school, not interested anyway, and I will be better off by dropping out of school and getting on with my life. Anyway, how much interest can the ordinary adding of simple sums and the dull spelling of words out of the *Blue Back Speller* muster up when you have faced Satan's legions, looked into the fiery pits of Hell itself, and emerged victorious?

However, I can't just up and quit school; that isn't the Lance way of doing things, for we aren't quitters, never have been, never will be. When we take ahold of something, we won't let go; we hold on with dogged determination. This trait has been brought about because of living a life of struggling for survival. It isn't that we suffer from hunger or are dirt-poor; we aren't and weren't—but it is because of Mom and Dad that we aren't. They are overachievers, hard workers, and planners who want us to have it easier and better than they did, just like their parents who wanted the same for them.

As of late, I'm beginning to better understand Dad and what he means when he says, "The blood coursing through my veins is the blood of my ancestors, and we're in this together." The very traits that made his father and mother, and their father and mother, Lances are in him, and these same traits, some good, others bad, are in me and will be passed on to future Lances. The good traits are nurtured and cultivated by our parents, we hope leaving no room for bad traits to take root. I pray no event will ever occur that will cause the bad to flourish at the expense of the good. Peter, my great, great, great grandfather, who came from Germany, though he has been dead for many years and his temporal body turned into dust, still lives through Dad and me. It's kinda eerie but comforting, for we are not ourselves, but small parts of our ancestors.

Therefore, a plan has to be thought of and implemented, whereby I don't quit on my own, but am forced to by being expelled. A lot of others have tried, but the schoolmaster is wise in the ways of students, and he won't be forced into making a hasty decision.

Remember, at this period of time in the mountains, there isn't that much emphasis put on educational matters, and getting expelled isn't looked at as being a dishonorable occurrence. In fact, the expelled student is kinda looked up to as a role model, signifying that a manly, daring act has been done, and the expellee has advanced from boyish pursuits to more manly undertakings.

This getting the schoolmaster to do a job for you, one that you want done but because of your raising can't do yourself, calls for an ingenious, imaginative plan, not just any old plan, but one befitting a proud family. I am entirely through and through a Lance. Therefore, I go on to school, don't miss a day, and think and think about a plan. Two weeks pass and still no realistic plan shows itself. Oh, some trite plans do; however, they are too simple to even think of trying on our teacher, for he has been subjected to many schemes in his years of teaching.

I am beginning to doubt my own abilities, doubt my own intelligence, beginning to have serious questions as to whether I have the brains to solve any problem, much less one requiring raw thinking ability.

We Lances, at this time, aren't noted for our scholarly attributes. We lean more toward what we perceive to be more honorable occupations, like looking after our own and fighting. We have never been called dumb, certainly not to our face, for if we were then we would revert back to the occupation that we think to be more honorable and bloody your nose. Hadn't Dad, with the help of a neighbor, taught himself to read? Hadn't Dad figured out a way to get water from the spring to the house by hewing out logs and connecting them? The water would then run down the logs, thereby saving Mom a lot of work. This accomplishment I know isn't big enough to change the course of history, but nevertheless it is big to my mom. Anyway, I don't believe a man lacking in smartness could have done it. Isn't it logical then to come to the conclusion that since my blood is Dad's blood, surely then I can't be all that dumb?

While I am absorbed with thoughts about the running water Dad rigged up, it brought to mind that I had seen about the same thing at Clark Dyer's, and to the best of my knowledge, the Dyers and we were among the first to have readily available running water. This recollection of my trip home with Clark Dyer's son causes me to remember how Mr. Dyer watched the soaring buzzards and solved the mysteries of flight by turning to nature for answers.

Since Mother Nature helped him to be the first man to fly, wouldn't it behoove me to do no less, to turn to her for an answer and listen and watch? I've heard Dad, so many times, caution us to heed, listen, live, and never violate her, for if we do these things, she will provide shelter, food, and solace. Therefore, I do.

On Thursday of the third week, on the way home from another hot, boring day spent at the Wild Boar Institute, a yellow jacket darts down, buzzing me in a threatening manner. I stop to swat at it and notice a multitude of them, persistently busy flying in and out of a hole. This brings to mind the time my brothers and some neighbor boys and me found a nest of yellow jackets. We cut branches and futilely attempted to beat them out, failing in a multitude of angry stings.

Then an idea—yes! A brilliant one begins to gather in the upper portions of my head, wafting from one chamber to the next, finally floating into being in the form of a plan of action.

This is it, a way to change water into wine, a surefire way to get expelled and at the same time garner more fame. Why, probably in years to come, when deeds of bravery and acts of notoriety are thought of, my act of pure brilliance will be remembered for what it is—an act of pure intelligence.

My bold plan calls for me getting to the school before anyone, especially the teacher. I get up earlier than usual and slip into Mom's can house to borrow a glass jar that has a tapered neck. When I am out of sight of home, I pull out my eternal companion, my sharp knife, and whittle out a wood stopper that exactly fits the opening in the jar. My next stop is at the yellow jackets' nest. I place the jar over their hole, hold the glass jar firmly, for the jackets aren't a bit particular as to whom they sting, and stomp around the nest. A horde of rushing, decidedly angry yellow jackets comes forth, and they are furiously stinging the sides of the jar. After catching an ample supply of yellow action, I quickly ram the stopper into the jar, sealing off their escape route, and speed on to school.

I arrive at the school and elatedly find that I am the first one there. If you recall, the school was built in a somewhat careless manner, and rocks were piled up and used for a foundation. This raises the floor level better than two feet. This enables anyone to be able to slide under the floor without any difficulties, but this is a no-no, strictly enforced by our stern taskmaker. I have noticed that strategically located, for my purpose, next to his desk is a hole where a knot fell from the green lumber when it dried. I slide under this ark look-alike and put the finishing touches on my grandiose plan. The rocks used to support the jar are placed one on top of the other so the jar when put in place will fit snugly against the hole. The stopper is tapped until it is flush with the mouth of the jar. All I have to do to activate this yellow lightning is to pick up the jar; give it a good country shaking, making the jackets real mad; tap the stopper once, thereby causing it to fall to the bottom of the jar; and rush back into the schoolroom without anyone seeing me.

I know that the teacher will be suspicious if he arrives at school and I am the first one there. I have never been early, so I walk back down the path and slip into the underbrush, letting nature conceal me.

You might be wondering why I am so secretive, if I want to be expelled anyway. Well, if my plan is picked up on before it is fully carried out, I won't receive the full honor such a brilliant idea merits. What's the use of doing a thing if you can't garner the credit? However, what if the plan is so perfect in nature and carried out to such perfection that the schoolmaster can't discover who the perpetrator is? Well, I know that is most unlikely because he has been subjected to many tricks in his teaching life. Anyway, the schoolmaster will be determined to find the culprit, for if he doesn't, he will lose stature in the eyes of the other students, and he will be asking prying questions. If he asks me, I'll not lie but tell the truth, for I've been taught that "nothing fits like the truth."

I wait until the rest of the Wolf Creek bunch comes by and stay hidden a few minutes more, giving them plenty of time to get to school before me. Then I saunter out of my hiding place and trudge on up the trail, barely getting to school before the classes start. Jane meets me and asks, "Where have you been, Jim? We waited and waited for you, but were afraid to wait any longer lest we be tardy for school."

"It's all right," I answer, "I had to do more work this morning than usual," which is the truth. I don't find it necessary to tell what kind of work I was doing.

Recess rolls around and as usual, the schoolyard is filled with clamoring students of all ages, each one trying to drown out the other by fully exercising their lungs. The time is at hand to bring into action the fruition of my ideas: "The Plan." Just before recess is over, I excuse myself from the others by saying, "I've got to get a drink," and I start toward the spring, hiding instead in the woods a short distance from the yard.

I hear the irritating dingdong of the bell, see the schoolmaster standing in the door, and watch as the other students rush toward the door, a-shoving and a-pushing all the while. I dart out of the woods, slide 'neath the floor, grab the jar of jackets, and give them a sharp shake. I tap the stopper, place the jar against the hole, and slither out from 'neath the floor. I rush back into the classroom and in my haste knock over my desk. The schoolmaster, the possessor of a caustic, rapier-sharp tongue, sarcastically says, "Jim, we all know you are an avid student. I know the rest of the students feel honored, even privileged, you've seen fit to grace us with your presence. However, I know of no reason for you to make such a debacle of yourself." Most of the students laugh, and the schoolmaster chuckles, proud of his wit aimed at me. I become angry and think, poke fun at me, you old buzzard, but let's see if you're laughing in a minute.

Then almost as the thought came, I hear an angry buzzing coming from the hole located next to his desk. I see the caustic-tongued teacher start swatting, slowly at first, then with a furious urgency, emitting cries of "Oh, Ouch, Oh, Dang" as the yellow thunder zooms in on him. They are holding him personally responsible for their torment, stinging him with ferocious delight. The students add to the confusion of the moment, not because they are getting stung, but because they are following the lead of their venerable teacher, who leads them screaming out of the room. Some of the students escape through the door, while others find it necessary to exit through raised windows. They all gather in the yard in a mass of confused, hollering humanity.

The plan works to perfection, and I feel good.

I turn away from the babbling confusion and start home. Before I get out of sight, I hear the incensed teacher shouting, "Jim! Jim Lance! You're expelled!"

I mutter to no one in particular, "I thought as much." I wave back to acknowledge that I hear, not giving him the courtesy of even turning around, and I leave the school to him and the yellow jackets.

Thus ends my foray into the field of scholarly matters.

Chapter X

START OF A NEW LIFE

What the future holds for me is uncertain, but I am eagerly waiting to start another chapter in my life. Moreover, I certainly hope the pages are filled with me and Jane, for that is what we both dream of, but life is filled with so many uncertainties. I've heard the best-laid plans of man often go astray, and I've seen it happen so many times that I somewhat believe it, but like Dad says, "Plan for the future, for without planning there is no tomorrow."

Therefore, Jane and I court and plan, dreaming idyllic dreams of a life together filled with complete happiness, lacking hardships and suffering. Young love and lovers are like this, and it is good they are, for to face reality completely might turn their dreams of sunny days into nights replete with thunder and lightning and governed by hordes of evil demons. But we don't have to worry about demons, for we have each other and our families and a merciful God that will tend to our needs.

Jane and I don't marry quickly. She wants to, and so do I, to be honest about it, but that's not the Lance way. I am, after all, a Lance, through and through. We believe marriage is a serious proposition and not to be entered into lightly. The head of the family should have enough means to support his bride and at least own a mule, for Dad says, "A mule is worth at least five acres of good bottomland." Now, don't think for a minute our families, Jane's and mine, wouldn't help us out in the "lean years"; they would, and gladly, but that wouldn't be right. They have enough hard work to just sustain all of us, and adding two more mouths to the mix would only increase their workload. I know you're already saying to yourself, "There would be no more mouths to feed"; however, Jane and I have crossed that bridge. We want plenty of children, for we love each other so much and want the same warm relationship that Mom and Dad have, a love that is not ashamed to be shown outwardly as well as inwardly.

I realize that the harder and longer I work, the quicker we can fulfill our love, so I light in working with a zeal that even amazes Dad, and he is hard to impress. I continue to help him because that is the right thing to do; after all, I am still at home partaking of Mom's delicious meals. However, when Dad doesn't need me, I look for work elsewhere.

I find that getting a job isn't that hard of a proposition, even though jobs are as scarce as hen's teeth. I was taught to give an honest day's work for an honest day's pay; our neighbors know that and that I am not afraid of work, hence they aren't a bit hesitant about hiring me, though I am still fairly young. Virge Waldroup is especially good to me, I imagine, because he likes my dad and is appreciative of the way I can easily muscle a hundred-pound sack of feed from the wagon into the store.

Citizens from other sections of the county see me working at Virge's store, notice that I am not at all allergic to work, and before long, I find myself getting work in Owltown, Coosa, and Arkaquah. This necessitates a long walk to and from the job, but when you are in love and have set a goal for yourself, why, this is viewed as just another opportunity to reach it quicker. Even though I have a definite goal emblazoned into my mind and desperately need money, there are some jobs done because it is the neighborly thing to do. I remember the many times I cut and haul wood for Aunt Cindy and feel good because of it. Doesn't the Bible teach us to look after the orphans, widows, and the less fortunate? It's just the right thing to do.

Some people have very little stick-ability, and find it hard to stay focused on a stated purpose for any appreciable length of time. Now, that's not like me, for when I set my mind and aim for something, I don't quit, come hell or high water. Why, I'll just grit my teeth, grip the plow handle harder, step closer to my mule, and plow on with dogged determination. If I tell you I'm a-goin' to do something, then I'm a-goin' to do it, no matter the time it takes. This trait is one thread woven into the fabric of my very being, and it mysteriously combines with the other threads, forming my framework, making me who I am, a distinct individual, yet uncommonly like my ancestors.

Four years later, to the surprise of some, I have managed to save fifty dollars and own a fine mule colt. I now have the means to provide for Jane in a decent manner.

Therefore, on November 7, 1883, our dream is brought to fruition by the exchanging of our wedding vows in a simple ceremony at her family home. As I kiss my new wife, I notice Mom and Dad standing quietly. A tear slowly trickles down Mom's face, and Dad gingerly reaches for her hand, holding it lovingly in comfort as only Dad can. No matter their age, when one of your offspring flies the coop and goes it on his own, there is some sadness, but it's tempered with gladness, for the union holds forth the promise of a new beginning, a new life, and opportunities created through the consummation of their love. I am twenty-two, and Jane is nineteen.

Our first home is little more than a shack when viewed in the vernacular of others' homes, but we don't care; we are young, in love, facing a bright future. After all, isn't a man's home his castle? Well, this is our home, and it is a castle to us, meager though it may be. It only has two rooms: a bedroom and a kitchen-parlor combination with hard-packed red clay for a floor. I have already promised Jane that my first project will be to build a front porch, because the house is situated in a pretty place alongside the banks of the Nottely River, about two hundred yards upstream from whence Choestoe Creek flows into the river. From the porch, you will be able to see and hear the whitecapping of the water as it splashes and roars across a natural outcropping of partially submerged mountain rocks, creating a cool breeze even on the hottest days.

We rent our little hovel and twenty acres of rich bottomland from Mr. and Mrs. Jim Allison, Jane's aunt and uncle, in exchange for me helping him work his fields. Blood is indeed thicker than water, and yes, we got a sweetheart of a deal, but isn't that the way it ought to be? Shouldn't kin look after their own? Why sure; that's just the natural progression of a caring family. Anyway, so I hear later, Mr. Jim said that was the best deal he ever struck because I made him more clear money than anyone he ever rented to.

So this is the honeymoon cabin where I take Jane, the place our love is finalized, the place we become as one, and the place that is home to us for several years. However, let me hasten to add, the simplicity of an ordinary shack is blotted out by the mere presence of Jane and her diligent work, 'cause she has for months been preparing, adding the special female touch that transforms the ordinary into the extraordinary.

If you stand at our house and look back toward Blood Mountain, as the crow flies, then Lance Cove and Mom and Dad will be about two miles distant and Jane's folks about three-fourths of a mile. Looking to my right and about one-half mile away is where my granddad, Sam, and my grandmom, Rebecca, live. Debarris lives across the road, and two hundred yards further down is Andy's place. I know this is of no concern to most people, but it is to us, for we are a close-knit family and intend to stay that way.

To the uninformed, it might appear that November 7 is a mighty odd time to be getting married. Everybody knows winter is tough sledding, and it is all a feller can do to keep body and soul together. I imagine the gossipy sisters are talking and expecting a woods colt in seven months or so. They better not let me hear this, or somebody will answer to me, for I have pledged to protect Jane's honor and that of my family with every bit of strength I can muster up. This is just the day that Jane and I set. It is the day the culmination of our work and dreams seems to point to and to come together in a planned pattern; hence November 7.

The tough sledding is avoided, not by some mysterious miracle, but by our preparation. Dad and I have mended the shed till it is in usable condition for the mule. We have cut and stacked enough fire and stove wood to last two years and have dug a cellar big enough to hold hundreds of cans and bushels of potatoes. The job of filling the cellar falls to Jane, and she doesn't shirk her duty. She cans beans, pickles, corn, kraut, beets, and hominy; strings leather britches; dries fruits; and makes jelly and jam from the wild fruits. She also finds and uses other mountain foods too numerous to mention, till the larder is strutted with these delicacies.

The first year of our marriage is as I have dreamed, and more. The joy of being continually with the one I love cannot be expressed by mere words. In the winter while fieldwork is slow, I build the porch as I promise, so Jane can enjoy it come spring, for she is expecting. I know that she will continue to work as hard as ever preparing for the next winter, even though she will be experiencing the rigors of carrying our child. Therefore, I want to provide a place where she can rest and be cool.

On a cold January night in the year of our Lord 1885, with a thousand stars bearing witness, our first child is born. Jane's mother and my mom serve as the midwives, and they are there helping Jane through all of the night-piercing screams that echo strangely upon Nottely's peaceful waters. The birthing of the first child is the most difficult. Even the nocturnal animals seem to recognize this, and they are quiet, providing an eerie stillness as the battle rages back and forth between life and death. I wage my own battle and secretly promise that Jane will never, ever suffer again like this. I pace and walk, making at least a thousand trips around our house, trying without success to halt the pent-up nervousness that wells up inside of me. That I failed is evident by the many times I open the door and ask, "How's Jane faring?"

Two hours later Jane's screams abruptly stop, and the little cabin reverberates with glorious shouts, mixed with the shrill cry of our newborn. I race into the cabin, almost removing the door from its leather hinges, so great is my haste, and behold new life, not just any new life, but life brought forth because of me and Jane. I see and hold our new baby girl for the first time, but it is not to be.

The thrill that we both feel is only temporary, for our new creation, our new life, our beloved baby, passes from us within the week and goes to be with the Heavenly Father, forever and ever.

Jane and I are both despondent, but she is even more so, for the seed of life that she carefully nurtured has been so quickly snatched, when it held forth much promise. We ask, "What terrible sin have we committed that caused the Heavenly Father to take her from us?" Dad provides the answer: "Everything works for good for those who trust in the Lord." Then we can see and are able to deal with the situation, fully realizing that our darling is in a better place, singing songs of happiness in an eternal Heaven.

It is comforting to Jane and me to think that our angel is one of the stars that gloriously fill God's sky, and now she too will bear witness unto us.

A few days later, I tell Jane of my secret promise, never again to put her through the tribulation of childbirth. She scoffs at me not in a manner of ridicule, but in a way to let me know that she will have none of that, for we both want a large family. This tragic experience in no way will deter her from being a fruitful wife.

Three months pass and Jane and I are blest when she finds she is with child. Experiencing the highs and lows that oft go with motherhood is bothersome for any woman, but Jane holds up like a seasoned veteran. She is determined to be a fit vessel and pass the Lance lineage forward with dignity.

So once again, on January 31, 1886, under the almost exact set of circumstances, Jane goes into labor. Now instead of one thousand stars bearing witness, there are one thousand and one. Her labor is easier, her contractions not as protracted, as if this time she has a special angel watching over her, and I too am strangely calm.

The calmness of the night is shattered by a fierce cry. I rush in and behold my son. He is vigorously protesting the sharp slap administered by Mom to his naked bottom. He is firmly dried off with warm blankets to stimulate his circulation and carefully placed in Jane's arms. The gentle touch of Jane's body against his and the warm milk flowing through his body brings peace. He stops crying, forgetting forever the difficulties he had in getting here, and a special bonding takes place. I am there to witness it, a bonding between mother and child that is so strong that no force can ever breach its strength. This then is what we hear of and sing about, "a mother's love," and it is priceless, not fully understood, but it still stands, thank God, as a bulwark in civilization's continual struggle for survival.

Our child is born under a "lucky star," and we proudly name him Thomas Jackson Lance. We daily find new joy, and now that Jack is part of our lives, we find that our main focus and concern has recentered toward him. Oh, the self-gratification of being parents is extraordinary, and the comfort and pleasure that he gives us can't be measured. Just to be there when he cries, loves, and learns new things will forever be etched in our minds. And now we are beginning to better understand what God had in mind when he commanded, "Be fruitful, and multiply."

All is peaceful in our neck of the woods, with everyone being in harmony and fellowship as God planned. Why, even the Yellow Mountain people seem to have fallen in line and are following the Golden Rule. Dad thinks they have, and if they have, it just makes for better living conditions for all concerned. I know the Lances are willing to let bygones be bygones, but I still have a nagging feeling about the Yellow Mountain bunch.

But in the last few days, I've come to believe that indeed our community is living in harmony and fellowship. And yes, the Yellow Mountain bunch may have forsaken their old roguish ways and fallen in line with the other citizens, creating an almost ideal living condition in our little valley. Why, yesterday Tom Swaim[3] came to Dad and asked him if he will marry his son, Frank. Dad of course agreed, and the next day he performed the ceremony, uniting Frank Swaim and his first cousin Mattie Swaim as husband and wife. The rest of the Yellow Mountain bunch was there, and everything went as smooth as silk. There was no mention of the previous encounter, but I wonder, can a leopard change his spots? Can a camel pass through the eye of a needle?

I still see Mom and Dad two or three times a week. Though I'm quite busy looking after Jane and Jack and sometimes am mighty tired, I make it a point to check on them, for I'll never forget what they've done for me, and I love them so. Anyway, it's a sorry piece of plunder that can't find time to look after his own family. I have yet to go back to Lance Cove and find Mom and Dad resting; they can't, for there is still a big brood of Lances that haven't yet gone it on their own. But if Mom and Dad could rest, I doubt they would, for there is not a lazy bone in their bodies. Mary, Lafayette (Fate), Sara, Jane, and myself have married, but

[3]Over the ensuing years, the name Swaim is gradually changed to Swain, so either is correct and interchangeable. This variation was chosen for the sake of consistency.

Joe, Rutha, Dora Lee, Anna, John, and Nancy remain at home. This is 1887; Dad is fifty-two, and Mom is forty-four.

The days have come and gone without any serious glitches, creating a routine of normality where time flies, and isn't this how it should be in a perfect world?

Our feeling of fulfilling God's command is further intensified in September 1888, when Juan[4] Bascom Lance sees the light of day and joins his brother Jack, who is now two-and-a-half years old, in the Lance household.

I can't find an appreciable difference in the workload with two more mouths to feed, but Jane can. She won't say so, but I know it to be. So, in an effort to provide her and our new children with a little more comfort, I buy lumber and floor our little house. For floors, red clay is mighty uncomfortable when the temperature drops to freezing and the north wind starts howling its cold, desolate song.

We awake the morning of December 10, 1888, to find the ground covered with a mighty big snow. It has to be in excess of a foot deep, for it is level with the porch, which stands a foot or more off the ground. Jane and I stand at the window and look out in awe at this spectacle of nature. For it is as white as angel wings and lies in level perfection upon Choestoe's plowed fields, creating a saintly illusion, an illusion so pure that surely neither Lucifer nor his legions will dare defile. How anyone can gaze upon this creation of nature and not see the working of a higher being is a mystery, for beauty such as this cannot be formed by mortal man.

This is an unexpected gift from God, for when we went to bed the sky was crystal clear; not a cloud could be seen, and a full moon, the long night moon,[5] cast a pale light, partially illuminating the fodder stacks that stand in the bottom looking like a sleeping Indian village. That this snow or any snow is a gift from God is sure, for another thing I've heard Dad say over and over is that "a snow is worth a good coat of fertilizer." I don't know the how's and why's, but I've seen the results too many times

[4]Pronounced Jew-an in the mountains at this time, thought to have been derived from Desota after he came through Union County on his explorations.

[5]So called by the Indians, for they recognized and knew that in December the nights were much longer.

not to believe it. Maybe the snow just warms the good earth and puts moisture in it, or maybe it somehow or other collects something from the air as it falls that acts as a fertilizer. Anyway, I'll just accept it and let it stand as another providence from God.

It turns bitterly cold, and our little cabin is anything but warm because of cracks between the logs big enough to stick your finger in. These cracks appeared over time, not because of shoddy workmanship but as a result of the natural warming and seasoning of the green-hewn logs used in the cabin's construction. So in order to provide a little heat for the rest of the house, it is necessary for me to keep a rip-roaring fire in the ingle, and this keeps me busy. As a result of standing backed-up to the fire and being too close to it, Jane's legs are pied. This is in no way harmful or detracts from her beauty, for it is a fact of life for her and all mountain women. I might point out that men aren't bothered by this because their homespun pants and the tightness of the weave protects them. So, my contribution of a new floor might seem pitiful, but it isn't, and Jane lets me know how thoughtful she thinks I am.

You might wonder and think it odd that I can so vividly remember the date, December 10, 1888. There is a reason the date is so prominent in my memory. I love and think highly of all my kin and will heed their call whenever necessary, but there is one that I've looked up to since I was a mere lad. I remember the many times that he held me spellbound with tales about his homesteading in Missouri before the war, and his stories about the war and his injury kept me mesmerized for hours on end. In addition, this is not a one-sided relationship, for there is a bond between us that goes beyond family ties. We are close, Debarris and I, not like Dad and me, but nevertheless close.

Debarris was born March 13, 1846. He was the eleventh child born to Grandmom and Granddad and Dad was the first. Debarris is a colorful figure, standing six feet and two inches, with naturally curly brown hair and a gift of gab that makes him popular in any crowd. He is like Dad in that he doesn't know the meaning of the word fear. He loves books and has a keen intellect and a fondness for grape wine. Debarris attended a boarding school in Dahlonega which is now North Georgia College for one year but had to leave because of white swelling.[6] He was an adventurous sort of fellow and went with Lid Wright to homestead in Missouri. After six months, he longed to walk again among his family in the friendly, fertile valley of Choestoe and left to come home. Debarris joined the Confederate army at the Union County Courthouse on September 18, 1863, and served under Robert E. Lee. To sum it up, let me state, "Debarris is a Lance, an adventurer, a soldier, a democrat, and my uncle and friend."

Our coziness is suddenly interrupted by a sharp rap on the door, and Jane says, "Who in the world would dare be out on a day like this?" I go to the door and open it, and there stands Debarris, grinning like being out in this inclement weather is the normal thing to do.

"Come on in before you catch your death of a cold."

Debarris responds, "Thought you'd never ask; I was beginning to think you were going to leave me out here to freeze." He stomps the snow off his well-worn boots, slaps me on the back, and walks in.

Our door isn't locked, never has been; Debarris knows this. He could have just walked on in without the formality of a knock; a lot of people would have. However, that isn't his way, or our way for that matter, for we are considerate of other people and their right of privacy. In fact, our privacy and the privacy of others is held in such high regard that sometimes we mountain people are considered unfriendly and standoffish. We aren't; it's just our inbred, suspicious mountain way.

"How about a good hot cup of coffee to get your blood circulating again, Uncle Debarris?" asks Jane.

"Never refused a cup of your coffee before, no need to start now," answers Debarris, "but I can't stay long, for this isn't a social call. I've got something to tell you." Debarris pours his coffee into the saucer, blows into it loudly to cool it, and sips slowly, enjoying the thick black coffee and the warmth it holds. He seems to be in deep thought and after a while says, "Jim, I've decided to make a big move. You know times are hard, and it's all a feller can do to barely keep body and soul together. I've been told there is a great opportunity to get ahead in Texas, and I've decided to go and see for myself. Land is practically free, so they say.

[6]An infection of the bone that won't heal because of a lack of circulation.

Elizabeth and I have talked it over; she doesn't fully agree, but you know a man's got to do what a man's got to do. I'll go, find a good place, settle down, and send for her and the kids later. You know I've got a restless streak in me anyway. I like to move around every now and then; sure hope I'm doing the right thing. Jim, I want you to be the first to know. I haven't even told your Dad yet; thought I'd go by tomorrow and break the news to him. Kinda figured you might go up and check on them today, so if you do, tell them what I've decided so he can kinda be getting used to the idea."

"Debarris, I'm sure going to miss you; when are you planning on leaving?"

"Jim, this is kind of a spur-of-the-minute decision. I plan on going day after tomorrow, if everything goes according to plan. I hate to rush off, leave good company and hot coffee, but I need to tie some loose ends together."

"Good luck Debarris; I'll miss you. I'll help look after Elizabeth and the kids until you send for them." Debarris puts his coffee cup down and gets up slowly. We shake hands and give each other a manly hug. Debarris walks out of our house but I hope not our life, for he is truly a fellow you can count on in a pinch. He looks back and waves a farewell, then disappears. A strange lump forms in my throat, and I fight back the dampness that gathers in the corner of my eyes. I turn around and try to hide my feelings but fail miserably.

"Jim, it's not right to bottle your feelings up inside; let go. I know how you feel about Debarris, and that's one of the reasons I love you so; you are a caring person."

Debarris knows me like Dad knows the pages of the Good Book. He knows that I will today face the elements, go back to Lance Cove, and check on Mom and Dad. It probably won't be necessary, for in all in likelihood they will be faring as well, if not better, than us, but I just have an overriding compassion and feeling for them that is hard to describe, especially to anyone who is not fortunate enough to belong to a loving family. I do know, though, my love is such that if anyone harms my parents in any way, then they will answer to me, for I will seek, demand, and exact revenge, over and over again, even for a lifetime, until I have complete satisfaction.

You can tell the temperature outside is starting to plunge, for you can see Nottely's waters beginning to freeze, first at each bank and then slowly creeping toward midstream; before long the river's water will be frozen solid. The wind is blowing with gale-like velocity, picking up shards of frozen snow and hurling them with evil intent. So I bundle up with the warmest clothes I have, kiss Jane goodbye, and step out into this no-man's-land with complete confidence.

My confidence is shattered when I am savagely flung backwards against the house by a swirling blast of snow and ice. It shrieks fiendishly, "Who are you? How dare you enter into my domain? This is our land. The day belongs to us. Go back inside then, you puny mortal!" I right myself, set my jaw in dogged determination, lean into the wind and surge forward, for I am a Lance. The two-mile trip that normally takes thirty minutes has turned into better than two hours when I espy smoke slowly curling from the chimney of the old homeplace. My pace quickens, and soon I am on the porch.

When I go into the cabin I am cold from my arduous journey, but I immediately feel the warmth of heat generated by a hickory fire in the fireplace and the warmth of love generated by my family, and I feel good.

Mom and Dad say in unison, "Jim, you shouldn't have gotten out in this terrible weather," but you know, they don't seem to be all that surprised to see me. And of course, they are all right. I tell Dad of Debarris's plans. His shoulders seem to momentarily sag a bit, but he quickly recovers and says, "I hope Debarris finds what he's looking for; he's deserving of it, but boy we're sure going to miss him." And it is then I notice for the first time that Dad isn't as young as he once was. His back has become a little stooped, and his shoulders seem to not be as broad. This probably can be attributed to three things. First, his love of God and his continual concern for sinners that weighs heavily upon his shoulders. Second, his continual struggle to provide the best for us, and third, his countless years of bending over the plowstock behind our plodding mule. Why, I bet right now it will push Dad to be five-eight, and he used to be around five-eleven. Why haven't I noticed before? I just don't know, and I feel ashamed, but I promise my God that I will be more attentive in the future, not in an intrusive manner, for Dad couldn't stand to be entirely dependent on anyone, but in a more helpful manner. Dad is fifty-four, and Mom is forty-five.

Let me add that today I did face the elements, and we did battle, the elements and I, but because of family love, I am able to meet it head-on and emerge victorious.

Debarris leaves for the Lone Star State as he says. He rides off in the very early morning hours of December 12, just a few minutes after the game roosters announce to all of Choestoe that a new day has dawned and there is work to do. His first destination is Gainesville, where he intends to sell his horse and catch a train to Texas. He hasn't planned out exactly which part he intends to settle down in, but this is typical of Debarris, for he is a man of action more so than planning. Anyway, he figures that will come later after he has thoroughly scouted the area out. No need to settle in one area when there might be a better one a few miles away. He promises to pick out a central location to serve as a home base and to check in to it often just in case an emergency arises at home. He does as he says and writes us, telling us how he can be reached.

Chapter XI

MOCKER OF WHAT'S
GOOD AND DECENT

Happenings in Choestoe are about as usual; however, the atmosphere of community goodwill seems to be changing somewhat. I seem to be able to pick up (and others have commented) that an air of looseness may be slowly invading our peaceful valley, bringing with it change. I do know that whenever a community of people fails to forcefully stamp out evil when it first appears and lets an aura of indifference settle in, no good can come from it. And I'm afraid if the good citizens don't band together and act for the common good before it's too late, evil will gain a toehold, and the entire citizenry will live to regret their indecision.

Dad has recognized the trend, and he preaches somewhere every Sunday. He feels it is his duty to sound the alarm and arouse the people, and he is doing so. It's as if there has been a tremendous burden placed upon his shoulders, and God is holding him personally responsible, so he's fervently preaching, pleading with a sense of urgency to the citizens, "Wake up, recognize this evil monster for what it is, a mocker of what's good and decent!"

The evil monster is moonshine, the floater of imaginary dreams, and we are warned about its effects, for doesn't it say in Proverbs 20:1, "Wine is a mocker, strong drink is raging: and whosoever is deceived thereby is not wise"? Dad has seen its effects, for it makes fools out of wise men and causes the closed mouth to open up and babble trite nothings. It does make the poor temporarily forget reality by offering them dreams of unattainable wealth, but when the debilitating effects of this purveyor of evil wear off, they awaken to find that they not only are as poor as they were before, but more so, for it has exacted a monetary as well as a moral price, dragging them further down into an abysmal pit. Proverbs 21:17 points this out: "He that loveth pleasure shall be a poor man: he that loveth wine and oil shall not be rich."

You might be curious as to my more than cursory knowledge of the Bible, and why I can cite verse after verse from it comfortably. There is no mystery surrounding this, for I was raised in a Christian home by parents who believe that food from God's word to nourish the soul is as important as food from the table is to nourish the body. They believe, and rightly so, that to develop the body and ignore the soul is contrary to God's plan. I can vividly recall sitting on the porch in the summer, watching the sun slowly dip below Sheriff Knob, listening to Dad reading from the Good Book. Then slowly the shadows of night spread over the valley, and the light of day is no more. Dad closes the Good Book, and we silently look out over God's creation. The whippoorwills are calling back and forth to one another, their calls echoing loudly in our secluded cove. We gaze out over the freshly mown meadow, and it is ablaze with the twinkling of a million lightning bugs, their brief flash looking like soldiers carrying lit lanterns and them on the march. In the winter, we would gather by the fire; Mom would sit on one side knitting, and Dad would be on the other with his well-worn Bible spread open. We would sometimes be inattentive, as kids are prone to be, and Mom would gently say, "Be quiet kids; listen to Dad, for he's reading to you from the Book of Life." We would heed Mom and listen to Dad, for he was wise and we loved him so. Therefore, my knowledge of God's word was not by accident but by design, for it had been sown and carefully nurtured by loving parents who still await a fruitful harvest.

Jane and I are doing as we have been taught, and every evening we gather Jack and Juan around us and read to them from the Bible. We know they are much too young to understand, but it is important for them to see their mom and dad pause at the end of a long day and give thanks to God Almighty. This is how it is with Mom and Dad, and this is how it is with Jane and me.

To add credence to the fact that the moral fibers of our valley are being stretched, notice the wildcat stills that have sprung up like jonquils in early spring on every river branch in Choestoe. They are busily churning out their illicit product and spewing forth bitter poison. If it isn't stopped, I fear no antidote, regardless of strength, will be able to neutralize its noxious effects.

The Yellow Mountain bunch (not in the least bashful when it comes to turning a profit the easy and illegal way) have thrown together a wildcat still on the branch that flows alongside the main road leading from Lance Cove to the church up on the river. It is near the Shuler place, in plain view to all traveling the road. Dad preaches at this church every Sunday, so he must pass this rotgut operation on the way to and from church, and he is furious. The Yellow Mountain bunch is openly flaunting the laws of civilized society, daring anyone to object to their illegal endeavor. Dad is not one to stand aside when principle is involved and let a wrong corrupt a peaceful people. He objects with a Christian fury by preaching from the pulpit of the pitfalls that await if the good people of Choestoe fail to stamp out this gangrene in our midst. Dad, being a straightforward man and possessive of a brand of courage seldom found, calls upon the Yellow Mountain bunch at their place of business. He warns them in no uncertain terms that he will not stand idly by and allow them to run their operation unfettered, so it would be in their best interest and Choestoe's to cease immediately their illegal pursuit.

Word has it that they are taken aback by Dad's demands and have started making veiled threats against him, promising to shut him up one way or the other. They shouldn't be surprised at the boldness of Dad's actions. I am not, for he is a fearless man, accountable only to God for his conduct. Anyway, most of them that are present when Dad calls have savored the results of tangling with a man of his mettle.

Dad doesn't seem to be all that concerned about their threats. He points out that basically they are cowards and won't do anything. I agree fully; they are cowards of the worst sort who wouldn't dare face Dad man-to-man, but that's what bothers me. I've felt the sting of their wrath before, and it wasn't a manly attack that did me in, but a cowardly ambush, aimed at crippling me so they could gain the upper hand and then carry out their fiendish perversions without fear of retaliation. I know they are like snakes in the grass, but they are far less noble than the rattlesnake, which at least has the decency to warn you before striking. They are more akin to the lowly copperhead, which strikes without warning, then tries to crawl away. When you are dealing with people such as this, is it any wonder I feel a bit uneasy about Dad's safety?

Today I hear about a chance meeting between Dad and Frank Swaim. It occurred several months ago at Charlie Henson's house, and it further raises my concern for Dad. Charlie came by for a visit, which was a little unusual in itself, for although we are neighbors and passing acquaintances, we are not bosom buddies. Even so, he cares about my family and Choestoe, and I appreciate what he tells me, for it is a neighborly thing to do. He asks if Dad has said anything about Frank Swaim threatening him. Of course, he hasn't. If he had been alarmed about the threats, he wouldn't have told us because he would have been afraid we would worry. That is just my dad and the way he handles things when it comes to family. Anyway, he probably remembers Frank from his first encounter, how he lay in a fetal position and babbled incoherently. I reply, "No Charlie, he hasn't. Tell me about it."

"Well, several people were at my house, Frank Swaim, Fed and Lizzie Cannup, Newt Spivey, and some others, when your dad came by for a visit. I asked him in, and he spoke to everyone as he always did. Everyone was glad to see him, except Frank. Frank was drinking, not yet drunk, but well on his way and feeling his oats. He started mouthing off to your dad, saying something about him marrying them illegally. He then picked up a chair and threatened to hit your dad, boasting, 'You damn old rascal, I'll bust your head.' [See Record of Trial, testimony of Newt Spivey (10).] Jim, as you know, your dad's not afraid of Old Lucifer himself, so he just grinned in a disarming way and told Frank to hush or he'd take him down a notch or two. This really got Frank's goat, got him into a real swivet, because he could tell your dad wasn't in the least scared of him, and it made him look foolish. I told your dad to go on home and come back to visit again when we could enjoy his company. After he left, Frank reaffirmed that he was going to cut his damn throat.

"Jim, I know Frank doesn't have the backbone to face your dad, for he's scared to death of him, and you couldn't melt him and pour him on your dad, but I also know he's awfully sneaky, especially when he's drinking, which now is most of the time. So tell your dad please be careful and not turn his back."

"Charlie, you'll never know how much I appreciate you letting me know about the threats toward my dad. I'll go immediately and have a talk with Frank, let him know that I've heard the threats and will be watching him like a chicken watches a hawk, but I'll not use your name in it, Charlie."

"Thanks Jim. I ain't afeared of him either, but I do have a family, and no telling what a sneak like him might do."

I tell Jane about Charlie Henson's visit and what he said about Frank, and that I plan on giving him a visit tomorrow. She is scared, scared for me, scared for Choestoe, and scared for Dad, for she has grown to love Mom and Dad almost as much as she does her parents.

Tonight I overhear Jane say her prayers: "Dear God, I pray that you will bless all of our loved ones. Look after Jack and Juan. You've called Jim's dad to be a messenger for you. You've molded Jim to be like him, to have faith and courage, to believe. You've given him a fighting spirit like his ancestors and like the disciples of old. Look after these gifts, I pray. Restore goodwill and common sense among your people. Keep Jim's spirit firmly channeled toward service for you, for I fear to think what might occur if anything bad happens to his dad. I ask this in your name and pray that it be in accordance with your will, Amen."

I arise the next morning, way before daylight as I always do, and make preparations to have a talk with a Frank Swaim. I am not in the least apprehensive in talking to him, for I will be on a mission concerning the one I love the most. I am six-foot-two and weigh better than two hundred and twenty-five pounds, and every bit of it is as hard as cured leather. You can render me out and not get one ounce of fat. Just the thought of someone threatening Dad raises my dander and a seething anger fills me. I am edgy, wrought up, and rarin' to go. However, before I can set out on my mission, I have to go to Virge's store to pick up an item or two for Jane.

I get to Virge's store around seven-thirty. The sun is just beginning to peep bashfully over the gap between Bald and Cow Rock Mountains, and its warming rays haven't yet begun to melt the frost that covers the ground in crystal profusion. I enter the store. "Jim, you're traveling mighty early. How's the family? Bet you've got a full day laid out."

"Virge, they're fine, and yes I do," I answer.

"By the way Jim, have you heard about the revenuers cutting down a still last night? It is the one that has so riled your dad and the other good people of the community."

"Did they catch anyone?" I ask.

"No, they scattered like flushed bobwhites and ran like their tails were on fire. Headed to the high mountains. They'll make themselves scarce around here for several days, for they'll lay low until they think the storm has blown over. It's a crying shame they got away, for everyone knows who owns it. Trash such as that is beginning to give Choestoe a bad name," Virge says as he shakes his head in disgust.

"Virge, that's the best news I've heard in a long time. I'm tickled to death, for as you say, they are giving Choestoe a black eye. We had nothing to do with having the still cut down. Our hands are clean, but I imagine that ignorant bunch will blame us. Anyway Virge, that shortens my day, for as soon as I left here and dropped the provisions off, I was going to pay Frank Swaim a visit. I don't know if you've heard or not, but yesterday I found out Frank's been shooting off his mouth about Dad—says he's going to shut him up for good. I'm goin' to look him in the face, eyeball-to-eyeball, and remove any doubt from his warped mind that I'll stand idly by and let Dad be hurt."

"Jim, I've heard; so has most of Choestoe, I imagine. Glad you found out before something happens. I was going to tell you the next time I saw you. Figured you might not have heard, even though the threats have been going on for several months. I might have known they wouldn't come to you or your dad, man-to-man; that's just not the way they operate. Jim, warn your dad, for I don't trust any of them. In fact, I wouldn't trust them in an outhouse with a muzzle on, so be careful and watch your back. They are very capable of an ambush, for that seems to be second nature to them."

"Thanks Virge; I've already been on the receiving end of more than one of their sneak attacks. I'll be careful, and I appreciate the advice and your friendship."

Most people in the mountains have the ability to read signs and predict what the weather will be like in the future. Thick shucks on ears of corn, wide stripes on a frost worm, hornets' nests built close to the ground, sheep with unusually heavy coats of wool, and thick hulls on hickory nuts all point to a cold winter. A ring around the moon means that it will rain within three days. If it clouds up on a frost there is sure to be a snow. If a fog rises after a rain, or if all the food is eaten at supper, clear weather is sure to follow. And all mountain people know that an east wind is an ill wind. I cannot see the wind, but I feel a slight breeze wafting in from the east, and it is still, slow, and soft. The leaves herald its appearance, for it has been humid and hot, and they are fluttering in its wake. Oh, how I pray that the wind stays a comforting breeze and no evil force turns it into a raging gale, causing it to destroy everything in its path. What worries me is I can read signs and see what the future holds, but I wonder if the Yellow Mountain bunch can do the same, for they alone have the power to stay the storm and calm the water.

Today is January 10, 1890, and instead of calming down, the ill wind of the east seems to be working itself into a full-blown storm. Today my brother Lafayette (Fate) came to me with some disturbing news that points out our troubles with the Yellow Mountain bunch are increasing to a dangerous level.

Fate was on his way to Fed Cannup's last night, walking along the ridge which leads to his house, when suddenly Frank Swaim stepped out from behind an outgrowth of laurels and said, "Fate, somebody's going to get killed over this."

"He had a Winchester rifle pulled on me before I knew what was going on. He cocked it, aimed it at my chest, and repeated, 'Fate you've been reporting stills, and I want you to know somebody is going to be killed over the matter.'

"I assured Frank that it was none of the Lances doing the reporting. Jim, when you have a cocked rifle aimed at your chest, it's hard and foolish to be brave, so I tried to talk myself out of a tense situation and finally did so.

"Frank replied sarcastically, 'It was you, Jim, or that old white-headed daddy of yours, and I can tell you right now, the matter is far from being settled.' Then he turned and skulked back into the laurels."

"Fate, I intended to talk to Frank the day after the still was cut down about the callous threats he was recklessly throwing around over at Charlie Henson's, but I knew that he would hide out for a few days, so I postponed it. I see now the situation has deteriorated to a dangerous point, so it is a must that I go tomorrow."

"Jim, I'll go with you to back you up, because when you go into their lair, no telling what they'll try to pull on you."

"Fate, I know you would; I can't stop you if you insist, but this is a job I feel compelled to do on my own, for I've felt their sting and been tricked by their pious attitude before. I think I'm wise to their ways and will be overly careful not to let my guard down and fall for their ruse again. Anyway, too many people in the community know I'm going to be calling on Frank for them to risk much of an altercation. They probably know also, for there seems to be no secrets anywhere anymore. I'll admit the numbers will be in their favor, but a frontal attack is not in their makeup. They prefer and demand to hunt and strike like a pack of wolves."

I have made the decision to meet Frank face-to-face, but I haven't yet decided on the course of action that I will follow. Should I go in without a specific plan and just let nature take its course, or should I go in with my mind made up, take the bull by the horns so to speak, and lay out in no uncertain terms what I will do should I not be fully satisfied as to Dad's safety? Then if I am not, let all hell break loose? Maybe I should get some of the other Lances to go with me and settle the matter once and for all. I have no doubt whatsoever about their being willing to come to the aid of one of their own, for I've seen the call go out, and I've seen the positive response. Nevertheless, it won't take all of us, for in a fight two Lances at their very worst are better than four of the Yellow Mountain bunch at their very best. This isn't bragging, because I've seen it tried and can swear to its truth.

The day dawns clear and cold. It is a typical Choestoe winter morning with a heavy frost hanging coldly upon everything, and I knew it would, because last night I gazed into the heavens and beheld a full moon, a wolf moon so named by the Indians for the red wolf packs that would howl hungrily outside their villages. It appears that God has touched every outside facet with a coat of perfection, thereby hiding any imperfections. But I know that everything isn't perfect, for as soon as the morning begins to warm up, the frost will slowly vaporize, and the façade of perfection will disappear with it. However, this is not a typical day for me, for I am once again going to face my nemeses and try to reason with them about what is right and wrong. I will do so with no illusions of great accomplishments, for it is as Cussin' Tom Henson says of them, "If a law were passed making it illegal to attend church, then the very next Sunday they would be there, sitting on the front pew, helping to lead the singing." This then is the caliber of people I am dealing with, but I must try, for so much hangs in the balance.

It is approximately a mile from my house to Tom Swaim's cabin, and even though the terrain is mostly up and down and not made for ideal walking, I am knocking on the door in less than fifteen minutes, so great is my concern. Tom comes to the door and says, "Who is it?"

"Jim Lance," I reply. "Is Frank in there? I want to talk to him."

"Yep he is here; come on in if'n you ain't skeered," Tom answers in a smart-alecky manner.

I've been taught by Dad to fight fire with fire and never let anybody get the bluff on you, for if they do, they will run you amok, so I step confidently inside and answer, "Tom, the man's not been made yet that I'm scared of, and I don't expect to find one here either." I quickly survey the room and see Fed Cannup, Ben Nix, and Frank Swaim sitting at the eating table, and the pushed-back chair indicates that Tom Swaim was seated before I knocked. In the middle of the table are the remains of what has once been a gallon of moonshine. The reeking smell of their foul breath and the putrid odor hanging like a cloud in the darkened cabin is proof of what has happened to the gallon of rotgut. That they had been equal partakers of the fruits of their labor is further enhanced by their slurred, guttural speech.

"The Winchester that Frank so boldly pulled on Fate leans in the corner within easy reach, and the shotgun that lies between Fed Cannup's feet partially sticks out from underneath the table. Tom Swaim has a knife belted securely around his waist, and it would be safe to assume that the others are also armed with knives. Moreover, it wouldn't take a brilliant scholar to surmise that this gathering isn't about doing the Lord's work." Then I continue with a decided edge to my voice, "And I don't see anything here that would make me change my mind."

This might seem like a stupid thing to say to a crew possessing little or no scruples, and to say it when you are facing them in the safety of their own domain probably looks like a case of stupidity personified, but in my own mind, I'm not stupid, just brazenly brash on behalf of my dad. I'm certain they can't believe I would have the courage to bravely walk into their stronghold and challenge them. This bold act creates doubt and enables me to meet them head-on and have my say.

"Frank, I have heard it on good authority that you think Fate, Dad, or me reported you for making whiskey, and this resulted in your still being cut down; now that's not so. I have also heard that you intend to get even by cutting Dad's throat. Let me assure you again that no Lance reported you. We are against moonshining, but reporting it is not the way we operate." Frank reaches for the rifle and picks it up. The rifle evidently gives him grit and boosts his courage, for he sets in to cussing.

"Jim Lance, you are a liar; so is Fate, and as far as I'm concerned your white-headed dad is a bigger liar than you both put together."

"Frank, if it's trouble you're hunting, I can assure you that you are looking in the right place. You can blackguard, call me and Fate liars, and you might get by with it, but I'll stomp the guts out of any low-down fellow that talks about Dad like that." I quickly lunge at Frank, fully intending to knock the foul-mouthed talking dolt into next week. He senses my anger, for he is no stranger to it, jerks the rifle up, and stumbles awkwardly back against the wall. I feel the others grab at me and I flail away, scattering them hither and yon, but my forward progress is impeded.

I hear Frank scream wildly, "Git out of the way; I'll gut-shoot the damn fool!"

108

I feel the cold barrel of the rifle being shoved against my stomach. "Frank Swaim, you don't have the backbone to shoot me or anybody else when they are lookin' you in the eye. Go ahead, pull the trigger, if you got the nerve."

Fed Cannup speaks up, because he can tell that things are getting out of hand, and says, "Let's calm down, we're all friends. Jim, have a drink with us."

"No thanks, I don't have a strong enough stomach to drink with Frank," I angrily retort.

Frank's courage surges when he realizes that I am vastly outnumbered and that he holds the trump card, the Winchester rifle, for I am unarmed. "Jim Lance, I still say you, Fate, and your dad are liars of the worst sort. I know who reported me; I'm no damn fool."

"Well you sure could have fooled me on that account, for I've always taken you for one," I answer.

"I don't intend to whip you or anybody, but I sure intend to cut some man's throat," Frank affirms.

"I'll agree; no, you're not going to whip me or anybody for that matter Frank, for you're not man enough to do it," I reply.

Tom Swaim steps in and says, "Jim, we know who reported us, and we ain't liking it a bit. You'd better leave while the leaving is good, 'fore Frank fills your belly full of lead."

"Tom, I know this: if you still think it is us, you're still wrong, and I'll leave, for I didn't come to stir up trouble, but to try and prevent it. But let me warn the whole kit and caboodle of you, just as fair and square as I know how. If any harm comes to Dad, they don't make a big enough place in the world for you to hide, for I will hunt you down like I would a mad dog and deal with you as I see fit. Do you hear me?"

"I hear, but ain't a-goin' to pay it no heed, for I ain't a-skeered of any yellow-bellied reporter," Frank replies haughtily.

I turn my back to them and slowly step out the door so they can't mistake my intentions and repeat, "I don't lie and don't have any use for anybody who does. I say what I mean and I mean what I say."

Newt Swaim, emulating his peers, chimes in, "You better git goin' 'for we'uns change our minds and start shooting reporters." My steps are slow and deliberate to reinforce that I am in no way afraid of the likes of them and start home. I think, what a waste; there's Newt, still wet behind the ears, just barely fifteen, and it looks as if he's well on the way to becoming as sorry as the rest of the lot. I imagine it's like I've always heard: like father like son. Anyway, in my case I certainly hope it holds true.

As I walk home, I can feel the wind at my back, pushing me forward. It is a strong wind, a contrary wind, and it seems to be increasing in force. I stop and look around to see the direction from which it is coming. It is from the east. I glance upward, see dark clouds gathering, and hear the distant rumble of thunder. When it looks threatening like this, can a dangerous storm be far off? On occasion, I have seen the dark clouds gather like this, and the storm will pass us by. However, most times when the clouds gather thickly, we can be assured that our valley will quiver and shake because of the intensity of the coming storm.

I walk slowly, ignoring the threatening weather, and try to unravel what has happened. Have I done any good, or have I wasted a trip? Did I get the message across that I wouldn't stand by in a passive manner if Dad be harmed? Do they remember how the Lances will retaliate if a member of the family is hurt? Do they know or care that Dad is the patriarch of our family and is revered above all others? I hope so, for if they didn't get the message or don't know, our peaceful valley will very well turn into an Armageddon.

When I near home I can see two people nervously pacing. I draw nearer and recognize Jane and Fate anxiously talking, trying to find comfort in each other. Fate has come to find out how the meeting went, and out of brotherly love. He is worried about Dad and about me because he too is under no false impression as to the moral uprightness of this lot. Jane has about worried herself sick about me going in alone to face them, but I would have it no other way, for there is no need at this time to draw others into a conflict that hasn't happened.

"How did you come out? Did you throw the fear of the Lord in 'em? Did you leave on friendly terms?" Fate rapidly asks.

"Well Fate, I don't think I came out too good; only time will tell. As for Frank, he's not changed a lot, still a lot of bluster and not much substance. When he has the upper hand, he will take advantage of it, but any way you shake him, he is still a coward, through and through. If being asked to leave makes it friendly, then I left on friendly terms. Jane and Fate, I would like to be able to report good news, but I can't, and I probably said some things in the heat of the battle that would have been best left unsaid. To be truthful, the feelings between us now may be worse than before if that's possible, but at least I have the satisfaction of knowing I tried." I recount to them what took place as best I can, and they shake their heads in bewilderment.

We are quiet for a few moments, and then Fate says, "Some people just don't know what's good for them. What do we do now, Jim?"

Jane answers, "I'm probably out of place in saying this, for I understand little about manly conflicts and what causes them. I know I'm not family by birth, but I am by marriage and for what it's worth, here is what I think. We need to immediately go to your dad and discuss the situation with him, for he's the one mainly involved. He has to know what's going on because it is community talk, and besides, he's older and far wiser than we are. You need to use his experience, for I understand that as a youth he was quite a fighting man."

"Jane, you certainly aren't out of place, because you are as much family as any of us, and of course we should get Dad involved, because he is, whether he wants to be or not. Fate, can you go in the morning to see Dad?" I ask.

"Sure Jim, no matter how early you come by, I'll be ready."

The day hasn't yet overcome the darkness of night when Fate and I bounce up on the porch of our old homeplace and holler out, "Anybody up in there?"

"Come in boys; you sure are up and stirring early. Bet you got up way before breakfast," Dad says. He puts his arms around both of us and squeezes affectionately.

Mom comes into the kitchen grinning in delight, for she is always tickled to see us. She has flour on her hands and apron, which serves to point out that she is making breakfast for Dad and the rest of the kids. "Boys, your timing is good; we were just fixing to eat."

"Mom, you never could knock me away from your table and you still can't. Set two more plates." She does, and we eat as if we haven't eaten in a month of Sundays, even though it is our second breakfast of the morning. The good-natured ribbing around the table brings back fond memories of the good times I have shared with Mom and Dad in Lance Cove. The love that flows through us for family cannot be expressed through words, but has to be shown.

After breakfast, we sit around the table and chew the fat for a while, fully enjoying each other's company. Nevertheless, since this isn't a social call, I can see it is time to get down to business, so I say, "Dad, we need to do some serious talking about a situation that has developed over the last few months."

Dad jokingly says, "I'll be danged; from the way you and Fate ate, I thought you were starving and came back to stuff your craw again. What have you got on your mind?"

"Well, I'll admit the breakfast by itself would have been worth the trip, and by the way we made the food disappear, you would think we were in dire straits. Nevertheless, the truth of the matter is we've come to talk about the Yellow Mountain bunch. I don't know if you are aware of what's going on; some of it I'm sure you've heard as community gossip, and if it were only gossip then it wouldn't matter all that much, but over the last few weeks we've become alarmed, for it seems to have taken a dastardly turn."

We tell Dad what we know of the sordid details surrounding Frank Swaim's tirade at Charlie Henson's, and about the run-in Fate had with him on the way to Fed Cannup's. I recount to Dad what was said and what took place when I paid them a visit at their dilapidated hovel.

"Yes boys, I have heard secondhand about what Frank said to my back at Charlie Henson's, but I hadn't heard about him pulling a gun on Fate or about you paying them a visit. I believe they were amazed when I walked in on them at the place of their ill-advised work; in fact, you could see it in their eyes, for they looked a lot like the cat that swallowed the grinding stone, but Jim, I bet they were more so when you had the gall to boldly go and face them man-to-man. The Lance way is not their way, and evidentially they have a hard time understanding how we have the guts to meet our adversaries man-to-man, face-to-face. This is just not in their nature!" Dad says.

"Now Dad, the question is, what can we do to protect you, for tomorrow when you go up on the river to preach, you'll be smack-dab in their territory the biggest part of the way. I say we call our family together and rid ourselves and the rest of Choestoe of this pestilence forever. I firmly believe this will bring back decency to our valley and allow our neighbors and us once again to live in harmony and fellowship. Dad, if you will say so, me and Fate will put out the word, and by late afternoon our clan will gather in force, and we will move as a family toward this end."

Dad sits with his chin firmly cradled in his callused hand and ponders. You can tell he is deeply engrossed, thinking about a decision that not only will affect him but his God, his family, and his community. After several minutes, he speaks: "Boys, it wouldn't be right to draw our family in right now, for if they come, and they will, they will come with fire in their eyes, and the Yellow Mountain bunch will be no more. If anyone in my family lost his life on my account, why, I would worry myself to death. No, I'd rather lose my life if it comes to it than take that chance."

"Then Dad, come tomorrow, Fate and me will go with you to your church."

"Jim, I know you and Fate would go with me, but you can't be with me all of the time. You all have a family and a life to live of your own. I'll just put my trust in my God, for doesn't He say in Psalm 23, 'The Lord is my shepherd; I shall not want. He maketh me to lie down in green pastures: He leadeth me beside the still waters. He restoreth my soul; He leadeth me in the paths of righteousness for his name's sake. Yea, though I walk through the valley of the shadow of death, I will fear no evil: for thou art with me; thy rod and thy staff they comfort me. Thou preparest a table before me in the presence of mine enemies: thou anointest my head with oil; my cup runneth over. Surely goodness and mercy shall follow me all the days of my life: and I will dwell in the house of the Lord forever'?"

"Dad, that's why we came, for you are so much wiser and more experienced in human nature than we are or ever will be, and I didn't want to go off half-cocked and make a bad situation even worse. You'll just have to forgive me for failing to trust in God completely as you do, because

I've not daily walked hand in hand with Him as you have, but I plan on it Dad, for I want to be as much like you as possible. I know I don't tell you and Mom oft enough how much I love you, but it's this love that sometimes blinds me and causes me to wildly strike out when it comes to protecting you all and the rest of the family."

"Jim, I couldn't have said it better," responds Fate.

"Boys, you need not apologize for love, compassion, and caring for others, for it's biblical, through and through. You can take the Good Book, study it chapter by chapter, and try to find the main thread that Christianity is based upon, and when it's all said and done, you will come up with the word 'love.' No boys, never apologize for love. Now, I'll admit, we Lances may be too headstrong and stubborn for our own good, but that's just part of our inheritance, and the best we can do is to bridle these traits and be headstrong and stubborn for our Lord," Dad says.

Fate says, "We feel better now, for though you will be walking through 'the valley of the shadow of death,' you won't be walking alone, for God will be walking with you every step of the way."

"You're right, Fate," Dad answers. "I'm not in the least fearful of what tomorrow brings, for I am compelled to believe in God and do His work."

We soon depart Mom and Dad's house and feel much better about the situation because of Dad's reassurance and his ever-abiding faith in God. The trip back home is more enjoyable, for a great load has been lifted from our shoulders, and our steps are lighter, for we are able to see God's love of life in the newly awakening season. Spring is in the air. If proof be needed, it can be found in the early blooming sarvis, whose white blossoms are splotched here and there. They contrast vividly against a background of gray, bare oaks that are still dressed in their drab winter garb. The dogwoods are beginning to bud, but they hold new life still securely bound within, just in case there is a late winter snap. And the tips of the maple limbs are turning red in response to some unknown stimuli. Last night I heard a whippoorwill rolling out his call, reaffirming to all that another spring has arrived. Yes, this is spring, the season of life, and now the Lances and all of Choestoe are ready to celebrate victory, for the shackles of winter have been cast aside.

When I get home Jane asks, "What we are going to do?" I explain what has been said, the decision reached, and she fully agrees, adding, "You know the Bible says that not even a lowly sparrow falls without God knowing it. A man as pure and saintly as your Dad is going to be protected by Him."

Tonight I hold Jane closely and feel good about my life, about my love for Jane, Jack, Juan, Mom, Dad, and the rest of my family. I silently thank God for all of his providence and wonder if I too might be called to be a messenger of His, just like Dad.

Sometime during the night, I hear a screech owl, the harbinger of death, calling out its sorrowful song, and I am alarmed. I snuggle closer to Jane, and the feeling of despair vanishes as quickly as the fog does after a fleeting summer shower. I feel guilty for doubting.

Sunday dawns. I arise from my warm feather bed and step out on the front porch. There is a nip in the air, and a light frost still touches the earth. The sky is clear, and before too long the sun will be making its daily journey from east to west and in the process touch every hidden cove in Choestoe and open them up to light and heat. Yes, this is going to be a pretty day, a beautiful Sabbath.

A little later, I hear the church bell at Old Salem Methodist Church, the church I am a member of. It is ringing loud and clear, calling the people to gather themselves for Sunday school. And in the distance, I can make out the faint tolling of the bells from the other churches in the valley. Most families do attend Sunday school, for Choestoe is a religious community. Oh, there are a few rotten apples, but surely not enough to cause the whole barrel to spoil. Normally we heed the bell's urging, but today Jane and I are staying home, because Jack and Juan both have a nasty cold that we are treating with pneumonia salve, and their persistent coughing isn't favorable to learning.

In a few minutes, Dad will be leaving home to go preach up on the river, a trek of four or five miles. I can just see him now, wearing the wool suit that Mom made for him. The wool came from our own sheep, and she wove it on the family loom. The coat is a Prince Albert-type and is adorned with two rows of shiny brass buttons which were taken from Debarris's Civil War uniform. Dad protested mightily that he didn't need such a fine suit, but Mom hushed him by saying, "A man of God needs to look nice," and that settled that. I will admit that Dad, of stalwart frame and with his long hair and flowing beard, will serve to be noticed in any crowd and yes, I am proud of him and have every right to be.

Whose Eye Is on the Sparrow

I saw a fallen sparrow
Dead upon the grass
And mused to see how narrow
The wing that bore it was.

By what unlucky chance
The bird had come to settle
Lopsided near the fence
In sword grass and nettle

I had no means to know;
But this I minded well:
Whose eye was on the sparrow
Shifted—and it fell.

—Byron Herbert Reece (1)

Chapter XII

THE LAMB IS SLAIN

After dinner, I go outside to walk around and check on things. I glance up at the sun, and probably out of habit, I pull out my pocketwatch to check the time. It is fifteen of one. I again think of Dad and know that the service will just about be breaking up, for Dad, like the other preachers, tends to be a little verbose and preach for a long time; they have a message from God, and it is too important to just skimp over. I know that if I leave now, I will intercept Dad midway his trip, some distance this side of where the Yellow Mountain bunch lives, and it is not all that unusual for me to do so. Often times, I will walk over to meet and accompany Dad home because I relish the time and conversation between us. Dad, when it is warm enough, always walks with his coat folded carefully over his arm so it won't wrinkle, for he doesn't want Mom to spend unnecessary time ironing it. But this day I'll not go, for Dad might think I'm "butting in on his business" and think he's too old to look after himself.

I piddle around the house for some time, and Jane brings Jack and Juan outside to soak up a little sunshine. It is warm, but there is a cool breeze blowing, which is typical of a sunny February day. Jane says it's too cold for the boys to remain outside and them with a cold. She starts to take them inside, but they protest mightily, so I find a sheltered, sunny nook on the west side of the house that is out of the wind, and it is cozy. And here we are, Jane, Jack, Juan, and I, contentedly lolling the Sunday afternoon away. I know one thing: Jim Lance has to be the luckiest man on the face of God's green earth. Just look at what God has blessed me with: a loving wife and two sturdy children, a Mom and Dad that I dote on, a name I can be proud of, and the most beautiful place in the world to live. How could anyone wish for more?

I glance up from my sheltered cote toward yon Yellow Mountain, and in the distance I espy a man coming toward me in a great rush. I stand up and shield my eyes from the glare of the sun to better see who it is that's in such an almighty rush, and then I recognize him, my brother Joe, running and screaming, but I can't yet make out what he's screaming about, and I become alarmed. I run toward him, and then I hear, "Jim, Jim, Dad's been killed!" and he falls prostrate on the ground screaming, "Why, why, oh why?"

I pick Joe up and hug him reassuredly and say, "Let me tell Jane, and we'll go." Jane, hearing the commotion, moves to us. "Jane, Dad has been killed; I've got to go." Outwardly, I seem to be calm; the reality and finality of Dad's murder has not yet soaked in, but soon there begins to well up in me an angry surge toward the perpetrators, and I feel as if I will burst. Then it comes out, a scream of such dimension that the dead must have twisted nervously in their graves, for such a rage has never before been unleashed upon Choestoe. "The low-down murderers that did this will pay!" I scream in torment. Jane holds me and Joe, and Jack and Juan clutch nervously at her dress tail as we cry our hearts out. Jack and Juan can't understand, for they have never seen me in such a state. Neither can I understand, for where was God when Dad needed Him?

We hear the church bells at Salem begin to toll again, for they are alerting the community that there has been a death. I don't count, for I know they will toll fifty-five times, one knell for each year of Dad's life.

We start back to Lance Cove, Joe and I, in a hurry, for I know Mom and the family will be in dire straits and looking to me for decisions. In addition, Dad will expect me to step forward and provide leadership, but how can I be a leader when it feels as if my heart has been forcefully wrenched out? However, I must; I owe it to Dad.

When we get close, we find Dad's body lying by the side of Wolf Creek. Mom and the rest of my younger brothers and sisters are there, as well as Joseph Ledford, Bud Miller, W. Y. Curtis, J. M. Reece, and others in the community. We family members hug each other, trying to find comfort and support among ourselves. Our gut-wrenching cries echo strangely back and forth upon Wolf Creek, for we are suffering. I reach down to hold Dad and start to clasp him to me, but his head stays strangely behind in a grotesque way. I can tell Dad's head is almost off, so I ease him back down and hope Mom and the rest of the family haven't noticed. I tell Fate to take Mom and the rest of the family back home, and I will stay with Dad and bring his body home after the sheriff and coroner's jury do their inquest. I cry openly before the other men that have gathered, noticing damp spots under their eyes also, for Choestoe too has suffered the loss of a great and saintly man.

The coroner's jury arrives and T. J. Butt, a member of the jury, examines Dad. I watch, even though it is torment to see Dad like this, for it would only be right to stay with him. Hasn't he always been there when I've needed him? Dad is stripped, I can see a deep stab wound in the breast, and his neck is horribly cut. It is cut almost entirely around, and his head is being held on by only one small strip of flesh. The cut is rough, of a zigzag pattern, and appears torn, and the windpipe is completely severed. Dad's face is bruised on the right side, there is a smooth cut on his right hand, and I notice his clothes that are scattered haphazardly are torn and cut in several places. This total carnage of Dad and the sight of his mutilated body makes me sick to my stomach, and I am about to throw up. "Who did this? I've never seen such a fiendish attack. Do you know, Jim?" inquires T. J. Butt.

"Yes, I know, but first I must tend to Dad." I feel like cursing God, the Yellow Mountain bunch, and anyone else who might have been a party, directly or indirectly, to Dad's death, but I just can't right here. Though Dad has passed on, there is still a reverence and an aura of goodness around his body that must not be defiled, and I stay to see that it is not.

Dad's desecrated body is carefully loaded on a wagon to be taken to Lance Cove for the last time. I sit on the wagon bed and hold Dad's limp hand the entire way. The mile ride is surely the longest journey anyone has ever taken, and the familiar sights bring back haunting memories of days and years replete with play, laughter, and good times, but now in its stead is sorrow, heartache, and evil. Over there is the big boulder the Yellow Mountain bunch was hiding behind when they launched their ambush against me, and right above it is the bluff Dad came sliding down as he came to my aid. Tears roll down my cheeks unimpeded and flow onto the wagon bed. I squeeze Dad's limber hand. There is no returned squeeze of affirmation, and I sob bitterly. "Why, oh why did God desert His servant?" The questions are many, but the answers are few and hard to come by.

By the time we get to Mom and Dad's house, the yard is filled with friendly and concerned neighbors; the news of Dad's untimely murder spread like wildfire, and the air in our little cove is permeated with cries of heartbreak.

We lovingly tote Dad's body inside to prepare for burial, for we know that the scavengers of death are already working on his mortal body, turning it back to the dust from whence it came. Joe, Fate, and I, under the direction of Mr. John Souther, who is experienced in preparing the dead for burial, wash the grit and sand from Dad's beard and hair and the caked blood from his ravaged body. We don't relish doing this, but it is for Dad, the one we all love above all others, and the tears of love that fall from us caress and sooth his maligned body.

Mom would have it no other way than to bury Dad in his Sunday "go-to-meetin" suit, the suit of love that she had so painstakingly woven, so she sets about to mend its material that had been rendered apart. It too is repaired with utmost love; every stitch taken, every broken thread repaired is stamped with Mom's tears. After Mom mends the suit, it is still wet, for Dad had lain in the icy waters of Wolf Creek for better than an hour, and wool will soak up water like a new ground, so Mom hangs the suit by the fire to dry.

When the suit dries, we boys dress Dad. Most of his unsightly wounds are hidden; however, his hands look terrible, for they are horribly disfigured. Virge Waldroup goes back to his store and brings back a pair of white gloves to put on Dad. The funeral arrangements are completed, and it is noted that practically everyone in Choestoe is at Mom and Dad's house, with the exception of Tom Swaim, Frank Swaim, Newt Swaim, and Fredrick (Fed) Cannup.

In the meantime, a search is on for the killers, and I join in. Tracks have been found of two men who came down the mountain, hid behind a fir tree, waylaid Dad, and then returned in the same general direction. Choestoe has some expert trackers, gentlemen who can read signs on the ground and make more out of them than a good reader can garner from an interesting book.

They are reputed to be able to see a honeybee fly over and track it back to the honey tree without a bobble, and if you ever saw them work, you wouldn't doubt it. The Reece men, J. B. and J. M.; John Souther; and W. Y. Curtis are hot on the trail. It is pointed out to me that the tracks are distinct and different. One is broader than the other is and makes no heel impression. The other is about a number seven shoe or boot with the heel a little twisted and set forward under the instep, and there are four large square tacks or nails in the front part of the left heel. Three of the tacks sit square to the front and one sits with the corner of the square to the front. These four tacks make a distinct and plain impression in the earth. We follow the tracks to a ridge across the road near Tom Swaim's fence and then across a path leading directly to Fed Cannup's.

Sheriff Jones comes up to me and says, "Jim, looks like the tracks lead right to Fed's house. Let's pay him a visit and see if he can account for his whereabouts. Is he involved, Jim? Do you have an inkling as to who the killers are?"

"Sheriff, I have more than an inkling, for I know for sure who killed Dad, and I promise you and all the world, that neither I nor any of the Lances will rest until the back-stabbing assassins are brought to justice."

"I don't know but what I would feel the same way if I were in your shoes, for your father was a good citizen and well respected," answers Sheriff Jones.

The time is five of ten, and what little light we have comes from the pale glow of a quarter moon and the occasional orange flash from a "ready roll" being lit and then dragged on. The posse sits hunkered in a haphazard sort of circle and listens to me recount the events of the past few months and the reason beyond a shadow of a doubt as to why I am certain it is the Yellow Mountain bunch.

"Well, men, I think I've heard enough. Let's go; we've got a long night ahead of us," says Sheriff Jones. We arise as one, and the only sound heard is the soft dusting of the dirt and leaves from our overalls; we know we must proceed quietly, because there is a distinct possibility that Fed will run.

We move silently, and in a few minutes we are in the yard of Fed Cannup. Sheriff Jones sends Bill Curtis and my brothers Joe and Fate around to the back door, just in case Fed lights a shuck, and the sheriff, the rest of the posse, and I stay in the front. The sheriff yells out, "Fed, Lizzie, this is the sheriff. Come out; we haft to ask you some questions."

In a few minutes, Fed opens the door, and the foul odor of his body rushes out to greet us. We step back involuntarily, for the smell of body odor mixed with mash is overwhelming. "Fed, where were you between two and three this afternoon?"

"I was at work, was there all day, and didn't come home until dark."

"Whereabouts?"

"I'd rather not say."

"Rather not say my . . . You'd better come clean, and fast, or you'll be in more trouble than you'll ever get out of."

"Ask Lizzie; she'll tell you I wasn't home."

"Lizzie, come out here and bring Fed's shoes with you."

Lizzie comes shuffling out, holding a pair of shoes in each hand, and mumbles, "He's only got two pairs—here they are."

"You men doing the tracking, look at these shoes and see if you recognize them as being the shoes that made the tracks." All gather around, examine the shoes at length, and to a man, agree that neither pair was worn by the killers. "Lizzie, you heard Fed say he was working all day; is that right?"

"Yeah, I reckon he was, for he shore wasn't here."

"Have you seen any of the Swaims today?"

"Yeah, Tom came by in the morning toting a tow sack that looked like it was filled with corn, and about two o'clock Frank and Newt came by for a little while."

"Do they visit often?"

"No, I ain't see'd them in a month of Sundays."

"Did anybody else come to your house?" asks the sheriff.

"Nobody, and Fed didn't git home until well after dark," Lizzie replies.

"Men, I've heard enough. Let's go arrest Frank and Newt," says Sheriff Jones.

Fed sheepishly asks, "Can I come along? I've always had a sneaky feeling about Frank myself."

"What about it, Jim? It's your call," says the sheriff.

There flashed through my mind Fed's association with Tom Swaim's crowd, for wasn't it his and Tom's still that was spurting out the evil shine when Dad called on them, and wasn't Fed at Tom's house a-drinking when I called on them to warn them about Dad? In all likelihood, the "work" that Fed didn't want to own up to doing was with Tom at their still, so I said, "Fed, let me warn you fair and square. If you do come with us, stay out of my way, for I don't have any use for the likes of you."

"I know you don't, Jim, but I'm your friend, and I'll swear on a stack of bibles that I had no part in your father's death."

"Fed, let's get one thing straight. You're not my friend, never have been, and never will be. If you get in my way, I'll grind you 'neath my heel like I would a copperhead."

I pull my watch out and note the time. It is ten after eleven. The posse, the righters of wrong, plus the one I have serious doubts about, hastily gathers for an impromptu meeting to plan the next move. The sheriff isn't all that acquainted with the habits of the suspects, Frank and Newt Swaim, though he's had to serve warrants and lock up Frank on numerous occasions for stealing and other petty crimes, so he asks, "Jim, where are they apt to be hiding?"

"There's not a bit of telling where that low-down, no-account Frank is, but wherever he is, you'll more than likely find Newt also. The members of the posse know Frank and Newt well. They are our neighbors, and we know that Frank in particular is a worthless individual, too sorry to provide a home for himself and his wife, so his whereabouts at any given time cannot be pinpointed. He meanders in and out of his kinfolks' homes, sponging upon them for shelter and food. Why, one week he might be at his dad's house, the next at Ben Nix's, the next at Newt Swaim Sr.'s, and so on, the length of his stay being determined by the amount of work that needs to be done. I don't mean to infer that he stays to help with the work, but that he leaves just before it commences." The other members of the posse nod in complete agreement.

"So where do we go from here?" asks the sheriff.

W. Y. (Bill) Curtis speaks up, "Sheriff, let's try his dad's place first. If he's not there, then we'll try the homes of the other folks he mooches on, and I'll bet you my hat . . . that when we do find him, the sorry filcher will be lying in bed."

We start out at a fast pace with me in the lead, for I am eager and chompin' at the bit to arrest Frank and Newt Swaim. I think how much I would like to face Frank again, just the two of us, and have a go at the conniving, low-down misfit. Why, I'd tear him apart limb by limb, do it slowly so he'd suffer the more, and I'd do it with total satisfaction.

Even though the terrain from Fed Cannup's to Tom Swaim's is steep, I quicken the pace, and at twenty-five after eleven, we are knocking on his door, calling him out. I notice the other men in the posse are almost out of breath, their chests rising and expanding rapidly—signs of a hurried trip, but I show no outward signs of exertion, for my body is shot full of some kind of force that drives me on and on. My teeth are clinched in decided anger, and my emotions are on raw edge, teetering precariously back and forth, edging closer to an eruption.

The sheriff yells out, "Tom, Tom Swaim, this is the sheriff. Come out here, we haft to ask you some questions." There are several minutes of muted talk and scuffling around inside. "Tom, we know you're in there. I'm telling you for the last time, come out."

"We're in bed. What do you haft to ask me?"

"Don't worry about that none; come on out, or I'll knock the door down and drag you out."

Tom can be heard saying, "Ah dang, it's getting where a feller can't do nothing. If it's not the old white-headed preacher a-pokin' his durn nose in other people's business, it's the fool sheriff." Then there could be heard the sound of dirty, stiff overalls being laboriously pulled on and the awkward noise of Tom fumbling around in the dark, trying to light his lantern, then foul-mouthed blackguarding as he says, "Hold your horses; I'll be out d'reckly."

This further defiling of Dad's good name angers me to no end. I nervously shift from one foot to the other, and my body twitches in uncontrolled fury as I anxiously await the appearance of Tom Swaim.

The rickety, ill-fitting door makes a scraping sound as it slowly creaks open, and Tom steps out. He holds the lantern in front of him, at arm's length, and it emits a strange, eerie light that portrays his scrawny face in an evil, orange glow. In this illumination, I can see what's wrong with the world. I see Satan himself and all of his legions wrapped up as one. "What do you fellers mean, getting a hard-working feller out of bed in the middle of the night?" Tom arrogantly asks. My hand moves involuntarily as if it is in the control of some unseen force, and I reach beneath my shirt for the secretly stashed forty-four. My fingers search out and eagerly wrap around the pearl handles, and I feel strangely good. I think now is the time to strike back at evil and remove its sinful force from the face of the earth forever. I quietly remove my hand from 'neath my shirt, cock the forty-four, aim it squarely at the face of the evil glow, and fire, but the click of the forty-four being cocked alerts Sheriff Jones. He hits my arm, ruining my aim, knocking my arm upward at the very instant I pull the trigger. The shot flies some two feet over Tom's head and cuts the top out of a sourwood. The retort echoes loudly as it glances wildly from mountaintop to mountaintop, and the heavy odor of gunpowder stains the night.

Tom drops to the ground as if he has been hit in the head with a maul and grovels about furiously, trying to escape this sudden assault. The lantern, having been slung aside by Tom in his hast to escape, lies about ten feet away, but its glow is somehow or other different; it shines out brightly because it has escaped from the hands of evil. I aim again, but Sheriff Jones steps squarely in front of me.

"Sheriff, step aside. I don't want to hurt you, but I'm a-goin' to pull the trigger."

"I can't, Jim. Come to your senses; two wrongs don't make a right. Now, I know how you feel, so I beg you, let law and order prevail."

"Sheriff, nobody knows how I feel. I don't know if Tom's directly involved or not, and really I don't care that much, for if he isn't, then he's indirectly involved. The still is part his, and he's the father of Frank and Newt, isn't he?" I say through clinched teeth.

"Jim, I know your reputation when it comes to the truth. If you'll say you won't take the law into your own hands, why then, I'll let you keep your gun."

"Sheriff, not being disrespectful of you or what your badge stands for, but if I don't want you to, neither you nor any other is man enough to take my gun."

"Jim, I know that's right, but just calm down. Let me handle this, for I promise you that whoever is involved will be brought to justice."

"All right Sheriff, I'll take you at your word, for I believe that would be Dad's way of handling it, but I'll promise you and the rest of the world that none of the Lances will rest in peace until the murderers are dangling from the end of a rope."

Tom lies motionless on the ground while the exchange takes place between the sheriff and me, but now he begins slowly to get up from his prone position, for he too knows my reputation and knows that I will not go back on my word or tell a lie, come hell or high water, and I can see a dark, wet stain resting in the crotch of his dirty overalls.

Tom's façade of bluster has been removed by my missed shot, and his cowardice lies exposed for all to see. He meekly says, "Sheriff, what do you want to know?"

"Are Frank and Newt in there?"

"No, they ain't."

"Do you know their whereabouts?"

"No, Sheriff, I really don't. I'm sorry." For once I agree with Tom as I think yes, sorry, and durn sorry at that.

We proceed relentlessly, for we are on the trail of two who have forever stained the name of Choestoe and who have brought grief and sorrow untold to the Lance family.

Finally, after several more dry calls, at about an hour past midnight we arrive at the home of Newt Swaim Sr. and strike pay dirt. The sheriff calls out, "Newt, we're looking for Frank and Newt Jr. Are they in there?"

126

"Yeah, they're here and in the bed," comes the reply. Bill Curtis, Joe, and Fate are again sent to the back door to prevent them from fleeing to parts unknown, for we know that Frank's wife has folks who live in Texas, and come first light of morning there is a good possibility that they will flee from Choestoe like scalded dogs.

Soon, Frank appears in the doorway, and his little brother Newt shadows him. He has on dirty, smelly clothes and presents an appearance of total filth. His boots are still wet and muddy. I glance down and notice a whang sown on one of his boots. I step closer to Frank so I can look the lowest of the low-down square in the eye. The sheriff steps with me, for he can feel the smoldering tension boiling within me, and he says, "Jim, be calm." He pokes me lightly in the ribs to get my attention, but it is unnecessary, for my dark brown eyes are focused on Frank as they pierce into the very depths of his soul, and all I can see is evil. At the same time as the sheriff, I spot an oval-shaped wound on Frank's face that has blood and matter oozing from it.

I step closer until we are within inches of each other, and I whisper, "Frank, you are a low-down backstabber."

Frank grins smugly through his prematurely rotting teeth and says, "Reporter, what's got your dander up?"

"Frank, shut your foul mouth before Jim knocks the rest of your rotten teeth out. You and Newt are under arrest," the sheriff says.

Frank is searched thoroughly. On his person, we find a hawk-bill-bladed, iron-handled knife. We give it an examination and find that the blade has been freshly scoured; there is sand inside the handle and blood on the knife itself.

A lump forms in my throat, and I try to hold back the tears that roll down my cheeks. I curse out bitterly, "Frank, you are a low-down—"

We start out with them, the low-downest of the low, heading to the law ground for a preliminary hearing. I can't help but notice that the fresh smell of the Choestoe February night is missing, for it has been overwhelmed by the dark stench wafting from the body and soul of these two perverts. I hope I haven't been contaminated by their filth, but I somehow realize better, for a cancerous hate has permeated every inch of my body, and the old Jim Lance is no more.

We have gone about a hundred yards when Frank asks, "Sheriff, what do you want with me?"

"Frank, you and Newt are wanted for murder."

"Well, what in the hell makes you think I done it?" [See Record of Trial, testimony of Sheriff Jones (12).]

And I think, just keep on talking, you nitwit; you are heaping more coals of fire upon yourself, for nothing up to this time has been said to you about who was murdered.

The sheriff pauses and says, "I need to be rounding up witnesses and gathering evidence; Jim, I'm going to turn Frank and Newt over to you, John Wellborn, Bill Curtis, and Ben Collins. Make certain they get to the law ground."

"Oh, no, ain't no way you can do that," Frank cries. "Just as soon as you're out of sight, Jim will kill us for sure; no way I'll agree to that."

Sheriff Jones jerks around as if he has been slapped in the face and snaps, "I'm callin' the shots. Your agreein' days are over. I can and will do as I well please, and you can consider it a done deal. Jim gave me his word, and that's good enough for me. I know you and your kind have a hard time understanding that there are still people left who follow the principle of 'a man's word is his bond,' but thank God, Jim is one of them."

It is two-thirty when the sheriff takes his leave from us and goes on to be about the business of sheriffing. We gather Frank and Newt up and start on our trek to the Choestoe law ground.

The pace is now more leisurely, for the job we set out to do is partially complete, and the sense of urgency has abated somewhat. Nevertheless, my sense of outrage at the heinous killing of my dad has not waned one iota, and there is still pent-up within me a volcano of fury just waiting for an excuse to erupt and spill its frustration out upon anyone who crosses my path.

After we have gone some little way, Newt complains about how hard it is to walk with his hands tied behind him. I know this is so, because the quarter moon is almost set, and what little light it gives out is soon dissipated by the dense forest; also, the mountain trail we are taking is steep and chock-full of rocks of assorted size and shape, and this makes walking difficult, even with arms swinging loose, so I cut their arms free.

Now, you might think this act of benevolence toward Frank and Newt is strange in light of the events of the past twelve hours, and on the surface, it is. If you were to pin me down and ask me what my real motive is, why, I'd tell you the truth. That, yes, I have an ulterior motive. I gave my word that I wouldn't take the law into my own hands, but what if the prisoners tried to escape? Now, that would put a whole new slant on things, wouldn't it? I am sworn and obligated to bring the killers to the law ground. We continue our journey in relative quietness, the only sounds being the huffing and puffing, the swishing sounds of overalls, the man-made sounds of a group of men on a mission. I am deeply engrossed with the unanswered questions of "What if?" and "Why?" What if I had met Dad? What if we had called in the other Lances and ended this before it began? Why did God turn His back on one of His faithful servants? The questions keep forming, and I keep grappling with them as best I can, but it is just too much for my young mind in its inexperience in handling matters of such magnitude. You can be assured of one thing: I'll not stand idly by. I'll act, and forcefully, with all of my might, for my very being, my soul, cries out "Retaliate, retaliate; seek revenge," and I will. I will over and over again, for I realize that I am a changed man. I know that there are many who will give up, many who put off doing things, and then there are some few who have the fortitude to go on; I, Jim Lance, will be one of the latter.

I lag a little behind the rest of the posse, hoping Frank and Newt will notice and try to escape. I know that I can catch them with no problem, for I am surprisingly agile and fast, despite the fact that I am a large man. Today, because of my fury, I am even more so. I give them every opportunity, but they refuse to take the bait and methodically plod on.

I see Frank engaging Ben Collins in conversation, and I am curious, for I would mightily like to know what is on his dirty mind. I notice Ben slowing down, not an appreciable amount, but gradually, as if he is getting tired, for it has been an arduous night. Before we have gone a quarter of a mile further, he is walking in front of me. I pick up my pace and close the distance to where I can hear what he has to say. "Jim, I thought you might be interested in what Frank said to me."

"You're right, Ben, I am. What did he allow?"

"Jim, he said that the damn reporting ought to be stopped or some more of the black sons of bitches would be killed." [See Record of Trial, testimony of Ben Collins (13).]

"Thanks, Ben." And I shake my head in bewilderment, because Frank still doesn't seem to think that he is in any kind of trouble. How ignorant can anyone be?

By the time we reach the law ground, a new day begins. Before too long, the sun will rise from behind Bald Mountain and the Low Gap and bathe Choestoe in warmth and goodness, but today, it seems to tarry in making its appearance, as if it has been desecrated and it too is ashamed of what it has been witness to. Why shouldn't it be? A Saint of God has fallen at the hands of Lucifer and his cohorts.

Some little time after we are at the law ground, Frank stands up and says, "I've got to take a leak."

I step forward and say to the rest of the posse, "I'll go with him." I take my forty-four, hand it to brother Fate, and say, "Keep this for me till I get back." The implication is plain and clear to everyone, including Frank, that it will just be us two alone out in the woods. Now is the time; try to escape if you dare.

I watch as Frank goes behind a big chestnut log. I see him wipe my dad's blood off his boots with frosted leaves, and I am incensed. Frank steps out cockily from behind the log and flashes me a sarcastic grin. I step up to him and say, "Frank, it's just you and me now." I say, "You are a cowardly sneak and have to squat to take a leak. Prove your manhood if you have any. Let's have a go at each other, see who the best man is. Why, I'll even give you the first lick." I wait, hoping and dreaming that he will take a swing at me, and then I can wrap my hands around his spindly neck and slowly squeeze, tighter and tighter, watch his face turn red, then blue, see his evil eyes begin to bulge out of their sockets, hear the snapping as the bone in his neck breaks; only then will I relax my grip.

Frank answers, "Ain't no way I'll let you get off the hook that easy. I heard what you promised the sheriff. I ain't big enough to fight you

130

head-up, but someday I'll cut your throat like I did your old white-haired daddy." Now I regret having made my promise to the sheriff. I think, surely there will come a time when it will just be Frank and me.

Around ten, Sheriff Jones makes it to the law ground with the witnesses. The hearing is held, and suffice it to say that there is ample evidence to bind Frank and Newt over to the Union County court system. The prisoners are taken to the Union County jail in Blairsville to stand trial for the murder of Reverend John Lance.

It is now noon, and Fate, Joe, and I start back to Lance Cove to be with our families. We have been without sleep for over thirty-six hours, and the strain of the ordeal, both mental and physical, has taken its toll. Yesterday we were carefree because we had Dad to turn to, but now our lives have been turned upside down. We have been shoved into positions of responsibilities not of our own accord, but because of the dastardly acts of others, and there are lines etched upon our young brows that weren't there before. We have fared better than the rest of the family though, for we were in the thick of the action while they were at home, not knowing what was taking place. This uncertainty breeds a kind of anxiousness that cannot be described.

When we cross the creek that runs in front of the house and step into the yard, there are our womenfolk, wringing their hands and waiting anxiously for us and word of what has taken place. I hug Jane and draw Mom near to me while the rest of the gathered family members and neighbors crowd closer. We all cry about Dad, for our hearts are broken.

I recount the events leading up to the arrest of Frank and Newt as best I can, for they are swirling around in my head like a crazy whirlwind. Whenever I skip over or omit any detail, no matter how small, Fate or Joe butt in, making sure that all of the family knows exactly what took place. When I tell about shooting at Tom and barely missing, Mom responds, "Too bad, Jim." I have never heard Mom raise her voice or hold aught against anyone; such is the depth of our hurt and rage. Mom feeling the way she does is easy to understand when it is considered in the light of belonging to a loving and caring family, for when Mom and Dad married, it was forever, and they became as one. Now

Dad, the sustaining light in Mom's life, has been snuffed out while it still is full of oil and burning bright.

I nod my head slowly and say, "I made a promise to Sheriff Jones that I would let the law run its course in dealing with Frank and Newt, but now I have come to regret it deeply, for no one knows how we (the Lance family) have been provoked by Frank running his dirty mouth, for even now he continues to brag and to blackguard Dad and all of us. If only I hadn't given my word, there would be no need of a trial, for I would have already judged and tried them, found them guilty and sorely lacking in the common principles of decency, and they would now lie as dirt beneath my feet. But I gave my word, and I will abide by it, no matter how bad it hurts."

Andy, Dad's brother, says, "Jim, I don't fault you in the least, but I didn't give my word, and if I can, I'll slaughter that bunch just like I would a pack of sheep-killing dogs, for that is what they are."

"And neither did I," responds John Frady, Dad's brother-in-law. "And if they want to stay healthy, they had best sleep with one eye open."

I also tell them about how I tried to lure Frank and Newt into trying to escape and about the bitter exchange I had with Frank when he was answering nature's call. How I baited and demeaned him, called him every kind of a name I could think of, even went so far as to offer him the first lick if he would only go head-to-head with me, but he refused because he knew what would happen to him should he fall into the trap, for even Frank is smarter than that.

"What about Debarris?" I ask. "Has anyone sent him word?"

"Yes Jim, Bud Miller has gone to Blairsville now to do just that, and there will be hell to pay when Debarris gets here," Andy replies. "John and Debarris were real close." And I know it to be so, for I have observed Dad and Debarris when they are together and noticed the special bond of love and mutual respect running through them both. Now the bond has been severed, and Debarris will hurt to the bone. Yes, there will be hell to pay when he gets here, there's no doubt about it.

Debarris, who has a passion for life, who has experienced the brutality of a civil war where brother sometimes fought against brother, will be coming home, and he will have fire in his belly, for the passion that burns just barely beneath the surface has been unleashed, flamed by the act of brutality against Dad, and it will be blazing out of control, ready to consume everything in its path.

I look down the road and see a stately-looking fellow mounted upon a sleek horse coming toward us at a steady pace. I notice the heavy beard, the confident way he sits the saddle, the determined tilt of his head, the chiseled set of his jaw, the appearance of a military man on a mission. As he gets closer, I make out who it is: Napoleon Hill, Debarris's good friend and ours.

With a steady hand, he guides his horse to a stop and alights. I walk toward him and ask, "Napoleon, how you been?"

"I'm fine, but how are you? Caroline and the rest of the family holding up? I came to be with you all as soon as I heard. Is there anything I can do?"

"Napoleon, it's mighty, mighty hard. I don't know what we're going to do without Dad. And Mom is grieving herself to death, for they were so close and loved each other so much."

"Jim, I know it's rough, for I felt the same way when we lost Charles. Is it all right if I go in and speak to Caroline?"

"Yes Napoleon, Mom would for sure want to see you." We go into the house and I call out, "Mom, it's Napoleon; he's come to be with us." Napoleon puts his arms around Mom, hugs her in a comforting manner, and tries to assure her that everything will be all right.

"Napoleon, what am I going to do? I don't believe I can live without John. Oh, we loved each other so very, very much; why did this happen?" And the tears flow freely.

I notice that Napoleon, the tough Civil War veteran who has been through many bloody campaigns and has seen death over and over again, can barely speak because he is so "choked up," and he whispers, "Caroline, we'll just have to take it a day at a time."

I do appreciate Napoleon coming. He is on a mission, a mission of friendship. I did not ask or expect, it but if I had given it any thought, I would have known Napoleon would be here, for when Charles was shot while fulfilling his duties as sheriff, didn't Debarris lay everything else aside and go to be with the Hills? So now, without asking, they are repaying the act of kindness.

And in the twenty-five years since Debarris and Napoleon became friends, the Lances and Hill families have become close. It is a friendship built to last, for it is built on trust, mutual respect, and a quiet acknowledgement of each other's independence, for both families are fiercely independent. After all, isn't this what friendship is, recognition of a need and then giving freely without having to be asked? Moreover, the depth of our friendship has not suffered, even though we live on opposite ends of the county and are separated by some twenty-five miles.

Our little cove is still filled with grieving family and friends who have come to be with us during this time of heartbreak, and the clay yard that Mom keeps so meticulously swept is packed as hard as a rock by the constant milling around, and my heart is too. It is hard for it is tempered like steel by the consuming hate that eats at my soul. So many people come up to me and ask, "What can I do? How can I help?" They tell me deeds of kindness done for them by Dad until I can barely remember who they are, and the day becomes a maze of confusion, a blur of activity, a nightmare that surely I will awaken from, but it is not to be, for Dad's death is final and absolute, and I will be driven and consumed by it until the day I die.

However, I do remember Jim Collins, a friend of mine, calling me aside and saying, "Jim, I'm awful sorry about your Dad. I was in attendance Sunday and heard your dad preach. Thought you would like to know what his text was and what his sermon was about."

"Jim, I would like to know."

"Well, his text was Matthew 25:1-13, the parable about the virgins. I have heard your dad preach many times, but Sunday he was at his best as he warned all of us about the perils of not being prepared for death and how we as individuals and as a community must not slumber but be alert, not stand idly by and be destroyed from within by bootlegging. Jim, as you know, your dad was so strong against moonshining that he could not preach a sermon without going into details about its evils. He warmed to the task at hand, and the 'Amen's' from the congregation were music to his ears as he waxed on and on. He preached with a fury, like he might have some sort of premonition about death and was afraid that he might not have much more time to speak out about this evil. When I heard that your dad was murdered, it brought to mind how he closed his sermon: 'Watch therefore, for ye know neither the day nor the hour wherein the Son of Man cometh.'

"Jim, there is something else bothering me a whole lot. I hate to tell you what it is, but I feel I must get it off of my chest and out in the open, for we have been friends for years, and I don't want anything to stand in the way of our friendship. I'm afraid that the knife Frank used to kill your dad was one I traded to him last Friday. It was a hawk-bill-bladed, iron-handled knife. Jim, do you know if that was the murder weapon?"

"Yes, I do, for when Frank was arrested he had that very knife on his person, and you could still see Dad's blood on it in several places, even though it had been scoured."

"Jim, I'm so sorry; if I had'a known or had an inkling as to why he so badly wanted my knife, then there would have been no way I would have swapped with him. And maybe Jim, I ought to have known, for I remember Frank saying he 'needed a man's knife, for he had a man-sized job to do.'"

"I know you wouldn't have, and I don't hold aught against you in the least for making a good trade; how were you to know?"

"But I still feel so bad and somehow or other a bit guilty," Jim Collins responds.

"Well don't, for the knife isn't responsible for Dad's death. It's an inanimate object only, an instrument that can be used for good or evil, according to whoever wields it. In addition, in Frank Swaim's hand it's for evil, for he is a sneaky bushwhacker and is rotten to the core. No Jim, the knife didn't kill Dad; it was Frank."

It is now seven o'clock, and I notice Dad's turkeys have already taken to the roost. This is much earlier than usual, and they too seem to sense, somehow or other, that not all is well, and they gobble excitedly. The sun has just gone behind the range of mountains that frames our cove, and before too much longer, it will be dusk. In fact, you can see it now; the tentacles of night are beginning to search out and catch hold of the last rays of the setting sun and pull them closer and closer, until they have been smothered, overcome, and cloaked in darkness.

The forces of nature have staged their daily duel and once again, it is night. If a tally were being kept between good and evil, if goodness is considered as light and evil as darkness, then the score would now be even, but in this instance evil is one up on goodness, for Dad, a good man, lies dead, but I can promise you one thing—the tally will not remain as it is.

I have been forty-eight hours without sleep, and it tells. I go to bed and fall exhausted into the feather bed that I slept in for years. This is the same bed that soothed and comforted my aching body when I was brutally accosted, and I seek comfort in its warmth. However, it is not forthcoming, because my sleep is fitful and constantly being interrupted by shrieking demons. I recognize who they are: Frank and Newt. I struggle, toss and turn, try to get at them, but my efforts are futile. Jane holds me and tries to comfort me as best as she can, but comfort is hard to come by when your dad has been killed.

The persistent crowing of Dad's game roosters announcing to everyone that a new day is dawning interrupts my fitful sleep. I turn over and smell the aroma of freshly perked coffee and the pleasing odor of country ham-meat frying. I get up, dress, and saunter into the kitchen to find the good women in our community preparing a sumptuous breakfast. "Jim, sit down at the table; I'll fix you a plate."

"No thanks Vesta, I'm not hungry; just a cup of coffee will do." I've not eaten a bite since I got word of Dad's death, and I'm mighty thankful for the kindness and consideration shown by these ladies, but my appetite has been stripped just as surely as one season following another. Why, I'll bet you that I've lost fifteen pounds, for I've taken up my belt a notch or two, and I notice in the mirror that my dark eyes seem to be darker and set further back in my head and are encircled by black rings.

I get up and go into the parlor to be with Dad, for I know that my time with him is short. The funeral is at eleven. I gaze lovingly down, pick up his gloved hand, and notice how pale he is, almost like the color of the white glove I am holding. I bend down and tenderly kiss his cheek, and I ache all over. I remain at his side, holding his hand, not wanting to turn loose, transfixed for several hours, absorbed in my own thoughts. I am in a daze, for my peaceful existence has been shattered forever by Frank and Newt Swaim, and possibly others.

Napoleon puts his hand on my slumped shoulder and says, "Jim, it's time to go." I slowly turn Dad's hand loose and gather with the rest of the family around the coffin and cry and cry.

Dad's body is loaded onto his wagon and the funeral procession to Old Salem church starts. It is long and stretches better than one-eighth of a mile, because Dad has so many friends that want to "go the last mile" with him. Now, the trip to the church is anything but quiet, for the wailing cries of despondent family and friends and the squeaking and rattling of the wagon as it bounces along the rocky road combine to create a tumult of sound that rolls surely and steadily along toward the church. I notice that the birds and the other creatures of the forest are abnormally quiet. I think it is because they recognize that a man who lived in harmony with nature has fallen. I believe they fall quiet because they are paying him their last respects, not because of the loud noise of the funeral procession.

As we pass the spot where Dad was murdered, I glance over to survey the scene once again, and I am further filled with a seething hate toward the perpetrators that boils and boils. I see that the icy water of Wolf Creek has washed away the evidence of Dad's blood that stained it, and it is again flowing pure and fresh. In addition, the sand where Dad lay when he was dragged out of Wolf Creek has begun to soak up and blot out the last remnants of his struggle to live.

It seems that Mother Nature is trying to cleanse herself quickly and revert to where life and conditions are the same, and it can be done, for I see it in the works, but I know that my life will never be the same. The consuming hate and the drive for revenge within me cannot be washed away by water or be healed by time.

The procession rolls slowly on, making its way steadily toward the church. When we get in sight of it, I see something astounding; the yard, the roads, and even the woods surrounding the church are packed with a multitude of people who have come to pay their respects to Dad, a man of God, a farmer, a father, and a friend to all.

We reach the churchyard at fifteen to eleven and the coffin is unloaded. Then it is taken into the church and opened up, for custom dictates that this is the time for friends and neighbors to file by for one last look.

We go in, sit down, and wait for the service to commence at eleven, but it's late in starting, for there are so many people in attendance that it takes better than thirty minutes for them to slowly file past, and we are so sad and our faces are ashen. This will stand as evidence of how much Dad was liked and esteemed. At fifteen after eleven, Dad's service starts with the congregation joining in and singing, "When the Roll Is Called Up Yonder," "In the Sweet By and By," and "What a Friend We Have in Jesus." Then the preaching starts. Mom has selected three preachers to speak at Dad's funeral, and each proclaims in some fashion or the other that Dad has already preached his own funeral, and I know he has. Moreover, from the size of the crowd in attendance, it is evident that he preached a noble one. To tell you the truth, I can't tell you anything they say, for I am so wrapped up in my own thoughts about Dad. At one-thirty, the last preacher finally winds down. We, the immediate family, plus Napoleon, gather around the open coffin for our last look at Dad, the greatest man who ever lived, in my estimation. Oh, the last look is so traumatic and final. We all cry our hearts out to no avail, for the hurt is not eased by tears. Mom tries to lift Dad out of the coffin and does manage to partially lift his body upward, but his head doesn't follow, and it tilts backward at a grotesque and awkward angle, for it is only attached to the rest of the body by a small strip of skin. Mom faints at this horrid sight, and the congregation gasps at this display of total disfiguration. My younger brothers and sisters scream and shout, "Get up Dad, get up, we don't want you to go, we don't want to go home without you!" I feel like crying my insides out and venting my frustrations out in the open, but I bottle them up inside, for somehow or other I know I must step forward and take hold, for Dad has trained me for it and he would expect it of me. I bend over the coffin and kiss Dad's cheek for the last time, nod to Napoleon, and we begin to gather the family together in a haphazard manner and try to sort out some semblance of control. The coffin is nailed shut and carried to the cemetery for burial. We follow behind.

A brief ceremony is held, and Dad's coffin is put into the wooden vault and gently lowered into the newly dug grave. Friends and neighbors take turns shoveling the dirt back into the grave. We stand helpless, not knowing what to do, as shovelful after shovelful heaps up, building a barrier forever separating us from the one we love. And we realize that even now Dad's mortal body is turning back to the dirt from whence it came.

Family after family comes by to wish us well, offer us their condolences, and inquire if there's anything they can do. They are sincere about it, but the sincerity has a way of fading with time. Families soon forget, quickly becoming occupied with themselves. It is natural that they do, for this is just another fact in the struggle of an ongoing life.

I know the facts of life, so to speak, and realize that it will be mainly up to our immediate family to cope and look after Mom and my younger brothers and sisters. So Jane and I, our two little ones, Fate and his family, and our friend Napoleon go back home with Mom to spend the night so we can begin to make plans about the future.

When we get back to Lance Cove, it is covered with a pall of sadness, for the one that has nurtured its resources, tended its fields, and caused them to sprout forth with abundant life, laughter, and love will never return. For Dad, the ever-sustaining force over so much and so many, is gone, and Lance Cove, Choestoe, and my life will change in its wake, because three days ago I was carefree, happy, and at peace with myself and the world, but now my peaceful existence has been shattered. I am being overwhelmed by a burning rage that must be quenched, for its depth and enormity promises to override everything else, and I will forever seek revenge.

The house we come back to is not as it was. It is filled with a strange quietness; where before its rooms were filled with laughter and happiness, the sounds of a happy family, now there is a silent void.

Still, we must plan for tomorrow. I recall the countless times Dad said, "Jim, plan for tomorrow, for without planning there can be no future." Then for some strange reason, I feel Dad's presence, and he says to me, "Jim, when you go into the woods and fell a tree, it doesn't destroy all of the rest of the forest, does it?"

"No Dad, it doesn't," I respond.

"Well Jim, don't let my death destroy my family."

"But Dad, the mightiest tree in all of the forest has fallen, and without you for guidance, it is going to be so hard."

"I know you may find it so, but look after your mom and the rest of your brothers and sisters. You can do it Jim; I know you can, for you are a Lance, and don't ever forget it."

I will do my best, Dad, and I promise that I won't ever forget anything.

Chapter XIII

PLANNING FOR THE TRIAL

Our family starts in to make plans. I suggest and want Mom and my brothers and sisters to move in with me, but Mom firmly says, "No Jim, I'm not going to move in with you and Jane. I believe your dad would want me to stay here."

I protest, but Napoleon says, "Jim, I know I'm not family and have no right whatsoever in voicing an opinion, but I believe your mom is right. She can't run away from what has happened, and she has too many good memories of Lance Cove just to pull up stakes and leave. Besides, if she did, that would, in itself, be a victory of sorts for Frank and Newt Swaim."

"Napoleon, you do have a right; you are as close to us as family. Yes, I understand what you are saying. I guess it is best that she stays here, and I'll come by every day to help," I say.

"And so will I," answers Fate.

John Frady, Dad's brother-in-law who lives in Frady Cove, the cove lying next to ours, says, "I'm closer than any of you. I'll be checking on Caroline and the family every day. It's just a hop, skip, and a jump from my place."

Joe, my younger brother, adds, "I'll put in the crops and look after things the best I can. I've always depended on Dad, but I'll give it my best."

"Joe," I say, "we have all depended on Dad, and he's always been there when we've needed him. He taught all of us well; you'll have no problem."

Napoleon adds, "Looks to me like you have got all the bases covered, for I can see everyone is willing to pitch in and do their share. And let me tell you now that if you ever need me, all you have to do is call; the day will never be too short or the night too long but what I will respond."

In any situation where there is conflict, it is important to have an individual on your side who cares, but who is not so emotionally bound as to have clouded vision. He needs to be able to separate himself from the crowd and step above spur-of-the-moment decisions. He needs to be able to discern with a dubious eye. He needs to instill confidence in those around him and be a natural leader.

Lucky are those who happen to be allied and associated with an individual who has this kind of experience. In this matter, the Lances are lucky to have Napoleon Hill as their friend.

Besides Joe, still living at home are Rutha, Anna, John, and Nancy.

We spend the night at Mom's. All during the night, I can hear cries of distress coming from her bedroom. This is the first night that she has been without Dad, and it is going to take a lot of getting used to before there is any relief, for she so much depended upon Dad.

We arise to a new day and a new beginning, a beginning not sought, but thrust upon us by the heinous actions of others. The day promises to be bright and sunny, with a decided nip in the air. We hustle around busily, trying to bury our sorrow by keeping busy; there are chores that have to be done and new routines to be established.

Sometime up in the later part of the morning, our friend Napoleon takes his leave and goes back to his home in Ivy Log.

At dinnertime, Mom calls me and the rest of the family together and says, "I've been doing a heap of serious thinking. Here's what I've come up with; see what you think. John's gone now, no use in trying to deny it, but we can't let him die in vain. I ache all over! My heart is hard, and I want an eye for an eye and a tooth for a tooth. Isn't that what the Bible allows? Frank and Newt, and any others that were involved in any way, must pay, and to the fullest. I want Fate, Joe, and the rest of the family to help out here until we can manage. Jim, I want you to take the lead in seeing that justice is served. Get the lawyers and see to all of that."

Fate responds, "Sounds to me Mom has it planned right. Jim, we'll take care of things around here if you'll see to the trial, for you're much more forceful than I am."

"Mom, if this is what you want, I'll promise you and the rest of the family that I'll not rest until the killers get their due. You can be certain on that account, and I'll help out here too."

Mom says, "Jim, we'll make it fine; the trial is the most important thing right now. See to it that Frank and Newt get what's coming to them!"

Now, this suggested course of action as put forth by Mom might seem a bit callous and unladylike in the light of how women are generally portrayed. However, here in the mountains they are not shrinking violets, and you will not find them drinking tea in the afternoon or being coddled by doting servants, for survival here is a combined effort, with the women doing as much as, if not more than, the men do.

Mom has lived, loved, and been loved in return. She has laughed and suffered the excruciating pain of childbirth with no outward sign of hurt, but no pain before has ever cut as deep or hurt as much as when Dad fell at the hands of the devil's henchmen. Her reaction is merely an extension of the deep love that she had for Dad.

The whole family feels as she does, and we will all be working to that end; besides, we know that even now the very bones of our ancestors are quaking in their graves, demanding revenge. And yes, until they are satisfied they cannot be quieted, and they will not sleep the peaceful eternal sleep.

Jane, our two kids Jack and Juan, and I leave Mom and the rest of the family at four o'clock in the evening and return to our home on the Nottely River.

I have to start making preparations, and I need to be by myself a little bit so that I can formulate a plan of action that makes sense. I have been given my marching orders, and I will march on until they are complete. And to tell you the truth, they are about as I would have suggested, except I planned on going back to Lance Cove every day and helping out. No man can honestly say that I, Jim Lance, ever shirked his duty when it came down to matters concerning the family. Now that the others are going to see to Mom and my brothers and sisters, I can more fully concentrate on the upcoming trial. I can see the wisdom of their course of action, for I would be stretching myself thin, and I might accidentally neglect some detail that would be important in seeing that Frank and Newt are convicted.

Jane recognizes my needs, and she promises to keep Jack and Juan quiet, for she too is a Lance, through and through, and her desire for revenge is almost as great as ours. Moreover, through experience, for she was the best student at the Wild Boar Institute, she knows that you think and learn much better when you are alone and things are quiet. So if in the next day or two, I go up on Blood and Slaughter Mountains to learn from them and to surround myself in the total quietness that only nature is able to provide, she will understand.

Now, Blood and Slaughter Mountains are not strangers to blood and gore, for they got their name from and were witnesses to the battle between the Cherokee and Creek Indians. Legend has it that the battle was so fierce and the action so brutal that Wolf Creek flowed red with blood for three days. Moreover, it is my desire that Wolf Creek flow again with blood, not as it did in legendary times, nor as it did three days ago, but with the blood of the Yellow Mountain bunch.

Dark comes, and with it comes the sounds and smells of an early Choestoe spring night. I can hear the croaking chorus of the frogs as they announce that the dearth of winter is over, and spring is indeed here; you can feel it in the air.

I step out on the porch, lean upon the railing, and smell the newly turned sod and the clean smell arising from Nottely's water. I inhale deeply and catch the faint, tantalizing odor from the early-blooming sarvis. I gaze up at the sky and behold a thousand and one twinkling stars.

Then suddenly, the peaceful serenity of the night is shattered by a blood-curdling scream rolling down from the height of Blood Mountain. I recognize the sound, the scream of the hunting black panther. Now, this scream sounds strangely like the agonizing cry of a woman in much distress, and it is given as a warning to others that she is the fiercest hunter of all. There is a sudden quietness that falls like a drawn curtain as the creatures of the forest and field also recognize the call and hurry about to heed its threat, for tonight all of Choestoe is under a "death threat."

I remember back to the time when I was fourteen, when Dad sent me and Joe to bring in our cow after we heard the panther scream. I thought we were alone, but we really weren't; Dad followed at a safe distance to make sure that we were safe. In this manner, he taught us to be self-reliant and have confidence in our abilities and ourselves.

A lump is in my throat, and a tear forms in my eye and slowly runs down my cheek. I don't bother to brush it aside because for the last few days, they are as common to my person as the frost is to a winter night. I realize that I don't have Dad, and I will have to get by and depend upon my own abilities, but in a way I do, for it was he who taught me and honed my skills.

An eerie feeling comes over me, and I feel strangely akin to the wily panther. I suck in mightily, pulling as much of the night air into my lungs as they will hold. I pause for a second, and then it comes forth, a scream of frustration and of challenge to the Yellow Mountain bunch of such magnitude and force that they will have to cringe in dread. It gets even quieter, for everything and everyone seems to recognize that now there are two hunters in Choestoe to contend with. Now the rules of old are cast aside, and I will do unto others before they have a chance to do unto me.

Jane comes out onto the porch, puts her arms around me, and says, "Jim, do you feel all right?"

"Yes Jane, I do. I don't know what in the world came over me. The scream seems to have come out of its own accord, but anyway, I want Choestoe, the Yellow Mountain bunch, and the entire world to know that this matter is not settled in the least!"

"I think they know now, if they didn't before," Jane answers.

We go back into the house and get ready to go to bed. Jane picks Jack and Juan up and puts them in the bed with us, and I am glad, for so much has been taken from us the last few days that it doesn't pay to take chances. They sleep between us, and we cradle them in a "cocoon of love." They feel secure and safe, and they are. After all, isn't this the way

145

it is meant to be—parents protecting and looking after their offspring, then in due time the offspring protecting and looking after their parents, a continuing cycle, bonded together by love? I think back and recall the many times Dad was there to protect me when I needed him. I feel awful because the one time when he needed me, I wasn't there, and because I wasn't, the bond has been broken. But what can I do to make amends? The bond is sustained by life, and Dad is gone. I think and cry for hours and hours, but nothing I can come up with offers any peace or comfort, and my pillow is soaked.

Sometime in the aft part of the night I fall asleep, exhausted, but what little sleep comes is fitful because it is filled with nightmares, and my entire body jerks in response.

When morning comes, I am eager to roll out of bed, not because I am rested and all is well, but because there are chores to do, more preparations to make, and questions of "Why?" and "What if?" running wildly through my head that demand an answer.

I am edgy, still running on a nervous energy that seems to have soaked into every nook and cranny in my body. My body is filled with hate, and I will readily admit that at this stage I am a troubled, dangerous man.

I don't mean I'm dangerous in the sense that I will strike out blindly and irrationally against my neighbors and friends and bring grief upon them such as we are experiencing. On the contrary, those who have been friends and befriended my family and me will still be treated in the same considerate manner as before. I will continue to be a neighbor and to be neighborly to them. This is a fact, for I will not tell a lie.

On the other hand, take Frank and Newt Swaim; they are such notorious liars that they will tell you that a black horse is a white one and you a-holding the reins.

What I really mean about being dangerous is that I will not be hesitant in striking back in the most brutal fashion possible at the Yellow Mountain bunch and all associated with them. In fact, I shall seek them out at every opportunity, and I promise that they shall fall, no matter the time it takes, just as surely as night follows day.

I know it says in the Bible to forgive, but there's no damn way that's a-going to happen, for neither I nor any of the Lances are in the forgiving business when it comes to one of our own. Anyway, I have serious doubts about the Bible now, for where was God when Dad needed Him?

This unforgiving trait is another characteristic woven deep into the fabric of my being. It combines with the other traits and makes me, Jim Lance, a distinct individual, yet I am uncommonly like my ancestors, for these traits have been passed forth from generation to generation. Moreover, they will continue to be, as long as one man or woman upon the face of the earth answers to the name "Lance."

This unforgiving spirit lay dormant in my body until four days ago, for it was covered up by the other traits that are perceived to be better. Now Frank and Newt Swaim have exposed it. They have plowed the soil of my soul, and it has sprouted forth, taken root, and is growing wildly out of control, fertilized by hate, anger, and malice. As the saying goes, "You reap what you sow." They sowed the seeds of discontent, and I will plow their fields until the Grim Reaper is ready unto the harvest.

Probably there are others who have an unforgiving attitude and can hide it, but I can no more conceal my hate and bitterness toward the Yellow Mountain bunch than a chicken can like a hawk. It's just there, plain and simple, for all the world to see. I'm no hypocrite, for if I hold aught against you, you'll know it, for I'll come to see you, face-to-face, man-to-man, and tell you about it and what I intend to do; then when it happens, you won't have to wonder who did you in, for you'll know. I don't believe in pussyfooting around when it comes to honor and family. The Yellow Mountain bunch don't see it that way, for they are yellow cowards and lower-down than snakes that grovel around upon the ground on their belly.

Too much has been taken from me and too much has happened in the last four days for me ever to be as I was. Whereas before, my life revolved around God, family, and love, now it is centered on hate and revenge.

I am a changed man. That much I know, for the die has been cast.

Even though my appetite hasn't returned, I force myself to eat a big breakfast; I know that I will need the energy to fortify myself for the planned day's activities. I finish the chores and go back into the house where I find Jane looking after Jack and Juan, busily doing the work which has been neglected for the last few days. Jane is a meticulous housekeeper, and she is hard at work, trying in one day to restore our little house to the spic-and-span condition it was in before. I chide her a bit by saying, "Slow down Jane; Rome wasn't built in a day."

She grins in a disarming manner and says, "Jim, I know it wasn't; you need to take some of your own advice." It's true; I do, for I've been burning the candle at both ends lately. I nod in agreement, but the swirling events of the last few days and my family's compelling drive for revenge doesn't leave any room for slowing down. It is necessary that I push myself this way, regardless of the toll it might take upon my body or me.

I say, "Jane, I think I will go to the big mountains today if you think you and the boys will be all right and if it's agreeable with you."

"Sure it is, Jim. We'll be okay. It will be good for you, because you need some time alone to sort out things. I'll pack you a dinner."

"That won't be necessary, Jane," I reply. She scoffs at my mild refusal and packs me a dinner.

I hug Jane, Jack, and Juan, pick up my rifle, load it, get my dinner, check my overalls to make sure I have my knife, and I step out the door. It probably isn't necessary to tote a gun and carry a knife, for I am not expecting trouble, but neither was Dad.

There are two main ways to get to Blood Mountain from my house. One is much better and shorter than the other is and is the customary route of travel. It follows Wolf Creek, up past the Reece fields to the foot of Blood Mountain, where the creek branches off into several smaller tributaries. The trail then follows the right prong that leads up to the gap between Blood and Slaughter Mountains. You take a left in the gap and follow the ridgeline to the top of Blood.

The other is much longer and is seldom used when your destination is Blood Mountain. To a seasoned walker, it would make no sense at all to take, but I take it anyway, for I have my own reasons.

I go a quarter of a mile, and just before I disappear from sight, I turn around to look at my family. They are standing in the door, waving. A knot wells up in my throat, and I wave to them in return, turn around, resume walking, and disappear from sight. I am on the trail that leads up toward Sullivan Cove. I go another one-half of a mile, swing to the left, and intersect the trail that Dad took from Lance Cove to the church up on the river. I pause to think. From here, it is approximately a half of a mile to the Tom Swaim place, and it would be a mile or more out of the way, but who cares; I have something to prove. I turn to the right and head straight toward Tom Swaim's house. Their house is situated so that the occupants can see anyone approaching from a distance. I might add that it was done so not by chance but by design.

As I approach, I see someone out in the yard; however, when they see me approaching, they get up and saunter into the house as if it is time for them to go inside. It is, for no telling what I will do if provoked, for the chip on my shoulder is resting lightly, just looking for an excuse to fall off. I stop directly in front of the house, sit down on a stump, and lean my rifle up against it. I take out my pipe, fill it with tobacco, tamp it in firmly, light up, and start smoking. I pull my knife out of my pocket, open it up, and start whittling away as if I am an innocent, tired stranger passing through an unfamiliar land, needing a rest. The meaning is clear. The heinous onslaught against Dad will never be forgotten, and I will never let the matter stand. I stay on the stump for over thirty minutes and glare at the occupants inside with a look as hard as steel, but no one comes out to greet or challenge me, for they are as quiet as church-house mice.

I get up, shake the dirt from my overalls, and saunter slowly on past the house until I am out of their sight. I follow a draw up a ways, fall back down, cross Spivey Creek, reach Chestnut Cove, and proceed on to Fisher Knob. From here, I can hear the roar of Helton Creek Falls. My pace quickens, and shortly I am standing by the falls and my body is being cooled by the floating wet mist.

I see the beauty of nature as the water plunges in a "free fall" down the sheer rock face of the mountain until its fall is broken by a gentle pool, and there it rests quietly, gathering its nerve momentarily before flinging itself once again over the cliff and continuing its deadly fall. I notice the transformation the water experiences, from a clear, soft-flowing peaceful stream one minute to a roaring cascade of rushing madness beset with danger the next. I think of how closely my life parallels the water of Helton Creek, for once I was quiet and peaceful.

I rest at the falls for thirty minutes or so and then start on. I climb steadily and at last reach Nance Ridge. I pause to take a blow and then proceed on. Before too long I reach the Level-lands and pause again to rest. I glance back down toward the way I came, and I see the settlement below. It looks so peaceful from here, because man's imperfections are hidden by the distance, but I know better, for we are awash in conflict or soon will be.

From the Level-lands, I take a right and follow the ridgeline until I reach Frogtown Gap. I sit down to rest for several minutes to gather myself, for the final push to reach the summit of Blood Mountain will be difficult; it is still some three miles distant, and the majority of my walking will be straight up. Now, there is a trail that winds back and forth and is not so steep, but the distance is much further. However, that is not the way I do things, for I have never dodged an object or an issue; I prefer to hit things head-on. I see the mountain's foreboding bulk looming in the distance, and it contrasts vividly against the paler blue of the sky. Blood Mountain is the second highest mountain in all of Georgia, and it plays second fiddle to Bald Mountain by only a few scant feet.

Its foreboding appearance is what draws me to it in the first place, and I feel no awe in its presence; rather I sense a strange force uniting us in a shared goal. I look up, and there it stands, proudly dominating the skyline, towering above the other, lesser mountains, meeting and rejecting all challenges thrown against it.

I get up slowly, inhale deeply to fill my lungs with the clean, fresh air, and continue my journey. I cross the long ridge that runs back down toward the Reece fields and Lance Cove and reach the foot of the Blood. I glance up again and notice its ominous height. Then I attack the Blood with the sustained vigor of frustration and youth and do battle for better than an hour before I at last reach its summit.

I sit down on the rocks that lace the pinnacle of the mountain to rest. I can't truthfully say that I conquered it or that it conquered me, but here I am on its summit. I am exhausted, and beads of sweat run down my forehead like little rivers. My shirt is wet through and through because the struggle was fierce, befitting two determined gladiators. I am being cooled by the winds that constantly buffet the Blood. I nod my head to the mountains in admiration. The wind picks up velocity and howls angrily.

Now, the curious might wonder how I can be familiar with and know the names of all the mountains, gaps, rivers, and streams in Choestoe. Well, there is no mystery in this, and I am not the only one who knows Choestoe like he does the palm of his hand, for my neighbors too are mountaineers, and we roam the mountains in search of food, medicine, and recreation. Why, we are as comfortable five miles from our homes as we are in our own back yards.

In fact, our livestock are fenced out of the homeplaces and taken to the mountains, where they fend for themselves and grow fat off of the wild grass, weeds, acorns, and chestnuts that flourish here in the mountains. They do flourish, for when they are brought back in off of the range they are sleek coated and are as fat as lard hogs. We go every so often to salt and check on them, and we know our own, for each family has a mark, and it is affixed to them. They may be miles from where they were driven, but we follow until they are found, and we become even more familiar with our surroundings, for it is our way of life.

Some of our mountains are named after and pay tribute to this way of life. Sheep Top, Grassy Ridge, Cow Rock Mountain, Cow Rock Creek, Hogpen Mountain, Hogpen Gap, White Oak Stamp, Roaring Calf Stamp, and Salt Rock, to name a few, and I might add they wear the mantle proudly.

The taller trees, the poplars, chestnuts, oaks, maples, locusts, firs, and spruce that are common to our area, prefer to grow upon the north sides of the smaller mountains and back in the coves where it tends to be warmer and wetter. They reach majestically toward the heavens above and furnish the earth with a shady retreat that is continually being cooled by gentle breezes, but here upon the Blood where the air is thin, none but the hardiest survive. It is covered with a brushy bramble of short, sparse vegetation, so I can easily sit upon the rocks and gaze out across the settlement below. To the uninformed, it might look as if nature has taken a giant brush and painted a beautiful picture. If I were uninformed, I might marvel at its beauty, but instead I gaze down and see a façade of the original filled with faults.

It is dinnertime. I can tell it is by the height of the sun in the sky and by the gnawing in my belly, so I open up the dinner Jane packed and eat every crumb, for the morning doings have sapped my strength, and I am hungry.

I think of Jane, Jack, and Juan back home, Mom, my brothers and sisters in Lance Cove, and my heart is filled with love for them.

My thoughts turn to Dad, and I recollect the many good times and the invaluable lessons he passed on to me, and I smile in love and appreciation, for no mortal man who ever walked upon the face of the earth can compare to him. I scowl in hurt and anger as I think of his murder and the ones who caused it.

In the days to come, I know I will call upon and use the lessons that Dad taught me many times, and without them, I wouldn't know where to start or how to carry on. I cry out again in frustration, and my tears mingle with the blowing wind and are hurled savagely down the steep slopes of Blood Mountain, to fall upon Choestoe.

There is a saying here in the mountains that goes like this: "When it rains while it is clear and the sun is shining, then it is the devil whipping his wife." Now, the citizenry could look up and behold a clear sky, the sun shining, and a soft rain falling, and they might say, "The devil is whipping his wife." However, Jane knows better, for she knows I am up on the Blood, and instead of rain falling, it is my tears of anguish.

I walk around the rounded top of Blood Mountain and survey the landscape spread out before me. Off to the right is the town of Dahlonega, a bit further is Gainesville, and Cleveland lies to the left. I can't see them, but I know they are there, for I see smoke rising slowly from their chimneys since winter hasn't yet seen fit to let go fully. I continue to stroll and to behold what is laid out in front of me. I see mountain range upon mountain range of assorted sizes, stacked neatly one upon the other, and in the distance I see the "granddaddy of them all," Bald Mountain, standing above the rest, and I am in awe at its primeval beauty, for its size denotes strength and durability.

Now, this is my land. I know it is, for my granddad, Sam Riley Lance, picked it out above all others, settled here, and helped tame it. He and the other Lances lent their names to some of its creeks, branches, mountains, and coves. Yes, I am proud that I am a Lance, a mountaineer by birth, and now by choice I call this place home. I know that in the days to come I will have to draw strength from its resources, for there is so much to do.

I climb up on one of the rock formations that are in abundance here on the top and sit down to ponder. There are many things to do and questions of doubt that need to be answered before I am satisfied. So I sit, motionless, and wait for the answers to appear, but they are not forthcoming. Here I sit, a solitary figure deeply puzzled, and I think and think as the wind cools and continually massages my strong young body.

The seconds turn into minutes, and the minutes roll into hours. The afternoon slowly waxes on.

I hear the bark of an irritated squirrel and the answering chatter from an excited crow, and I look around to see what the commotion is. A rattlesnake has crawled out of its den and is sunning on an adjacent rock, no further than ten feet away. Most days, I would make quick work out of him, but not today, for in reality this is his home, and I am the intruder, so I let him be. Anyway, I hold some respect for them, for they will not strike without warning. And my emotions focus again on the Yellow Mountain bunch. I look down into the settlement, espy Yellow Mountain in the distance, and curse out again in frustration. Nothing pays me any mind, for everything else is occupied with themselves and theirs.

I pull my watch out to check the time. It is four o'clock, well on into the "shank" of the afternoon. The day is almost spent, and so am I, but there are still things that I must do.

I pick up my belongings and start back home; however, before I go fifty steps and fully leave the summit, I pause to reflect on my accomplishments. I realize there are not a lot on one hand, but yet quite a few on the other.

My puzzlement as to why God would forsake His faithful servant and throw him to the wolves has not been answered. In fact, if He is a caring, loving God, as He is portrayed and as Dad believed, then how in the world could He let this happen to him, a most faithful servant? My doubts haven't been answered, and I begin to realize that I will probably struggle with this issue until the day I die, for I am a bitter and confused man.

However, I did formulate a plan of action in regards to the upcoming trial that will begin unfolding tomorrow, for I intend to see Virge Waldroup and then go on to Blairsville to see Attorney W. E. (Buck) Candler.

This time I take the shorter preferred route home. In less than an hour and a half, for I have pushed myself, I am to the road that leads up Lance Creek into Lance Cove. I take it because of love and a need to check on Mom and my brothers and sisters. When I get there, everything is as I expect; the rest of the family are doing a yeoman's job in holding up their end of the bargain. I now more fully realize the enormous responsibility that has been cast upon my shoulders: the rest of the family are depending upon me to see that justice is served.

I stay a while, and we bring each other up-to-date on the news, for any information garnered may prove to be useful in the upcoming trial. Now, some of the information being passed back and forth can be counted as community gossip, but we don't turn any of it away, for our neighbors are also mighty interested. Dad's murder has given Choestoe a black eye, and they are trying to help erase the stain and restore its good name. It is our job to separate the chaff from the wheat, the true from the untrue, and it will be done.

I leave Lance Cove and strike out for home and Jane, Jack, and Juan. I walk fast, for any time spent away from them is too long; I love them so. I realize in the coming months I will have to be away for extended periods, for I am duty-bound to avenge Dad's death. This vengeance is a personal matter involving principle and the honor of the Lance name. Jane also realizes this, because we have talked about it, and she is more than willing to take on and shoulder more responsibility even though she has a full-time job looking after Jack and Juan.

In fact, I say it will be too much for her and I want to get her some help, but she quickly turns down my offer by saying, "Jim, I know you mean well, but I can handle it. I don't want anybody else messing around in my kitchen." She can handle it, there's no doubt about that, for she is as tough as whet leather, and anyway, you know how women are about their kitchen.

This is another manifestation of the love that we have for each other, where each one respects the other and is willing to go the extra mile. It's like Dad said, "It's not the big things that cause problems in families, but the accumulation of little ones."

When I get within sight of our home, I see Jane standing in the yard looking up the road toward me. She waves to me, and I wave back. It's as if she can sense when I am coming and which road I am taking, a premonition, for she has this ability. But don't think for one minute that this is odd or eerie, for it's not. It's just that when two people are truly in love and consummate their marriage, then they become as one, and they are united in spirit, body, feeling, and thought. Mom and Dad were once, and so are Jane and I now.

I hug Jane, kiss her tenderly, bend down, and pick up Jack and Juan. I pull them to me in a protective manner because now that Choestoe's veil of innocence has been rent, no one can tell which other family will be ripped apart or how long it will take to mend the tear. I certainly don't, for I am not a tailor but a young man beset with trouble, and I silently vow to protect them with all my might. I squeeze them tightly as an outward sign of an inner pledge.

I think, if the truth be known, that Choestoe as I once knew it will not be fully restored until the Death Angel personally removes the principals involved. I have no lie to tell. I can promise you that Choestoe is not big enough to dilute the anger I feel, especially when we live in such close proximity to the Tom Swaim family.

They may be willing to let bygones be bygones. I can't answer for them and will not try to, but I can for myself and the rest of the Lances. I'll personally promise that there is no way in hell that I'll ever forget. I will push forward until they are forced to act or to move out of the county in disgrace. Then the Lances will celebrate in glee.

And to be fair about the matter, even though no degree of fairness was displayed by Frank or Newt, I consider myself as one of the principals. I know that I will stop my quest for revenge only when my body is laid out

155

and pennies are put over my eyes to hold them shut. Therefore, you see Choestoe can expect to see many dark days ahead. As long as the Grim Reaper delays his coming, there is the constant threat of bloodshed.

Chapter XIV

THE TRIAL

I go to bed early, knowing that I need to rest and enlighten my body and mind, for the task ahead will not be without difficulty, but no matter how difficult it is, I have the fortitude to carry it out. I am determined to avenge my dad's brutal killing, and I will persevere and continue until the shadows flee from the mountains. This I have promised to Mom and the other Lances, and it will be done. The rest I need is not to be as I toss and turn, having nightmares of evil against good, of Dad and me facing this evil again, of good gloriously triumphing as before.

Several hours after midnight, when the very first hues of morning have come to break the dearth of night, I awake early and prepare to slip quietly out of bed. Jane is awake also and says, "Jim, I didn't sleep much either, knowing what lies ahead for you. Do whatever you have to, and I will do my part by taking care of things here."

I answer, "I know you will, and because of that, it frees me up to take care of things for Dad."

"I'll fix breakfast real quick, for I know you are anxious to get started," Jane replies.

With Jane and me, it's like it was with Dad and Mom; we are as one and instinctively know what to do for each other. I can't explain it; it's just a perfect understanding between two people who are genuinely in love.

So, even before the sun has a chance to wipe away the darkness that has shrouded Choestoe, I step out of the house and head to Virge

Waldroup's. Virge Waldroup is an influential and wealthy man in Choestoe, has studied and practiced law, and is a good man to have on your side in a confrontation of any kind; I know this will be more of a lengthy battle than a confrontation, and I want to be prepared.

My steps are swift; there is an urgency within me, and soon I am knocking on Virge's door. The door quickly opens, and Virge says, "What took you so long? I've been waiting on you."

"Virge, will you help us see that justice is served, that Dad's killers get exactly what they deserve?"

"You're durn right I will. It will be a privilege to do so, for your dad was a man you could count on in a pinch, a real friend, not just to me but to countless others. This dark stain on Choestoe must not be allowed to stand. It must be stamped out with force or we as a people will forever be seen as a community of ruthless ruffians like the perpetrators," Virge says.

"Virge, when I get through here, I plan on a-goin' to Blairsville to see Buck Candler, a good friend of mine, about also representing us; is that all right with you?"

"It certainly is; I've worked with Buck on other cases and have found him to be sharp as a tack and especially brilliant on cross-examination," he replies.

Virge loans me his saddle horse to ride to Blairsville. I am most appreciative and tell him as much. I saddle up, take my leave of Virge, and start to Blairsville. The mare is smooth, fast, and ready to run. We light out in a fast trot because she seems to sense the urgency of the trip, that this is a business trip and there is no time for capers. Shortly we are in Blairsville, and I am rapping on Buck's door. Buck answers the door with, "Jim, I'm so sorry about your dad. I know how close you were to him and how much you loved him; please come in." We sit down, I ask if he will join with Virge in prosecuting this bunch, and he readily agrees. "Jim, I've never seen such a large crowd as there was at your dad's funeral. The church was filled to overflowing, and even the yard was as crowded as could be. I know it is no consolation to you, but that points out the complete respect that people had for your dad. Jim, I remember distinctly the William Townsend murder case of 1880, which your dad sat on as a grand juror. Other members of the panel told me later that he was a stabilizing influence for good in seeing that justice was served. Can we do any less for your dad?"

Buck and I discuss the case for about two hours, because it is important for him to be filled in on Dad's tragic murder and the sordid details leading up to its actual occurrence. He doesn't take notes, doesn't need to, for his mind is as sharp as the tip of my honed knife. Buck keeps his mind honed by continually reading and studying the finer points of lawyering.

After two hours of rehashing the tragedy that has befallen us, I am worked up, fighting mad again at the ones who committed the dastardly act against Dad. I try to conceal my anger but can't. It shows through my body as plain as the nose on my face. Buck says, "Jim, I somewhat know how you feel, don't blame you a bit for feeling like you do. In fact, I would act the same if the shoe was on the other foot, but you mustn't do anything rash just now; it would only work against us. Let me and Virge handle it."

I reply, "Buck, I'll promise, but if things don't go like I feel they should, and I don't see why they won't, I'll hunt them down and get even until the last breath is pulled from my body. This is just my promise, Buck. I can't speak for the rest of the Lances, for Debarris is already on his way back from Texas, and I imagine for a certainty that when he gets here, there will be hell to pay."

"Jim, I know you will do as you say, for the Lances are noted for their truthfulness. Let me make a suggestion: go back home, take care of chores there, then what say you and Virge come back and meet me in my office first thing Monday morning."

"Sounds good Buck; we'll be in Blairsville just a bit after the 'crack of dawn.'"

I thank Buck for his kind consideration and step out the door, stride quickly to the saddled mare, and mount. She whirls in a fluid, well-practiced motion, and we head back home. The rhythm of a well-bred mare as she does what she is bred for brings on a feeling of controlled perfection, and I wonder if I am in control of the situation involving Dad. Yes, I know that I have gotten off to a good start; I have Virge and Buck to represent us, and that in itself is a good beginning, but I know also that the kin of Frank and Newt Swaim are working, trying to free them from the arms of justice. I don't have much strength money-wise, because Jane and I are just getting started. What little I've made has been spent on our beginning family, but I do have an unlimited supply of energy, love for Dad, my immediate family, the other Lances, and justice. I vow that my pent-up energy will be spent in its entirety if it takes it to avenge this horrible deed.

To those who haven't been around beasts of burden, it might seem untrue, but they will always make the return trip far faster than the initial trip, and we do. Shortly, I am again in Virge's yard. He is resting on the porch, and I say, "Got Buck to agree to help us."

"That's good news Jim; I thought he would agree, for he deplores uncivilized behavior just as much as we do."

"Virge, he wants us to meet him at his office next Monday to go over the evidence and to start making plans about the trial."

"Jim, that's not just a good idea but a necessity; we must be prepared in every way. I'll have my buggy hooked up and be ready to go before dawn."

"Virge, have it ready; you'll not have to wait on me. Thanks again for the use of your mare. That was the smoothest ride I've ever been on. What do I owe you for her use?"

"Not one red cent; I'll never forget the many times your dad has helped me. No way I'll ever be able to repay him or the rest of your family, so just consider it a down payment on a very large debt."

"Thanks Virge, we certainly appreciate your friendship. See you come Monday morning," I say, and I start back home.

When I get near home, I can see smoke rising slowly from our fireplace. I know that Jack, Juan, and Jane are inside where it is warm and that the boys will be playing and having fun with Jane. Little do they realize the turmoil that is churning within me, and I don't want them to know; they are so young, innocent, and loveable.

The sun is beginning to dip lower and lower in the western sky; it has been a long, hard day. I haven't noticed until now, but the lengthening shadows begin to cast a coolness round about, and I am getting cold. I pull my coat tighter around me; my steps become longer, my pace quicker. Before long I step into the yard, bound up on the porch, carefully open the door, and go inside. Jane, Jack, and Juan rush to meet me. Jane hugs me lovingly, and the boys grab me by the legs, wanting to romp as we so often do. I oblige them for a while, but the tantalizing odors drifting from the kitchen remind me that I haven't eaten a bite since I left home early this morning, and I am famished. "Jane, what smells so good?"

"Chicken and dumplings, because it's one of your favorites. I knew you would be tired and hungry; it's been a long, hard day for you." We eat, and I fill Jane in on the day's events, recounting to her that I have gotten Virge Waldroup and Buck Candler as our lawyers.

"Each seems to be very optimistic about the outcome. However, Buck seems to worry about one aspect of the upcoming trial, even says as much, but won't tell me what it is, says he doesn't want to worry me needlessly because it might not happen anyway. Jane, I wonder what it is?"

Evening time is coming on. Night is drawing nigh when I say, "Jane, I must go to the cemetery and visit with Dad. There is so much I need to tell him and to ask about. I don't want to leave him up there by himself. I know he must be terribly lonely."

"Of course you must, but take the lantern; it will be dark before you know it." I pick up the lantern, feel in my pocket for my knife, go to the corner, get my rifle, say goodbye to Jane, Jack, and Juan, and go out the door. These are troubling times in Choestoe. A fire has been lit that promises to consume all that it touches. It has touched me in a very personal manner, and I vow to fan it until satisfaction is garnered. So I know I must be careful, be prepared, for haven't I been entrusted by my family with this job?

I go a short distance, look around, and see Jane holding Jack and Juan, and they wave to me. I know what to expect, know they will be waving to me. That's just the way it is with a loving family, and I return their wave, turn around, and start toward Old Salem Cemetery to visit with Dad.

When I get there, I sit on the ground at the front of the grave adjacent to Dad's head. I begin to tell him how much I love him, how much I already miss him, how things are going with Mom, about the plans I've

161

made for looking after her, and the decisions I've made concerning the bringing of the scoundrels to a just fate. However, Dad doesn't answer! He doesn't respond in any manner. All is deathly quiet in Old Salem Cemetery, and I finally begin to realize that Dad will never speak to me or reassure me again, for the Death Angel has taken Dad for his own and deposited his lifeless body here to lie. Tears fill my eyes, run down my face unimpeded, and pool up at my feet, and I sob until I shake uncontrollably. I can't help it, so great is my sorrow. A slow drizzle starts softly falling. I know what it is; it is the mountains weeping, for they seem to sense that these dales could be turned into the valley of slaughter. Here I sit in wretched misery contemplating the fate that has been assigned to me, and I am quiet, listening to the sounds of a North Georgia mountain night. A breeze stirs the fallen leaves that have banked up against the gravestones, and they make a rustling, ghostly sound as if the interred bones are trying to escape the dark confines of the grave. The gentle breeze wafting up the cemetery hill is slowly beginning to scatter the gathered clouds. Soon the drizzle stops altogether, and the stars begin to appear in the February sky. I can't help but notice that one star is much brighter than all the others and is brightly twinkling. I gaze upward and focus on it, for I know who it is. I wave lovingly toward it and pull out my watch to check the time. It is fifteen of ten, fairly late for a short February night, and I arise, tell Dad good-bye, and promise him I will be back soon, and I will, for as long as I live. I start home and realize how tired I actually am, but despite my tiredness, I soon am home. Jane already has Jack and Juan in the bed, and I am ready to hit the sack soon myself. I remember that Dad always said, "One hour of sleep in the fore part of the night is worth two in the aft part." However, there is not much of the fore part left, so I'll just have to take what's left of it and make do. Yes, I'm tired, really tired, but I feel somewhat good about the amount of preparations that I have made, and I think that Dad would be proud and so would the other Lances. I fall into the bed. Jane puts her arms around me and holds me, as she so knows how to do, saying, "Jim, I am so proud of you and love you so much; when I'm in your arms, I feel so good and secure."

I answer, "Jane, I love you too." I sink further into the soft feather bed, and its softness and Jane's arms cradle my tired body in love; then magically, I'm out like a light.

The next thing I remember is being awakened by Jack and Juan jumping into the bed with me. "Get up Dad, get up!" they scream. I rise up on my elbows and see light filtering into the room. I quickly jump out of bed in alarm, look at the clock, and see that it's already seven o'clock. What will the neighbors think? What will Dad think?

And I remember what he once said about being in bed late. One rainy, cold winter morning a neighbor came by our house at four in the morning and found Dad a-sittin' there by the fire. He said to Dad, "John, with the weather like it is and you with nothing much to do, why do you get up at this ungodly hour?"

Dad replied, "If I don't have a darn thing to do, I want to get an early start on it." This then is the Lances' attitude about getting up early. We are early risers and proud of it. What was I thinking, staying in bed until seven? Here it is less than a week and a half after the death of Dad, and I have already let him and the family down.

I smell freshly perked coffee and hear the distinct sound of country ham being fried, so I hurry to check out what is going on in the kitchen, and there is Jane cooking up a breakfast fit for a working man. She turns around and sees me. Her hands are covered with flour, and she comes to me, puts those floury hands around my neck, and gives me a big kiss. "Jim, I thought you were going to sleep all day."

"I'm sorry Jane; a Lance or no man worth his salt should be in the bed after four in the morning."

"Jim, it's all right, you need the rest; no man except you could do what you did yesterday, and I don't hardly see how you did." It is amazing what a little bragging from the one you love does to a feller, and I lift my head a little higher, stick my chest out just a bit more.

We eat a big breakfast together, and Jack, Juan, Jane and I and chat about menial things: the weather and who is sick. After breakfast, I say, "Jane, it looks like it is going to be a warm, sunny day; I need to check on Mom. Do you think it will be warm enough for you and the boys to go with me? I've not had enough time to devote to you and the boys lately, and I know Mom will want to see you and them."

"Yes Jim, I do, I'll bundle them up real good. We'll be ready in a bit."

We start the two-and-a-half-mile walk to Mom's. I carry Juan, Jack runs alongside Jane exploring everything around, and I hold Jane's hand. We walk along together, a perfectly happy family from outward appearances, and I promise to make it so, but still lying just 'neath the surface is a boiling anger that eats at me continually. I've heard it said by my ancestors that in a place where the law is ineffective because of its remoteness, it is necessary to have kin that are true and faithful until death. I am, and I will be until my body is lowered into my grave and it is covered with dirt.

When we get to Lance Creek and start up the road that is covered with a shade of matted laurel, the temperature drops appreciably. I pull Juan closer to me. Jane catches Jack and makes him put his coat back on, the one that he carelessly tossed alongside of the road. We let them dip their hands in Lance Creek, and they scream in childlike wonder at its stinging coldness. Oh, the joy of being young and learning.

The road to Mom's follows the meandering flow of Lance Creek as it runs from higher up in the cove. We continue on, and in minutes we step out of the damp coolness of shade into the warming rays of the sun beating down on the bottomland that Dad cleared. Soon we see the cabin, with smoke winding upward from the chimney to mingle with blue sky and disappear. We are a noisy group. Mom hears us coming and is outside waiting on us to get there. When we do, I immediately inquire, "How are things a-going?"

"Fine Jim, but that's not the main question; how are you, Jane, and the boys?"

Jane and I answer in unison, "Fine," but it isn't, I know and Mom knows. However, there is an inner toughness with mountain women that is hard to explain. They birth their children with little outward sign of pain, work alongside their men in the fields, and keep going long after the men sit down to rest. They are as willing to fight as any man and can hold their own. Why shouldn't they, for the same fierce blood runs through their veins as does through the men. They tend to be private, quiet, and a settling influence on their family, but do a dastardly deed to one of their kin and they will strike out with a fury that belies their size. Mom is a mountain woman through and through, born and bred, proud and independent. This is just how she is, and neither she nor any other mountain woman will apologize for it.

"Come in; we're about to eat dinner."[7] Mom immediately gathers Jack and Juan up, and we go in and sit down at the long table that has nourished the family for so long. We all eat heartily, thoroughly enjoying the sumptuous meal and loving companionship of our caring family.

"Jim, tell us what's going on, about the progress you've made in bringing justice to the cowardly killers of Dad," Mom says.

I tell her all of the particulars, how Virge and Buck have agreed to represent the Lance family in the court trial, and that they too were incensed that something like this could happen. "Jim, I'm proud of you, and I know if anybody can step forward and bring some semblance of order, it will be you. I know you worry about me, but you need not. Fate, your other brothers, sisters, and our other kin are really pitching in. In fact, Fate is here every day, so are Andy and John Frady, most every day. I'd much rather you take care of the aspects concerning the trial. We must avenge Dad's death! That will be small compensation to us for such a huge loss."

"Mom, consider it done. I guess we best be getting the boys home before it starts cooling down too much."

"Just a minute Jim, let me get a poke.[8] I want to send some tea cakes home with the boys." And she does.

"I'll see everyone shortly." We return to our home. I am tickled to find that Mom and my younger brothers and sisters are doing fine.

Several days pass, and it is Sunday. I've taken care of my family, visited Mom every other day, and gone to the cemetery to be with Dad every day. I've heard people say that time heals, and with them, it might, but I haven't found it so, for I still miss Dad so.

[7]Dinner is the noon meal in the mountains. The evening meal is supper.
[8]A sack.

I know that tomorrow is the day Virge and I go to Blairsville to meet with Buck, and I am eagerly looking forward to it because I have always been a man of action, not one of reaction.

Sunday night finds me in bed early, way early. I must be as rested as possible. Tomorrow is a big day in my life. It is then that we can start making some positive plans about the upcoming trial. Surprisingly enough, I fall to sleep quickly, so when the clock strikes three o'clock, I bound out of bed eagerly. I am wide awake and raring to go! Jane gets up as I do. I try to get her to stay in bed, but she won't have any part of that. She heads to the kitchen to fix breakfast. I protest, but not vigorously. Shortly, I smell breakfast being cooked. Soon it is ready, and I eat heartily, for I have yet to see Jane fail on cooking or for that matter anything else. I think how lucky I am to have found a helpmate like Jane.

By four I have broken the ice in the wash pan, washed my face, dressed, eaten, and am ready to step out of the house. Jane stands at the door and wishes me "good luck." I kiss her good-bye as I always do, and I am off. I am in a hurry, my normal long stride even longer, and I cover the ground like there is no tomorrow. I check my watch for the time. It is reading four twenty, and I am almost at Virge's; another five minutes finds me there. It is as he said; the hitched buggy is in front of the house, and the team snorts in anticipation, ready to travel. I knock on the door. Virge comes to the door holding two steaming cups of coffee and says, "Nothing like a hot cup of coffee to wake a feller up," and I agree. "Jim, I knew you would be on time; that's why the buggy is hitched." Mountain people are noted for never being late. I've heard Dad say that if he was a-goin' to a hangin', and it was him a-fixin' to be hung, why, he'd want to be on time so as not to disappoint the gathered crowd. I remember Dad, and tears form in my eyes. I think, Dad, this is for you. I hope in a few months that I'll be a-going to a hangin'. There's nothing more I'd rather see than Frank and Newt Swaim dangling by their necks. Why, I'd be thrilled to be the one kicking the trap door open, and I would laugh in fiendish delight as they kick and swing wildly in the thin air!

We get in the buggy, and I find that Virge has heated two rocks in the fireplace, wrapped them in a blanket, and put them on the floor of the buggy so that our feet will stay somewhat warm, else we will get cold, since it is February and the temperature early in the morning is still hovering well below freezing. This is another example of the kind of neighbor and friend Virge is.

We get to Blairsville in a hurry because Virge has hitched up his fastest team; both of us are keenly anxious to arrive at Buck's on time. As a matter of fact, all of Virge's teams are fast, and he uses some of them every day, since he has several stores scattered around the county, and if he is to continue to prosper as he has, it is a necessity that he check on them regularly.

Buck is already in his office when we arrive, and he has a pot of strong coffee going. We exchange pleasantries, and Buck pours us a piping hot black cup of coffee. Then we get down to business. I stay quiet while Virge and Buck discuss various points of law that more than likely will come into play. After they finish with their discussion, they begin to question me thoroughly about the evidence, about what I actually know concerning the circumstances preceding Dad's killing and the events and evidence leading up to the actual arrest and bringing in of Frank and Newt Swaim. They caution me to be sure in what I tell them, because in the heat of the battle you might skip a pertinent fact that could be of major importance in the final verdict. To the best of my knowledge, I do as they wish. Virge and Buck both take notes, pages of them, because the outcome of this case is mighty important to them also.

"Buck, who will be the lawyers for the defense?" I ask.

He answers, "Jim, you remember I told you the other day that there was one thing worrying me, and I wouldn't tell you what it was, thought it wouldn't happen, but it has! Well, the judge is Carl J. Wellborn Sr., and they have retained his son, Carl J. Wellborn Jr., to represent them, plus they are also using an M. G. Boyd from Dahlonega who is reputed to be a crackerjack attorney. He has served in the state senate and the state house, as have the Wellborns. I imagine they are the ones who got him in on this case."

"Is this legal?" I ask.

"Don't know if it is or not; I'll try to find out, but it certainly isn't ethical," replies Buck.

Virge adds, "I studied law under Judge Wellborn; I don't think he will be partial in any way, for I've never found him to be. I've always gotten along real well with him."

"Did you pay him?" asks Buck.

"Why, of course I did."

"Then he didn't do you any favors, Virge. You know the saying, 'blood's thicker than water.' I'm just leery of this kind of a setup."

"You might be right, but I can't quite bring myself to believe that any shenanigans will go on; anyway, we'll just have to play the cards that we've been dealt," Virge says.

"Just thought we need to be aware and keep in the back of our minds this little quirk," Buck answers.

I am worried! The deep furrows on my brow, my white knuckles, the hard set of my jaw, the glazed, icy stare, my total silence—all serve to point it out. I remember how it is with the Lances, the many times they've banded together to right a wrong. I recall the time in August of 1870, when my grandfather Sam Riley Lance; his sons James, Debarris, Andrew, and John (my dad); and his son-in-law John Frady did call on Joseph Henson, and as the indictment in court did say, "fight, whoop, holler, and curse, and attempt to go into the house of said in a violent and tumultuous manner" because of what he said about one of the members of the family. I also recall the times they've come to my aid. Blood is much thicker than water; I know it to be so and yes, I worry, for I know that somehow, somewhere, the Wellborns are apt to act as I would.

Virge and Buck plainly can see that I am troubled. Virge says, "Jim, let me and Buck worry about this matter; that's what you have us for."

"I know it is. I am satisfied. I have the best lawyers anywhere, but you see, it was my Dad that they so brutally killed, so I have to worry."

Buck, probably in an effort to ease my concern, says, "Now, about their lawyer Boyd. I'm not all that scared of him, for he's from the other side of the mountain. I don't care if he is a crackerjack, why, we'll just have to bring him down a notch or two. You know how independent our people are and how they resent outsiders coming in, pretending they are smarter and better than we are. I say they've made a grave tactical mistake, and it will work against them just as surely as night follows day. I've seen this tried before; it didn't work then and it won't now."

Buck continues, "Let me tell you about it. A man was on trial for stabbing a neighbor in a landline dispute, and he made the mistake of hiring counsel from outside the county. There was an eyewitness to this wild altercation who happened to be a man in his early eighties, a quiet, distinguished, well-respected citizen.

"This dapper, nattily dressed lawyer walked into the courtroom with an arrogant air about him that seemed to hint, 'It's far beneath me to even be here; I'm better and certainly smarter than you mountain hicks.'

"The eyewitness was put on the stand and recounted in vivid detail exactly how the incident occurred. He stated firmly that he was about fifty yards away and saw the defendant, in a fit of rage, pull out his knife and stab the accuser.

"The pompous lawyer, in his cross-examination, tried to portray the witness to be an almost blind, senile, country bumpkin. He said, 'Mr. Jones, how old are you?'

"'Eighty-two,' Mr. Jones replied.

"'I suppose because of your age, you've slowed down some.'

"'Yep, a little bit,' answered the witness.

"'Can you see as well as you once could?'

"'No, sure can't,' he evenly replied.

"'I imagine that you have to wear glasses now, don't you?'

"'Yes I do,' came his reply.

"'Come, come now, Mr. Jones, you've just testified that you've slowed down and have to wear glasses because you can't see. Why, at your age, I'm shocked and mortified that you would have the audacity even to pretend that you could see a knife at that far a distance. Mr. Jones, just how far can you see, anyway?' The lawyer strutted in self-satisfaction because he had made a fool out of a mountaineer.

"The eyewitness, not being in the least bit intimidated, replied, 'Well I don't rightly know, but last night I stepped out on my porch, looked up, and saw the moon; how far's that?'

"Jim, does it surprise you that the defendant was found guilty?" Buck asks.

"Now that I think of it, I'm not all that worried myself about Lawyer Boyd, for we all are, as you say, fiercely independent and resentful to a fault concerning outsiders. However, I am still deeply concerned about the Wellborn connection, and if there should be some secret conspiracy that affects justice being served, then I promise you that I will . . . " Then before I can finish what I am about to say, Buck breaks in.

"Jim, let's not go there right now, okay?" And in my heart, I know he's right.

We've had a constructive session. Issues have been raised, discussed, and somewhat resolved that will be important in the upcoming trial. Though I'm not altogether satisfied with some of the issues that have been brought up and discussed, I still have complete confidence in Virge and Buck.

They have agreed to meet weekly so they can keep abreast of what's happening concerning the trial. They ask if I would like to be in on every meeting they have, and I answer in the negative, but I promise if I hear anything that will be beneficial, I will surely let them know.

Virge and I return to Choestoe, and I try to resume some of my normal activities. I know that the fields need to feel the point of a plow soon because spring will be arriving shortly, but it is hard to regain normality when your life has been turned upside down because of the actions of others.

Two weeks pass, and I have been wondering where Debarris is. I know as soon as he hears about Dad's murder, he'll be out of Texas and on his way home like a raging bull!

I hear a sharp knock on the door. Jane goes to the door, opens it, and I hear a familiar "Howdy Jane, where's Jim?" I don't have to wonder anymore. I jump up and meet Debarris just as he enters the house. We hug each other, and the tears start flowing openly. The sobbing of two grown men is gut-wrenching, and Jack and Juan become upset and start to whimper in confusion. Jane takes them into another room. Now, words are useless in a situation like this, for we both have lost one dear to us. After a few minutes, we are more composed, and Debarris says, "I've already gone by and spoken to your Mom and the others. Jim, this is almost more than a feller can stand; I know how you must feel. Brother

Andy and me haft to go to Blairsville to take care of some unfinished business. We'll be back late tonight. We'll get together again tomorrow." Debarris says a quick good-bye. He seems to be in a mighty big hurry about something. I'm puzzled by his complete rush, for it is contrary to his turn, but I guess if he wanted me to know, he would have told me.

Early the next morning, I am outside splitting stove wood when I see someone coming toward me that looks familiar, but he is so far off, I can't tell for sure who he is. As he gets nearer, I see that it is Fate, and he is in a big hurry. I keep on splitting, and when he gets near enough for me to hear, he yells excitedly, "Jim! Jim! Have you heard?"

"Heard what, Fate?"

"Debarris and Andy tried to get into the jail and kill the low-down rascals!"

"Did they get it done?"

"No, but they came in a gnat's . . . "

Now I understand about the unfinished business and the cause of Debarris's big rush. I wish I had been there. I was right; I knew there would be hell to pay when Debarris got here.

Later in the afternoon Debarris comes by. I am anxiously awaiting his arrival so that he can fill me in on the try on Frank's and Newt's lives. He saunters in and announces, "Jim, we came within a hair a-getting the sorry sons of guns, and we will afore this is over."

"Debarris, tell me what happened!" I anxiously reply.

"Well, after I left your house, I went by Andy's, and we headed to Blairsville. We knowed what we were going to do and what needed to be done, had it all planned, tried to save the county the cost of having a trial. We got to Blairsville around five-thirty and knew one of the deputies would be going to eat supper soon. We watched, and when he did, it was almost dark, so we waited a few minutes more until it was pitch black. We knocked on the jail door, and the jailer came to the door. I didn't recognize him, and he didn't us, but Andy knew who he was: Taylor Cobb, who lives in the lower end of Ivy Log. Cobb asked, 'What can I do for you fellers?' I said, 'We're friends of Frank and Newt, and we need to see them real bad.'

"'Well come on in; they're the only ones back there. I'll get the keys. Go on back, and I'll open the door.'

We went to the door, and I saw Newt peering through the bars. Then all of a sudden, he let out a blood-curdling scream and yelled, 'Don't let them back here! That's the damn Lances, they'll kill us for shore!' My hand remained in my pocket, tightly wrapped around the handle of my pistol.

By then, Deputy Cobb had his shotgun leveled on us, and he calmly said, 'Men, I think it would be best if you go back out that door,' and we did, for we can recognize a stacked deck when we see one, and there will be other times. Jim, look at my hand; it's turning blue."

You can see distinctly the print of the pistol in his palm, so tight was his grip and so great was his desire to wipe the scoundrels off the face of the earth and even the score for Dad.

"Great try, Debarris," I say.

"Thanks Jim, there will be others."

The Lances keep a constant vigil on the jail up to the time of the trial, tryin' to snipe a shot at the murderers, but to no avail, because the sheriff doubles the watch, and even Frank and Newt are smart enough never to show themselves before a window. I can assure you that every day there is one of our clan in Blairsville trying. Now, we might not be seen, but believe you me, we are there.

On March 29, Jane again presents me with a new offspring, a little girl that we name Lenor. Yes, my days leading up to the trial are awfully busy with me looking after my family, helping to see about Mom, visiting Dad's grave, and going to our lawyers to pass on tidbits of information that are passed to me by neighbors who are genuinely interested on our behalf. In addition, yes, I take an occasional turn at watching the jail, just in case.

I get together with Virge and Buck a few days before the grand jury is to meet for the April term of court in order to wrap up how they are going to prosecute the case. Everything seems to be in order, and Virge and Buck are well satisfied as to the preparation that has been made.

Monday, the day that the grand jury is to meet to consider worthy cases, finds me in Blairsville again, as the one bringing the charges against

Frank and Newt Swaim. Virge and Buck are with me just in case the grand jury should need to ask me anything. The attorneys for the defense aren't here, because only the parties bringing the charges can appear before the jury.

I am called in by the bailiff. The foreman of the grand jury reads the charge and then asks me to tell what happened on February 17. I do, and I graphically describe the heinous actions of the murderers and the sadistic desecration of Dad's body. I notice that there are tears in the eyes of some of the jurors and there are in mine also. I am excused by the grand jury, they go into deliberations, and then take a vote as to whether there is enough evidence to prosecute. Shortly, we learn that by a unanimous vote, a true bill of murder has been issued against Frank and Newt Swaim. I know this is just a beginning, but at least it is a start.

Buck appears before Judge Wellborn and makes a motion to the court to return John J. Berry to this county as a witness. It is granted and reads thusly:

> *State v. Frank and Newt Swaim*: Charge of Murder in Union County Superior Court, April Term 1890. It being shown to the court that John J. Berry of said county is now confined in Fulton County jail on a charge of violation of the United States Alcoholic Beverage Laws and that he is a material witness for the State in the above case. It is on motion ordered that upon the approval and discretion of the Hon. Judge of the United States District Court that the sheriff or jailer of Fulton County deliver the body of said John J. Berry into the custody of H. T. Cobb, a deputy marshall of the U.S., to be brought to this court to testify in the above stated case.
>
> C. J. Wellborn, Judge
> April 7, 1890

The first Monday in May finally comes around. On this day, with thunderheads boiling up over the mountain ranges, the trial for Frank and Newt Swaim, accused murderers of my dad, begins.

Now, in Union County, court week is the social event of the year. It is the time to catch up on gossip, renew friendships, get acquainted, swap horses or dogs, and buy and trade in the stores. Our clan and lots of our friends form a sort of a caravan coming down from upper Choestoe, and before we even get close to the square, we find a mass of curious humanity already there, anxiously awaiting the spectacle of Dad's trial. It seems that most every family in the county has laid aside everything they've been doing and are in attendance. Why not, for the murder of Dad is the most notorious killing that has ever taken place in Choestoe and for that matter, in all of Union County. It might be pointed out that all of the Lance men are armed to the teeth, just in case there is any kind of a ruckus. Should there be, we want to take our part in it. In the last few months, we have suffered greatly, and our nerves are frazzled.

Our family and friends enter the courthouse and proceed toward the courtroom, but before the men can go in, we are searched and made to leave our arms. This is no concern to us; we know we will have to turn them over, but I'll admit the size of the confiscated weapons pile is impressive, and the deputies smile in deep admiration. This ought to point out how serious and unforgiving we are when it comes to Dad. I take Mom and my younger brothers and sisters inside and help them to be seated on the right side of the aisle. I turn and walk back out because Fate, Joe, and I are witnesses and will not be able to hear the testimony, but you can be sure we will know exactly what goes on and is said, for we have friends and family. Mom wears the long, big-collared black dress that Dad liked so well. It is appropriate, for she is still in mourning over her loss. As I start to leave Mom, I glance over and see Napoleon and the other Hills seated by Debarris. I'm not surprised; I knew they would be here in full support—why, they're just like family. I smile at them, and they nod in friendship and support.

Even though I'm not inside the courtroom, I know how the proceedings go. The judge enters, and everyone stands. A prayer is said, and then the jury selection begins. They are questioned, and in my mind, I hear the lawyers as they ask the potential jurors: "Are you close friends with the accuser?"; "Do you have a preconceived opinion as to the guilt or innocence of the accused?"; "What part of the county do you live in?"; "Have you ever sat on a murder case before?" Then I imagine the booming voices of the lawyers as they say "Strike" or "Let him be seated." And again I am glad that I have Virge and Buck representing us, for they know almost everyone in the county and are familiar with the quirks, peculiarities, and strengths of each potential juror. I know the selection of a favorable jury is one of, if not the, most important ingredients in any trial.

In any group, for a decision to be reached, there has to be a leader, someone to step forward and sorta take charge, and if that someone looks kindly toward you and your cause, then you've got a head start. Buck is acknowledged by his peers to be absolutely brilliant in striking a jury.

The jury selection process takes all day, and when it is finished, the jurors chosen are: S. Nichols, foreman; A. M. Cook; S. A. Erwin; R. B. Mauney; Thomas C. Lewis; Thomas G. Kelly; Wm. L. Chapman; Frances M. Owenby; Hodge Raburn; Ben Logan; Jacob I. Posten; and Morgan A. Brackett.

We arrive the next morning fairly early. I need to meet with our lawyers once more to see if everything is in order, and they confirm that it is.

Because of the county-wide interest that Dad's murder has generated, the courtroom is crammed full, every bench filled to overflowing. This May morning is unseasonably warm, and by midday it promises to be hot, so the windows have been raised, and they too are filled with curious spectators.

The trial starts promptly at nine, and the first witness called to testify is Joseph Ledford, the one who found Dad killed, his body lying motionless in Wolf Creek. He tells that he recognized the body to be that of Rev. John Lance, and when he did, he thought it was best to notify the Lance family. After going in the direction of the Lance home for some distance, he met Rev. Lance's wife and children coming to look for him. They were clapping their hands, screaming and hollering.

T. J. Butt is next to testify, and he states that he was a member of the coroner's jury, and when he heard John Lance was dead, was murdered, he went to Virge Waldroup, and he went with him to the scene.

Attorney Buck Candler asks Mr. Butt, "What did you do when you got to the scene of the murder?"

He answers, "I stripped the deceased."

"What did you find?"

"I found he was stabbed in the breast, and his neck was ghastly cut."

"How bad was his neck cut?"

"Ghastly, for it was cut almost entirely around and looked like it was done with a dull knife."

"Were these his only wounds?"

"No, his face was bruised on the right side, and there was a smooth cut in the right hand."

"How did his hand come to be cut?"

"I suppose he grabbed the knife."

John Souther is the next to take the witness stand, and he tells how he probed the wound. He says, "I examined Lance and saw the wounds on the body and breast; they were bruised. The flesh was bruised where the knife entered the body, and the cut on the throat was a zigzag cut. The windpipe was cut, and his head was turned back. I did not know that the cut extended to the back of the neck until I attempted to move the head and my middle finger slipped into the gash. The head was almost entirely cut off."

These are the only three witnesses to testify on the first day of testimony.

The third day of the trial begins promptly at nine o'clock, and my brother Joe is the first called to testify. Joe points out the boots that Frank Swaim had on when he was arrested, for they are distinctive and made an unusual, peculiar, easily identified track because they are run over at both sides, with the tacks extending through the heel. He also testifies that on Frank's neck and cheek there were fester scratches that looked like fingernail scratches.

J. M. Reece is next on the stand, and he is an acknowledged tracker, having a unique, uncanny ability to identify and to follow the faintest of tracks till the quarry is either found or treed. And he positively identifies the boots that Frank wore as the boots making the tracks. He also confirms that Frank had scratches on his face, which looked to him to have been freshly done.

My brother Fate is next to testify and he says, "I heard Frank Swaim say that somebody was going to be killed."

"Where were you when this occurred?" Attorney Wellborn asks.

"I was at the time up on the ridge, and he was about to shoot me."

"Why was he about to shoot you?"

"He thought I was reporting stills—and he then said someone would be killed over the matter."

"When did this take place?"

"This happened two or three weeks before the murder of Dad." Court breaks for dinner after Fate testifies.

After dinner, I am called on to take the witness stand, and after the usual swearing in, "Raise your hand. Do you swear to tell the truth, the whole truth, and nothing but the truth so help you God?" and the "I do," my dark eyes are riveted on Frank and Newt, for I want the worthless defendants to understand fully and without any doubt whatsoever how I so hate and detest them. The cowardly rogues drop their heads and won't look me in the eye. Virge questions me. "Jim, I know you were in the posse that arrested Frank; what did you do?"

"I helped to guard Frank."

"When did you first see him?"

"On Monday, after the killing."

"Did you recognize his boots?"

"I sure did, and I noticed they had something on them. He said he had to answer nature's call, and I saw him go behind a big chestnut log and squat down, saw him rubbing his boots. I saw him wipe my Dad's blood off of his boots with frosted leaves while behind the log."

"Before the murder, did you have a confrontation with Frank?"

"Yes, after I found out he had threatened Dad, I went to see him and warned him of the consequences if he touched one hair on my dad's head."

"What did he say to you, Jim?"

"You know Frank's brave, if he's in a crowd, and there was his dad, Tom; Fed Cannup; Ben Nix; and Newt, his brother. He said I had reported him, told me that he intended to kill me, and that he knew who reported him.

"He said I was brave and a reporter, said he did not intend to whip anybody but would cut some damn man's throat." [See Record of Trial, testimony of James Lance (7).] I hear Mom crying, for this reminder is more than she can stand up to, and then I arise quickly from the witness chair and shake my clinched first at Frank and Newt, the meaning of which is obvious.

"Did you say anything else?"

"I had no further conversation with him."

"When was he arrested?"

"He was arrested at one o'clock in the morning."

"Who lives in the house closest to where your dad was killed?"

"Simpson (Si) Reece."

Virge rests. Then Carlton Wellborn, one of the lawyers for Frank and Newt, begins to question me.

"When did you have the talk with Frank Swaim?"

"Before Dad was killed, when he accused me too of reporting him."

"Were you on bad terms with Frank?"

"Yes, the feeling at that time was not good between us. No, I did not in the least like him."

"When was Frank behind the log?"

"It was daylight."

"Who was guarding Frank at this time?"

"Fed Cannup and I."

"Was the sheriff there?"

"No."

"Who else was there?"

"Bill Curtis, John Wellborn, and Joe Lance."

"Who else saw the blood?"

"I don't know, didn't ask."

"Did you tell the coroner's jury about the blood?"

"No."

"Why not?"

"Thought there would be another trial when I could tell it."

"Did you tell anyone else about the blood, or are you just telling a lie?"

I glare at Wellborn and think, why you damn fool, how dare you to think that a Lance will ever tell a lie. I feel the anger beginning to rise, but I know now is not the time or the place, and I rein it in as best I can. I told the circumstance to several, including Virge Waldroup," I state firmly.

He turns around slowly, as if he has caught me in a trap of my own making, and he seems to be enjoying it immensely and smartly asks, "Virge, is that right?"

"It sure is," Virge replies. That exchange ends my cross-examination, but it doesn't end the sudden contempt that I now hold toward Wellborn.

The court session for the day ends on this sour note, and I promise you I will never forget what I consider to be the unfair questioning of my integrity.

The fourth day of the trial begins with Ben Nix testifying first. When questioned by Attorney Candler, he admits that he was at Tom Swaim's on Sunday.

Attorney Candler asks him who else was there and he replies, "Frank and Newt Swaim and my father-in-law, Boots Swaim."

"Were they drinking, and what did they say?"

"Yes, Frank and Newt took a drink before they saw Rev. Lance and afterwards. They said to him 'Amen and amen' as he passed and also laughed at him."

"Were there any other remarks made about Reverend Lance?"

"Yes, my father-in-law, Boots, said, 'Yonder goes the Preacher.'"

Attorney Boyd questions Ben Nix for the defense, asking, "Have you heard anyone else saying 'Amen' when referring to Reverend Lance?"

Ben replies, "Yes, I have heard others say 'Amen,' I suppose referring to Reverend Lance."

Lizzie Cannup, the wife of Fed Cannup, takes the stand and swears that Frank and Newt were at her house about forty-five minutes after the killing of Dad.

Lizzie also swears that one year before the murder, she heard Frank say he wished he had thrown an ax at Reverend Lance, and Frank's wife, Mattie Swaim, told him to hush. He affirmed that he would have thrown it had he not been afraid that someone would see him and tell on him. Lizzie confirmed that Frank told her on another occasion, shortly before Reverend Lance was murdered, that he would have followed and cut him with a knife if Charlie Henson had not stopped him.

Newt Spivey is next called and he verifies what Lizzie has testified to, and so does the next witness, John J. Berry.

The next to be called is John W. Jones, the sheriff, who testifies and gives damning evidence against Frank Swaim. He says that after he arrested Frank, they had gone one hundred to one hundred and fifty yards before Frank Swaim asked what the sheriff wanted with him. "I told him murder. He then asked, 'What in the hell makes you think I done it?' Nothing up to that time had been said about who was killed." [See Record of Trial, testimony of Sheriff Jones (12).]

Sheriff Jones also states that Taylor Cobb told Frank that blood had been found on his knife. When asked, Frank told Taylor that he had not used the knife in cutting up hogs or squirrels. 8-10 days after this, and after the report had gone out over the county that blood had been found on his knife, Frank's father, Tom Swaim, came to see him for the first time and asked if he did not remember that they killed hogs on Saturday before Lance was killed on Sunday and how they used his knife, and he said, "Yes." This indeed was the first time his father saw fit to visit him. Sheriff Jones confirms that Frank had a scratch on his cheek, oval in shape, and there was blood or matter oozing out of it. "When I took the knife from him, it looked like the blade had been scoured, and there was sand inside the handles and mud on the outside. I saw blood on the handles."[9]

Ben Collins is called next, and he states that he was a guard over Frank and Newt Swaim, and also saw a scratch on Frank's face and several on his neck with blood oozing out of them. [See Record of Trial, testimony of Ben Collins (13).]

Dr. F. J. Erwin is sworn in and states that he saw the defendant after he was brought to town. He had one mark on his left cheek about half an inch long, oval in shape, and Frank's knife had blood on it in three places, on the jaw and back spring. It also had sand and mud on it, and the blade looked like it had been scoured.

Frank Swaim then makes a statement. He isn't under oath, but it wouldn't have mattered if he were, for never in his life has he EVER told

[9]The knife was reputed to be a large hawk-billed knife. The blade, when closed, was encased by two handles.

the truth, and now that his neck is at stake, he's not about to begin. Frank says, "I don't know much. I don't remember how come the scratch on my cheek might have been made, with a brush, or it might have been a small scratch. I don't remember. I don't remember that anyone said anything about it." This winds up the day's portion of the trial and the judge says that closing arguments will begin in the morning, and after that, he will charge the jury and dismiss them to make their decision.

Friday morning comes, the fifth day of the trial, and we hope for a quick decision, for we know that usually this bodes well for the accuser.

I get to Blairsville early, because I need to meet with Virge and Buck before the closing arguments; I want to feel them out as to how they believe the decision will go. I was needing some reassurance, and they give it to me, because they both are highly optimistic and both feel strongly that in particular, Frank offered little or nothing in his own defense.

The crowd on the square and in the courtroom has dwindled a bit during the week, but today it is as big as it was on Monday, the first day of court. There is an excited buzz stirring through the gathered populace. They think, as we do, that a verdict will be rendered today.

Court starts and Judge Wellborn gets right down to business, for the trial has been hard on everyone, and he seems anxious to wrap it up. Therefore, without much ado or fanfare on his part, he calls on the plaintiffs to begin their closing arguments.

Buck rises and confidently walks over to the jurors and commences. "Gentlemen of the jury, it's been a long, stressful trial. I promise that I will make this fairly short, for you have heard the evidence, as have I. I want to personally thank you for being willing to spare the time to serve on this jury, to enforce and see that our justice system and freedoms survive. This, pure and simple, is what this trial is about. Are we going to continue to allow our ministers to minister to us, to be able to walk to their church without fear, to be able to preach the almighty word of God without trepidation, or instead are we going to allow the laws of our land to be usurped by a few individuals willing to thwart the system that we so love for their illegal unlawful activities? I say no, and no to them, for our ancestors fought and died for these very principles, and now they have come under attack by the likes of Frank and Newt Swaim.

"Doesn't the preamble to our constitution say, 'We hold these truths to be self-evident, that all men are created equal, that they are endowed by their Creator with certain inalienable Rights, that among these are Life, Liberty, and the pursuit of Happiness'? Now the light of life that the Lances loved so dearly has been snuffed out. And by what authority was it done? Who gave them this right, the right to deny Rev. John Henry Lance the right to life, liberty, and his pursuit of happiness? I say no one. If we allow unprincipled individuals such as these to run rampant and to tread on our liberties without severe penalties, then we are certain to fall into anarchy, just as Rev. Lance fell at the hands of the devil's henchmen. Now, I'm sure that our distinguished colleagues will tell you that the evidence is purely circumstantial, and I ask you, what's circumstantial about having the God-given ability to track accurately? Nothing, for I look in the jury box and I see and know men who can easily track the wily black panther for miles back to its hidden den. What's circumstantial about seeing the knife of Frank Swaim covered with the innocent blood of Rev. Lance and knowing how it got there? What's circumstantial about Frank not knowing how the blood got on his knife, but after being told by his father that he stuck a hog with it, miraculously remembering? What's circumstantial about clearly visible scratch marks being on his face and him not remembering how they got there? Gentlemen, I would remember, and you would, and so does Frank. Gentlemen, I want to again thank you for your consideration, and I firmly believe that as sure as there is a God in Heaven, you have a duty to go into the jury room and reach a just verdict, and I close by saying, it must be guilty!"

The defense attorney, Mr. M. G. Boyd, is next, and he fairly bounds toward the empaneled jurors and announces, "My name is Col. Boyd from Dahlonega, which is in Lumpkin County," as if we didn't know. "I've just heard Attorney Candler say that we will claim all of the evidence presented is circumstantial, and we will. But thanks anyway Colonel, for your foresight, though it won't be needed, for we have our own." He grins in self-appreciation at his learned wit.

"You've heard the witnesses say that Frank and young Newt are good men, only concerned with making an honest and honorable living, and that's all they want. Let me point out that no one saw Frank or Newt kill

Lance. No one saw how the very small, minute scratches came to be on Frank, no one. The evidence is entirely circumstantial, and I don't believe you can convict a person solely on this kind of evidence. It just wouldn't be right. Now, I don't claim that they are Sunday school teachers, for they are not, but they are young and prone to make mistakes in judgment because of their youth. However, let me assure you that murder is not one of their youthful mistakes. Jurors, it is your honored duty to find Frank and Newt not guilty. Thanks again."

Judge Wellborn gives the jury their charge, and then they retire to the jury room to begin their deliberations.

The courtroom remains crowded, because the spectators fortunate enough to have gotten a seat in the first place aren't about to get up and chance losing it. A low murmur slowly arises in the crowded room, brought about because the curious are asking among themselves, "What do you think the verdict will be?" We Lances talk among ourselves and ask the same, for we are confident, but we know that one dissenting vote will cause a hung jury. The whispers gradually become louder until it reaches a crescendo of unabated confusion. The judge raps his gavel and sternly says, "Order in the courtroom!"

The jury has been out about one and a half hours when the bailiff approaches the judge and tells him that the jury is ready to come back in with a decision.

They come in, take their seats, and Judge Wellborn asks, "Mr. Foreman, has the jury reached a verdict?"

"We have, Your Honor."

"And what is your verdict?" the judge asks.

"We the jury find the defendant Frank Swaim guilty, and recommend him to be imprisoned in the penitentiary for life and to the mercy of the court, and Newt Swaim not guilty."

Frank Swaim lowers his head, not in shame, but in dread as the thought of life imprisonment and hard labor drifts through his head, for he is not accustomed to labor of any kind, much less hard labor. Newt grins stupidly from ear to ear at his good fortune, brought about probably because of his age.

The Lances gather around Virge and Buck and thank them for a job well done, for we know without their help and acumen, Frank might have gone free also. I think of the sinister connection that we have been exposed to in the court and shake my head in disgust. However, I feel some gratification in that Frank will be in prison doing hard labor the rest of his life, for that sorry rascal has never done an honest day's work in his life.

The sentencing of Frank is set for May 23. That day finds me and most of the Lance men in attendance. We owe it to Dad to be here when the sorry misfit gets just a little bit of what's coming to him.

The judge's sentence is:

> Wherefore it is considered and adjudged by the court that the said defendant, Frank Swaim, be taken from the bar of this court to the common jail of this county, and that said defendant be securely kept in said jail until he shall be demanded by a guard to be sent to the penitentiary of this state for the purpose of conveying said defendant to the said penitentiary or to such other place or places as governor of this state shall direct for and during the full term of his natural life.
>
> C. J. Wellborn, JSC
> May 23, 1890

Chapter XV

THE PETITION

I go back to Choestoe and try to resume a functional life and to be a more devoted parent to Jack, Juan, and Lenor, who is two weeks old, and a better husband to Jane. It is difficult, for I have added responsibilities with helping to take care of Mom and the almost daily visits I still feel compelled to make to the cemetery to sit by Dad's grave a little while.

It is now late in the spring, much too late to be getting my crops in the ground. My neighbors realize this also, and they have pitched in and already have my fields plowed and are going to help me in the planting. I don't have to worry at all about the garden, for somehow Jane has taken care of it, and it is up, weed free and growing lushly. I still am amazed by Jane, her work ethic and the way she manages to get so much done without much fanfare. Even though the life of the Lances has been decimated by the treachery of a few, we still are fortunate to live in a community where the vast majority of the people are God-fearing, Christian individuals. Yes, we are indeed fortunate in so many ways.

The cool nights and warm days of a typical North Georgia spring turn into the hotter, humid, dog days of summer, and the pace of life becomes slower for some because the hectic days of spring, where so much has to be done in so short a time, are over. But not for me.

Now, I don't mean to imply that there is never any time for fun and laughter. I enjoy the humorous things that happen as much as anybody, but the main focus of my life is still the total avenging of Dad's murder, and I don't have as much time to find humor in everyday life. However, I do recall what I heard down at Virge's store and find it funny.

Arguments can occur about anything, and because of frivolous petty differences can take bizarre turns. Two women who were both expecting got around to talking about what they were going to name their offspring. Somehow, the conversation deteriorated to the point that an argument came about as to which one could saddle their baby with the longest name. This in itself is unusual because all women always agree on everything. A little girl was born first and was given the imposing name of Violet Louvada Matilda Carolyn Georgian Victoria Lorane Haseltine Mary Ann Kansada Ruthie Adeline Stephens. The next born was a little boy, and the mother, determined not to be outdone, promptly labeled him with this calling card: Jonathan Jonah Soloman Saul Jeremiah Jacob Lazareth Paul Shadwick Simon Malachi Nat Joshua Joseph Timothy Pat Weaver. I can find the humor in this in particular because I have an aunt named Sarah Harriet Nancy Artillary Saphrona Martha Ann, and we all affectionately call her Aunt Harriet.

I receive a letter from Buck, and he requests that the next time I'm in town, he needs me to come by his office, that there is no rush, but a matter has come up, and we need to talk about it. The next day finds me in Buck's office, and he doesn't act surprised when I show up. In fact, Buck says, "Jim, I was expecting you." This is another trait of the Lances—punctuality, for I was taught by Dad and him by his ancestors never to put off till tomorrow that which needs to be done today.

"What's come up, Buck?" I ask.

"Jim, I was notified by Judge Wellborn the other day that the attorneys for Frank Swaim have filed an appeal requesting a new trial."

"Buck, what does this mean? Do you think there is a chance he'll get out?"

"No Jim, I don't, but I see this as a first step in a long, protracted effort to get Frank loose. And as you already know, the Wellborns and Boyd have substantial pull down at the capitol because they have served as legislators. They may be due a favor or two because of past votes. Moreover, when the time is right, they'll call them due. I guess what I really want to know is, do you want me to write a letter opposing a new trial?"

"Heck yes, Buck, I do, and any other appeal they make, now or forever. Why, I'll spend what little bit I have left or what I ever expect to have to see that the low-down scoundrel stays in prison."

"I thought that would be your answer, but I wanted to be sure before I marched on. If I were you, I know I would do the same."

Buck forwards the letter, and on August 12, 1890, he receives this reply: Frank Swaim was taken to Fulton County jail to await motion for a new trial. It was not granted. He was ordered to be remanded to principal keeper of the penitentiary.

For the next eight to nine years, I lead a fairly normal life as a farmer and a father, and my immediate family increases substantially as Jane gives birth to Ed and Docia. This gives us five living children, and we are so proud of them. But I ask, how can you continue to lead a normal life when your insides are torn asunder by an overwhelming need for reprisal, and when you know there is a strong undercurrent flowing and working deceitfully against you, trying to free Frank Swaim? As of now, it hasn't reared its ugly head openly, but I sense and feel this apparition.

Even though we live in the same community as the Swaims, in fact as neighbors, I have never been able to see Newt, for he dodges me like the plague. It's likely good that he does, for truthfully, I do not know for sure how I would react to him. I know he wasn't convicted, but I do know for a fact that he was with Frank when he murdered Dad; he is a mooncalf, a follower who looked up to his worthless brother. I do know that my body and heart have hardened, along with my reputation as a man not be tinkered with. These attributes I have not searched and strived for, but they seem to go with the territory.

As for Tom Swaim, the father of Frank and Newt, I have no use for him whatsoever, for wasn't it he and Fed Cannup running the illegal still that turned out the rot-gut moonshine that poisoned the air of Choestoe, thereby bringing on the unfortunate murder of Dad? He knows for certain how I feel about him, and so does the rest of the populace of Choestoe, for I make no secret of the fact, and I have no apologies to make concerning the matter. Why, when he goes to visit his brother-in-law, Fate Fortenberry, who lives practically within shouting distance of me, he goes the long way around, not daring to pass my place. In no way will I ever countenance his existence.

This particular day finds me at Virge Waldroup's store, along with several other people, and Tom just happens to be in the crowd there. He has been drinking, as is typical of him, and I imagine the moonshine bolsters his nerve enough, because he, in the company of others, sidles over to me and innocently asks, "Jim, will you sign this petition to get Frank out of prison? If you will sign, I'm shore they will let him out."

I am dumbfounded by the boldness of the ignorant son of a gun, and my body trembles in a sudden, uncontrolled fury. I quickly reach in my overall pocket for my knife, thinking all the while, I'll settle this once and for all.

Virge sees what is a-fixin' to take place and he says, "Jim, if you don't mind, I need to see you a minute." I walk over to Virge, and he says, "Not now Jim, not now."

"Okay, Virge," I answer.

I turn around and walk back to Tom, who it seems has miraculously sobered up. "Tom Swaim, if you ever mention to me again about signing your petition, I'll kill you faster than a feather will burn in three hells. Do you understand?" His goozle bobbles up and down, and he weakly nods his head. Tom, petition in hand, quickly leaves Virge's store and hurries back to his hovel situated at the foot of Yellow Mountain. I think he realizes that he has just looked death in the eye and escaped only because of the quick action taken by Virge Waldroup.

Judson (Judd) Duckworth, who drives a team for Virge and is Dad's brother-in-law, says, "Thought you were going to gut him there for a second or two."

"I would have, Judd, if it hadn't been for Virge," I reply.

Shortly thereafter, I am in Blairsville and stop by to see Buck; I make it a habit to do so, for our respect and friendship for each other continues to grow year by year. Buck says, "Heard about your little face-to-face with Tom the other day at Virge's store. Thought you ought to know, in case you don't, that Tom's carrying the petition all over the county, getting people to sign it. Jim, you know as well as I do that most people will sign anything put before them without reading it or caring really what it says, just wanting to get rid of the one presenting it. In law it has no validity whatsoever, but if you're lookin' for an opportunity to do something, it might be used as supporting evidence or as an excuse to do it."

"Thanks, Buck," I reply.

Elections in the mountains are a big event, almost being on par with court week as a social gathering. Most men, whether it be by custom or excuse, seem to be of the mindset that it is a necessity to drink on election day. An election is being held, and a feller can count on practically every man in Choestoe being at the voting precinct and staying all day in vigorous support of his candidates. I am there, and so is Tom Swaim, but he is careful to avoid me. However, he is a liberal participant in the time-honored tradition of the bending of the elbow, and he has become quite happy and brave. Now herein lies one of the dangers of drinking: one gets bold and may forget what he has been told. Evidently, that's what happens to Tom, for down in the shank of the evening, he walks up to me and says, "Jim, have a drink with me, and will you sign this petition?"

When I tell a feller something, I'm a-goin' to do it. I don't answer Tom, don't need to; my mountain toothpick will answer for me. My hand flies into my pocket, and I quickly whip it out and go to work on him. The vision of Dad lying lifeless in the cold waters of Wolf Creek flashes through my mind. I intend to take care of Tom Swaim, exactly like his boys did Dad. I start at the belt line, cutting and slashing, working my way up to his throat. With every cut, I feel the flesh tear, hear bone being met by knife; the blood in bright profusion covers him and me and pools up 'neath our feet. I am ready to finish the job, so I grab him by his shaggy hair, jerk his head back, and press the point of my knife to the base of his ear just 'neath where the jawbone ends. Tom is a-kicking and screaming for help, but it is useless, for I have him in a vice. It's as if I'm possessed by some strong unseen force, and I am. It's my love for Dad. I feel someone grab my arm; others jump on my back. I make a quick cut, bringing my arm down in a circular motion, intending to sever his windpipe, but the men ahold of my arm thwart my intent somewhat, and the cut only goes about a quarter-inch into his throat. Even though I am above six-one in height, weigh in excess of two hundred and twenty-five pounds, and my body has been honed to a strength and hardness of steel by years of hard work, I am no match for the number of men pulling me away. As my grip weakens somewhat, Tom falls flat on the hard ground, his body crumpling, comatose at my feet. I yell, "Get up, Tom; you're not hurt all that bad!" and I struggle in vain to get loose, intending to finish him off.

Then I hear a voice from afar yelling, "Whoa, whoa, Jim!" It sounds familiar, and I see that it's Debarris. He draws near, and it is then and there for the first time that I notice how much he resembles Dad. I stop struggling in deference to him. I give him a nod, and he says, "Fellers, it's all right; it's over for now." I am released, for they know when we say a thing it's exactly as we say.

I look back to where Tom is down. He is still there, but he is weakly trying to crawl away. His overalls are cut and ripped where my knife slashed feverishly as it sought and found his flesh. Two of his kin are kneeling beside him, trying to quell the flow of blood by applying pressure, administering as best they can. A wagon is speedily procured, and Tom is carefully loaded into it. He is taken home and the doctor sent for. Dr. Berry sews him up. Tom doesn't die, though it was my intent, but he will forever carry the scars as a continual reminder of February 17, 1890, the day my Dad was killed.

I go home, clean up, and burn my clothes, for I don't want ever to wear again any article of clothing that has been defiled by their rotten blood.

Chapter XVI

THE COURTHOUSE

I sit and wait. Some time later, Sheriff W. L. Bowling arrives and informs me he has a warrant for my arrest, the charge being attempted murder. I tell him, "I've been expecting you." Sheriff Bowling gathers a coroner's jury to seek evidence against me, and I am escorted to Blairsville jail and locked up by a deputy.

Buck has heard of the events of the day and comes to the jail to talk to me and find out how much my bail is going to be. While we are talking, I hear a commotion of men on horseback riding hard, then many voices crying "Whoa!" as they come sliding to a quick stop in front of the jail. I glance out the window to see who is in such an all-fired hurry, and then I see that it is the Lance men in force, armed to the teeth, leading one horse with a saddle but without a rider. They knock on the door and are let in. Before anyone even asks the amount of the bail, Granddad hollers back and says, "Son, we've come after you." There is no doubt, bail or no bail, I'm going back with them. They make bail, and I say good-bye to Buck, walk out of jail, mount, and we ride out of town, a-whooping and a-hollering.

The coroner's jury meets at the Choestoe law ground, and they compile the evidence against me. You may wonder why I'm not taken back there for the setting of my bail. They do hold trials there, but these are for minor infractions such as landline disputes, disturbing the peace, breaking up public worship, and petty theft. And I know that my fight with Tom Swaim, if you can call it that, for he put up little fight, certainly doesn't fall into the petty category. I had full intentions of killing him. When brought to trial, if asked, I know I will be compelled because of my upbringing to testify that "yes," I meant to kill him. I desired to rid this land of his kind. I realize also there is the strong possibility that I might serve prison time for this act, but I'll have a fighting chance 'cause I will again have Virge and Buck to represent me.

I find the next several days after I get home to be very interesting and somewhat unexpected. Instead of being scorned, as one might imagine, I am welcomed back as a victorious hero. I have many people coming by to visit me, wish me well, and to tell me, "Good job, Jim." I know this outpouring of sympathy and praise isn't really all for me, but is instead out of respect for Dad, for he was genuinely liked by most.

This attitude toward me might seem strange to some, but not to the populace of our mountain region, for you must remember that we live in an isolated area; outside influences have not yet penetrated our isolation. Law enforcement is far away, and it fails to serve effectively, so it's up to the immediate family clan to protect his own. In fact, it is not written but fully understood that if family is harmed or perceived to be, then it is the moral duty for kin to rise up in support and to retaliate. You will find this loyalty to kin throughout the Appalachian Mountains. This devotion toward family might be considered odd, but not to be so would be odd to us.

A few weeks pass, the grand jury meets, and a true bill is returned against me for attempted murder. I am to be tried next week for this serious offense.

Debarris calls a meeting of the Choestoe Lances to decide how to best respond to this threat against me. We meet at Mom's because it's more isolated, and I tell them up front that I don't want anything done that might get any of them in trouble, for we have gone through enough already. Granddad speaks up, "Trouble, they ain't seen trouble yet."

A decision is reached, and riders are sent out to bring in the other Lances: Martin's bunch from Lumpkin County, John's clan from Dooly and Ivy Log, James's bunch from Shooting Creek, North Carolina, and Napoleon Hill from the lower end of the county. We are all to meet two days hence at Mom's house in Lance Cove. I know this makes for a tight schedule, but when it comes to one of our own, we will immediately lay everything else aside and come.

Your curiosity might be aroused as to why Napoleon is included in this meeting. It is pure and simple, for ever since he and Debarris became friends, he has been there for us and us for him, and he and the Hills are as family. We need Napoleon's expertise in helping to formulate a plan of operation; he has experience at such, gained by serving as a major in the Confederate army and helping them make and carry out battle plans. His experience as an elected official in Union County, having served as sheriff from 1875-1877 and 1877-1879, can't hurt either. We are under no pretense that what we want to accomplish will be easy, knowing that to be successful, it will have to be kept quiet. It will be a battle and has to be planned accordingly, down to the smallest detail; thus Napoleon.

In Union County, in two days if you are in a centrally located part, you will notice an unusually large number of riders passing through Blairsville on the way to Choestoe and then proceeding on up Lance Creek, finally congregating at Mom's.

The meeting begins, and let it suffice to say that after much give-and-take and heated discussion, all agree upon a plan of action. It is complicated, takes coordinated timing, is to occur over a large area of the county, and it is to be put into action at once.

The citizens of Union County as a whole are early risers, getting up way before daylight, and on this morn' as they awake and begin to stir, they notice a strong, overriding odor of smoke. They step outside and see the mountains burning hotly, stretching as far as the eye can see from Choestoe to Town Mountain and into the Gum Log Mountains, lying close to and almost surrounding Blairsville, then extending on down to the Ivy Log Mountains, into the Rocky Top, then on near to the North Carolina line. A general alarm is sounded, and the inhabitants of Blairsville and the surrounding areas rush out to fight the fiercely burning fire. The city of Blairsville is practically deserted. Some men arrive on the square, dismount quickly, and can be seen going purposefully into the courthouse. They rush back out, mount, and head toward Choestoe to help fight the spreading fires. Then mysteriously, the courthouse begins to burn. Soon it is totally engulfed in flames. When the residents of Blairsville get back from fighting the fires, the courthouse is almost gone, evidently burned because a spark from the fires must have blown up on the roof, causing the roof, which is as dry as a tinderbox, to ignite.

Rumor has it that some people think the Lances might know something about the fires. I answer them truthfully that we were in Blairsville on business, and when we heard that the mountains were on fire we rushed back to help fight the fires, which we did.

A few days later I receive a letter from James L. Haralson, clerk of Superior Court, notifying me as the defendant that due to of the accidental burning of the courthouse, my trial will be postponed because of a lack of a suitable facility in which to hold court. Tom Swaim, as the accuser, gets a similar letter.

Sometime later, Jim Collins goes by the Tom Swaim house on his way to see Si Reece. He notices a flurry of activity and inquires, asking, "What's up, Tom?"

"We're packing, I've got kin out in Texas, and I'm taking my family out there before the crazy Lances kill me. There's nothing they won't do, and I know for a fact the courthouse didn't accidentally burn. It was some of that damn Lance clan that set it afire."

This is news to me, and I need to know what this does, if anything, to the charges pending against me of attempted murder, so this necessitates another trip to Blairsville to see Buck. It seems that I have been having business in Blairsville right regularly lately.

Midmorning of the next day finds me in Blairsville, and immediately I go to Buck's office to confer with him.

After telling him of Tom's departure to Texas, I ask, "In light of recent events, when do you think my trial will be?"

"Since the accidental burning of the courthouse," he looks at me and slyly grins in a knowing manner, "and the fortunate or unfortunate leaving of Tom, I believe you are home free. The reasons being: first, there just isn't a place now big enough to hold the trial, and there won't be any time soon. Second, Tom is the accuser, and in all probability, he will never set foot in Union County again, and there is no way you can have a trial without the plaintiff."

On my way back home, I get to thinking about one thing Buck said: "the fortunate or unfortunate leaving of Tom." Now just what did he really mean? I ponder, turn it over and over in my mind; yes, this and the accident probably frees me from the prospect of a prison sentence, but it also frees Tom from me. I still abhor him, almost more than anything in the world, and now that he's in Texas, he's gotten beyond my reach. Now I believe I've figured out the subtle message of Buck's statement, but sometimes I'm still amazed at the keenness of his mind.

The other day at Virge's store, Virge calls me aside to report on something that has been floating around the county as gossip. "Jim, as one of your counsel, I need to let you know that there is an undercurrent of talk about the courthouse burning not being an accident; some are speculating that the Lances set it deliberately to save your hide. Debarris in particular is getting blamed, and there is talk of a grand jury investigation. Don't imagine you've heard, because I don't believe many folks have the courage to face you with malicious gossip such as this."

"No Virge, I haven't heard, but it's not a complete surprise."

Before I go home, I know I must swing by Debarris's and warn him of what I've found out. I do so, but he's already heard, for he seems to always have a sixth sense about what's happening and what's about to happen that stands him in good stead, gives him a leg up on almost any situation. Thus it is with a fighting man, and he certainly is that. "Jim, glad you dropped by, I was a-goin' to come see you later in the afternoon anyway; need to talk to you. Tell you I've decided to move over about Hayesville, in Clay County, North Carolina. Here are the reasons: we've taken care of your problem about the trial just as we intended, and now that I'm the one mainly getting the blame about the accident with the courthouse, if I move, neither you nor any of our other kin will ever be accused, and it's all over. If I stay, there might be an investigation, and I can't chance drawing them into it. Jim, I'm so proud of you; you've become a man among men. I'm glad that you are a Lance and my nephew. If anything else ever comes up, send a rider, and I'll beat him back."

"The same goes here," I reply. I am choked up and want Debarris to stay here in the worst way, but I know there's no use objecting because he said he has decided and that's the way it's going to be, for he's a Lance.

"Wait a minute, Jim; before you go home I need to tell you how come I decided on Clay County."

"I'd like to know," I answer.

"Well Jim, I'd been sensing something was wrong, felt a bit uneasy, then when I heard what was being said behind my back, I knew that was what was a-causing my jitters. I needed some advice, so I turned to Napoleon again, told him I was thinking of moving out of Union County, explained the reason for doing so, and asked him what he thought. For a while Napoleon didn't answer, just sat there with his head down, real quiet-like. I could tell he was in deep thought and didn't want to say anything till he thought it through and through. Then after a bit, he responded by saying, 'Debarris, seems like you've made a solid decision. Can I throw something out for your consideration?'

"'Why sure,' I answered, 'for that is the reason I came to you in the first place.'

"Then Napoleon continued, 'My oldest son Ben lives in the Hayesville, North Carolina area just a short distance from where Fires Creek flows into the Hiawassee River, and he likes it a lot. Says the people there are friendly enough, but not too much; they mind their own business, from what he says. Sounds like that might be a good place to light, and there just happens to be a two-hundred-acre tract available that abuts up to his place. I know Ben would like to have a man like you, Debarris, as a neighbor.'

"'Well Napoleon, I've been a Missourian, a Texan, a Georgian, and I don't guess it would be too bad to become a Tar Heel. I'm certainly interested. Can you go with me to look at it?'

"'Sure can, name the time,' Napoleon said.

"'What about tomorrow?' I asked.

"'Suits me; I don't have any fodder down. You can spend the night with us; that way we can leave early in the morning.'

"Napoleon and I talked late into the night, remembering times past, the Civil War, and the eerie similarities about the tragedies that have befallen our families, the murder of his brother Charles and the murder of my brother John.

"It didn't matter any that we talked late into the night. Early morning daybreak found us on our mounts heading to North Carolina. We sat ramrod straight in the saddle, rode swiftly, and it reminded us of charging into battle, but I hope never again, for I've had enough battles to last any man a lifetime. All I want now is to live in peace and harmony.

"Jim, the property was as I had been told, flat fields ideally suited for farming, mountains big enough to hunt in and a river running swift and deep to fish in. I liked it so much, I just up and bought it."

"I'm tickled for you, Debarris," I answer.

I go home sad. We are going to have to make do without Debarris, and he will be sorely missed, but I am also glad, for he has earned and deserves nothing but the best.

It's been ten years since Dad's death, and it seems that there is somewhat of a closure for me because Tom Swaim, his son Newt, and the rest of the immediate family have seen the value in moving out of Union County. His worthless son Frank is safely ensconced in the penitentiary in Dade County.

Let me point out that there are many more Swaims that are living here that are closely akin to Tom's bunch, some even marrying into the Lance family. I hold no aught against them, for they are principled people and make excellent neighbors and trustworthy friends. It is aptly said, "There is one rotten apple in every barrel." Thus, it is so.

But there will never be complete closure when it comes to Dad's murder, for though it has been ten years since his untimely death, I still miss him as much as the day he was so tragically killed, and even though I don't visit his grave every day now, I do so at least once a week, for my loving memory of the life he led and his love for his family and neighbors cannot be forgotten.

Chapter XVII

THE PARDON

Just when it looks like I can devote more time to my wife, Jane, and our children Jack, Juan, Leanor, Ed, and Docia, I receive a letter from Buck saying he needs to see me again at once. I show it to Jane, and after she reads it, she without a minute's hesitation says, "You must go," and I know I must.

I leave Choestoe at once. Midafternoon finds me again in Buck's office. "What's it this time, Buck?" I anxiously ask.

Buck pushes a packet toward me and says, "Because I am one of your attorneys, I received these letters from the prison board asking my input on the matter, and as the attorney for the accuser, we have a right to know and to appear when it comes up."

I start to read the packet of letters, and quickly the temper I've inherited takes over, and I spill out curse words in a seemingly endless torrent of vile, harsh profanity. I go on and on, the venom of my words filling the office with a poison so vicious that it threatens to destroy everyone in reach, finally ending with my maul-like fist pounding down on Buck's desk with a resounding thud. When my outburst is spent, Buck calmly says, "Jim, would you tell me now, how do you really feel?" I am taken aback by such a question. I have to grin, for he seems always to know how to handle me and bring me back to my senses.

The letters read (and are typed as written):

December 2, 1899
To the Board of Prison Commissioners:

I learn that the case of Frank Swaim, who was convicted before me some years ago in Union Supreme Court of the murder of John Lance, will shortly be brought to your attention through an application for pardon, and I have been requested to make a statement in reference to the case. The conviction rested entirely upon circumstantial evidence that contained some points of weakness.

Ex. Judge C. J. Wellborn Sr. (1)

Choestoe, Georgia
June 25, 1900
Mr. C. A. Evans
Dear friend:

I will write you wanting some information as to whether C. J. Wellborn Jr. has got Frank Swaim case before your Board of Prison Commissioners for pardon and whether he has before you in this instance or not.

It would be very much appreciated if you could recommend his release as he has bin in prission a long time and the evidence all week. The people at large have grave doubts as to his guilt and think he ought to be released. I would be glad to hear from you as to what Mr. Wellborn has don.

Signed,
James C. Dyer Jr. (2)

Blairsville, Georgia
Gen C. A. Evans
Dear General:

J. C. Dyer, who is interested in the application for pardon of Frank Swaim has shown me your card of the 19th in which you say "further arguments will be heard by the board any day next week"; as you of course know, I am counsel for Swaim. You will remember that I have made one formal argument and have talked with the board on other occasions in regard to the case.

Truly Yours,
C. J. Wellborn Jr. (3)

Sommerville County, State of Texas
July 9, 1900

Personally appeared before me the undersigned, Newton Swaim, who on oath says that he was with F. Swaim in Union County the entire day on which J. H. Lance was murdered, and that neither he nor Frank Swaim were at any time nearer the place where the crime was committed than the road leading from his father's home to the house of Fed Cannup. I make this statement in the full light of the past and that justice may be done and Frank Swaim be released from the punishment inflicted for a crime of which he is innocent.

His Mark,
C. N. Swaim (4)

July 10, 1900
General C. A. Evans
My Dear General:

Received your form in regard to the matter of Frank Swaim, application for pardon. I will file some affidavits with the board during the next few days, after which I will ask the board to pass upon the matter. You have seen that there is room for grave doubt, and the judge who tried the case has never been satisfied about the matter. I trust the board will grant the pardon, but if not, then at least reduce the sentence to a term of years.

C. J. Wellborn Jr., Lawyer (5)

"Jim, from where I sit it appears that the political paybacks have been called due, and they are going to be paid in full by the granting of Frank Swaim a pardon. I was scared that something like this might happen when we elected Carlton Wellborn Jr. to represent us at the state capitol, and from the letters you see, he is also getting strong pressure from some of his supporters up here. He even admits in his letter to Gen. C. A. Evans that he has talked to the board about this on other occasions, but you may note also that he doesn't see fit to reveal to them that the judge who heard our case and has so-called grave doubts is his father. Actions such as this are what make politics unseemly, and if it's allowed to continue, it will destroy our system as we know it. It makes one wonder if his father's judgeship was earned on merit or is it also a political payback! Now, I don't know, but I do wonder. What I need to know from you is, do you want me to go before the board, represent you, and argue against the granting of Frank a pardon?"

I answer without hesitating, "You're dad-gum right I do. It appears that it's getting about time for me to face Wellborn 'eyeball-to-eyeball' and explain the situation to him, and when I do, I'll put it in a way that he can understand fully."

Buck replies, "Jim, be careful; remember that his father is the judge."

"It's him better be careful. I'll not cut him any slack if his father is a judge."

Buck Candler does go before the board as the Lance representative and argue against the granting of Frank Swaim a pardon. It is not granted.

Could this be the last we hear from them on securing a pardon for Frank Swaim? I certainly hope so, but I agree with Buck that probably this is wishful thinking. He believes that we must be ever-watchful, for the next round could be more deceitful in scope, 'cause Wellborn is down at the capitol as our representative. We have nobody down there to keep an eye on him, and I'm sure he's buddying up with the prison commission on a regular basis.

Life must go on. I realize this and try to cope as best I can, but for me there can never be a regular routine, because a slithery reptile struck my very being on February 17, 1890, poisoned my body with its noxious venom, and even now its coils are wrapped around my soul, threatening to deliver a fatal strike to me and the Lances.

The next three years brings some small semblance of getting ahead. We have been able to save up a little money, and we are beginning to look at buying a place that we can call our very own. Jane and I have found that by toiling from sunup to sundown somewhat eases the pain of our loss. Because of our love for each other, we again are blessed by the addition of Frances into our home. This gives us six living offspring. We love each equally but continue to learn better how they are alike, yet how they are unalike, each having a unique personality.

Then I think of Jack and the way he's turned toward scholarly matters. Why, at an early age, Jane, who in school was the acknowledged best speller in all of Choestoe, recognized his keen intellectual ability and guided him in spelling words taken from the *Blue Back Speller* and taught him to read even before he went to the Wild Boar Institute. I recall how he studied and prepared his lessons by the light of a kerosene lamp while his brothers and sisters played. With Jack, there's no foolishness about him, and I'll guarantee you that he will someday bring honor to our family and praise to Choestoe in scholarly circles.

In late January of 1903, I meet with W. A. Charter as the now solicitor general for our county and apprise him of the situation regarding the murder of Dad. I request that if he hears of an effort to pardon Frank Swaim, would he please notify me? He replies in the affirmative, and a few days later, I get a copy of a letter he writes on February 2, 1903 to the prison commission saying:

Honorable J. S. Turner, Chairman, Prison Commission
Mr. Turner:

I am advised that an application for pardon may be made for Frank Swaim, convicted, Union Superior Court, for murder. I know nothing of the case, the conviction having been before I came in office. The relatives of the man killed desire to be heard before the application is passed on, and I write you to ask that an opportunity be given them to be heard. If you will give me timely notice, say ten days before you take up the application, I will notify them.

Sincerely Yours,
W. A. Charter (6)

I hear nothing further about the matter until Buck sends me a message, delivered by a rider, telling me that he needs to see me at once! "It's urgent!"

I immediately rush to his office, and I am appraised of a nasty turn of events. He received a letter forwarded to him from W. A. Charter, solicitor general for our county, who received a letter on March 31. The letter from a Goodloe Young to W. A. Charter was prompted by a letter sent to Mr. Young by N. A. Morris, speaker of house, which reads:

Dear Solicitor General:

I have your card in reference to the Swaim case. I wish you would please arrange to have the relatives of the deceased, or such representation as they may desire, to be present Monday, April 6, so this matter can be disposed of.

Yours Truly,
N. A. Morris, Speaker of House (7)

"I'll read you the letter forwarded from W. A. Charter, solicitor general, to me," says Buck.

Honorable Goodloe Young
Dear Sir:

I beg to acknowledge receipt of your letter notifying me of the hearing of clemency petition of Frank Swaim: I have forwarded your letter to Honorable W. E. (Buck) Candler of Blairsville, who will doubtless notify the people of interest on the other side. (8)

"Jim, I took the liberty of replying, and did so immediately, knowing that it was too late. Here is my reply."

Blairsville, Georgia
April 4, 1903
Dear Sir:

Your kind letter in regard to the hearing of the application of Frank Swaim, Union County, for pardon was duly received and noted. John H. Lance was the murdered man, and then Sol. Gen. Howard Thompson and myself prosecuted Swaim for the murder. The family of John Lance are honorable, hard-working, poor people and have done all they could in an honorable way to punish Swaim for the killing of their father, who was a local Methodist preacher and who I have no doubt was killed on account of an honest effort on his part to benefit his immediate section and people. His boys got me to confer with Howard Thompson of Gainesville about representing them before you all and for him to resist the pardon. Howard Thompson has agreed to do this, and when the matter is taken up, I suppose he will be present and ask to be heard. The record of this case will be before you. All the testimony in the case satisfied the jury of the guilt of the defendant and they so found. Not a single thing has occurred in the county from that day until this going has shown that the defendant is not guilty, and in my opinion, no good reason can be given why he is not. That being said, he ought to remain where he is.

With kindness and best regards for you personally,
I am truly yours,
W. E. Candler (9)

After reading all the letters shown to me by Buck, my Lance temper that is so short-fused anyway is seething just beneath the surface. It starts to take hold of me, and I angrily storm out, muttering, "Why the dirty, conniving son of a . . . " Just as I am getting started real good, Buck breaks in.

"Jim, before you go completely off the deep end, let me summarize what I think has happened, and then you can finish your tirade; can't say that I blame you really."

"I received the letter written to Sol. Gen. Charters from the prison board on April 4, 1903. It was written to the prison commission on March 23, 1903 from Speaker H. A. Morris, asking that relatives or representatives of those opposed to pardon be notified of a hearing on April 6, 1903. As you noted in my reply to the board, I stated, 'I can't go, because court will be in session here next week, and I have several cases pending, and Attorney and Representative Wellborn know this.' At your request, I made arrangements for former Solicitor Thompson to represent you. I had no idea the hearing would be held in two days. Jim, it took seven days for the letter to get from Dahlonega here to me. How do they expect us to notify Attorney Thompson and for him to make plans and be at the hearing in two days? They don't, pure and simple! I believe this is a political setup between Representative Wellborn and N. A. Morris, who is speaker of house and is also representing Frank, to prevent you from appearing, thereby probably assuring the pardon of Frank because there will be no one there to point out that Judge Wellborn and Attorney Wellborn are father and son. If it works for them, and under these circumstances I see no reason why it won't, well, all I've got to say is shame on those involved for using an elected public office to free a guilty man and to unjustly manipulate our justice system at the expense of the Lances."

Then the tirade that has been temporarily interrupted by Buck comes full circle, and the blackguarding words erupt like a volcano spewing forth its scalding, molten lava, so hot that it expends everything it touches. But my eruption is more so, as it rolls on and on, finally ending with a chorus of "Durn the Wellborns and durn Frank Swaim, for my day will surely come!" and then it is spent.

On May 11, 1903, we are notified that because of the recommendation of the prison commission, it is ordered that the said Frank

Swaim be and is hereby pardoned and that he be discharged from custody forthwith.

J. M. Terrell, Governor

The reasons for executive clemency are as follows:

The evidence discloses enough facts and circumstances to create grave doubt in the mind of the judge who tried him, as well as in the minds of a large number of citizens of Union County, as to his guilt, and the judge who presided recommends clemency. Frank Swaim has served with good conduct thirteen years, and in consideration of grave doubts as to his guilt, his meritorious conduct, and the recommendation of the judge and over 300 good citizens of Union County, the board recommends a pardon. (10)

Neither I nor Buck are surprised at the outcome. Rather, I am expecting it because of the covert actions of some before and at the April 6 hearing of the prison commission. Even though I expected as much and am somewhat prepared for it, there is still deep-seated resentment and disappointment because of the mitigating circumstances by which it is accomplished. During these hectic times, our family is blessed by the birth of another son, Carter Paul, who later is nicknamed Tom.

For some reason, I think of what I once heard Dad say, "It's always darkest right before daylight." Though he has been dead going on fourteen years, I still so vividly recall the many sayings he used so often to make a valid point.

I sit and think, ponder and think. Now it seems to me that I do much more pondering than thinking. And why not? For most of my adult life has been about asking questions of "What if?" and pondering how life would have been if Dad had not been so brutally murdered by Frank Swaim. Now Frank is free, pardoned to go on living as if Dad's murder never occurred, and yet Dad still lies motionless in Old Salem Cemetery with the fallen leaves still packing up against his headstone. Others may forgive, and they may want me to forget about the fateful day of February 17, but I won't, I can't, never, ever, for my teeth are still on edge, and they have hit a nerve that I can feel to the quick.

When you have been so engrossed for more than thirteen years on one objective, that being total satisfaction for your loved one, it does become an obsession, embossed upon every nerve in your body, making it extremely difficult to focus on anything else.

Then I see the darkness fading, the veil of its total blackness being slowly lifted, revealing a rising sun that carefully reaches into every hidden cove, and Choestoe is alive, filled with light and goodness. I begin to imagine that I can see this light. Could it be possible that now that he is a free man, Frank Swaim will come back to Choestoe? I grin to myself in fiendish delight, dreaming of an encounter, a personal meeting with him so that I can have a go at exacting the total revenge that I and the rest of the Lances long for.

So I set in planning, sharpen my knife to a keenness that will split a hair, and clean my hog rifle until it shines as new money, just in case, as a last resort if I can't get to him any other way. That's not the way I want it though, for I want him face-to-face, eyeball-to-eyeball, a fight to the finish; only then can I have some sort of closure. I laugh in eager anticipation!

I immediately start patrolling all of Choestoe, but pay particular attention to his former haunts, the areas he is most familiar with. I do this night and day, sleep very little, and what sleep I get is short catnaps, snatched while in the saddle. I patrol for going on a month until I become distraught, finally realizing that I have been thwarted again. Even Frank is smart enough not to show himself here, and now he has departed for parts unknown without the formality of saying a cursory good-bye. Oh, how I did want to greet him and to welcome him back in a special way!

Chapter XVIII

My Nemesis

Life is peculiar in so many ways; why, you can be in deep despair one minute and then an event occurs, and your mood turns to optimism.

This year it's been like that for me; on the one hand, there is the total despair of the granting of Frank's pardon and him not returning to Choestoe, and on the other hand, there's the joy of welcoming Tom into our family and also the possibility of finally having a place of our own.

The owning of our own little farm has long been a secret dream of mine and Jane's, but it has seemed so far out of reach because of the cost and time associated with Dad's murder and the providing for our family, which now numbers seven.

Jane and I are finally able to make our dream come true. Mom has continued to live in Lance Cove for going on fourteen years, just she and my remaining brothers and sisters. But they're growing up, marrying, and moving out on their own; however, most remain in the general vicinity. But Joe, who married Laura Souther—they've moved all the way to Colorado. He wants to start anew, get away from the nasty reminders of Dad's murder and the continuing struggle to right a wrong. I can't really blame him, for sometimes I think of the same, but the memories I have of my dad won't let go, and I know I must struggle on.

We are urging Mom to sell Lance Cove and move in with some of us. She doesn't want to, says she has too many fond memories of her and Dad in Lance Cove. She's afraid if she leaves, these memories will somehow become dimmer, and she wants to hold on to them tightly, till the Lord comes in all of his Glory and calls her home, and then as she walks through the Pearly Gates, Dad will be there a-waiting for her They will embrace again, and he will say, "Caroline, what took you so long? It's great up here, but I've missed you so."

Mom is now sixty. I wish I could say she is a young sixty, but she's not, for there's been so many struggles in her life with Dad's murder and the raising of the rest of her children by herself and the keeping up of Lance Cove. Oh, we've all pitched in, but in the final say, it has been her and her alone. Her fortitude has prevailed, but it's taken its toll.

Times are still hard here in the mountains. It has always been this way; money is scarce, and people save up from one year to the next just to pay their county taxes. Finding a party willing to purchase your property is somewhat of a dream, but Mom is lucky in that she has a buyer for Lance Cove. Vogel Land Co., based in Milwaukee, Wisconsin, has recently started to buy up land here, and they've approached Mom about hers. We urge her to sell, and reluctantly she agrees to do it. On April 27, 1903, she completes the transaction, leaves the old place, and moves in with us.

Virge Waldroup knows that Jane and I want to have a place of our own, and probably because of our friendship, he gives me the opportunity. The Campbell men, J. H., T. L., and D. G., come to Virge and offer to sell him their property that adjoins some that he owns. He comes to me and offers to put the deal together if I am interested; I certainly am, and he does. We close on it August 17, 1903. There are 225 acres, and I pay $225.00 for it ($1.00/acre). I don't have that kind of money, but Mom chips in and helps me pay for it. This is just a typical example of how my family looks out for each other in all matters, whether it be physical or financial.

Virge tells me that he has had many chances to sell this piece of land and turned them down because it is considered one of the best farms in all of Choestoe—and it is.

Wolf Creek boldly runs through it, and for about three-fourths of a mile on each side of it, there are fertile, flat bottoms just waiting to be plowed, eagerly wanting to provide a bountiful crop to whomever is fortunate enough to own it. Now it belongs to us.

There is a good-sized house on the property, but it needs some fixing up. We set in and soon take care of this little problem. At last, we have a house big enough for our growing family, and there is ample room for Mom also.

Mom is more satisfied than she ever imagined she would be; she has told us as much because when she is with us or at Fate's, she is still close enough to easily walk back to the old homeplace and remember the good times. She does this on a regular basis, and it is refreshing to behold Mom and her grandkids walking beside Wolf Creek hand in hand, laughing continually on their way to rekindle fond memories.

We are prepared now in every way to turn our farm into something that we can all be proud of. My team of mules that I bought two years ago as colts have grown up, and they are sleek, fat, and hardened, ready for real work. I have broken them to work so that they obey my every command.

Most people seem to prefer a horse over a mule, but I don't. I guarantee you that a mule will work any horse half to death. I've also been told that you can't ride a mule; they are too rough, will shake you to pieces, but my mules will ride as easy as can be because they have been taught to "single-foot" as good as any horse. I've also heard that a mule is stubborn, mean, and will work for you a lifetime, just to get a chance to kill you. I can't find fault with them for that because that's a whole lot like I am.

I thought that Jane and I, while we lived at the Allison place and sharecropped for him, did all that was humanly possible to give "an honest day's work for an honest day's pay." We did improve his place enormously, but when you look at our own place now, after a year's work, and see what tremendous progress has been made in cleaning it up, we have to admit that we might have shirked our duties just a bit.

The house has been cleaned and fixed up, and we are thinking about adding on. The barn has been repaired, another one built, also the creek and branch banks have been cleared so there is more productive land. The hedgerows and wood lines have been trimmed back to where they become too steep to plow; the split-rail fence has been mended so that the cattle, sheep, and hogs have to forage in the mountains where they belong. They have become fat on the mast provided by the oak and chestnut trees. At night we are so tired that when we lie down we fall asleep immediately, satisfied by what has been accomplished, and we awaken each morning rested, keen to get back at it.

I am the happiest I've been since Dad's murder, probably because of the thrill of seeing something that you own increase in value as a result of hard work done by you and your family.

In the spring of 1904, however, my happiness is shattered by a visit from Attorney Wellborn, who I have no use for because of his actions in Dad's trial and the subsequent pardon of Frank Swaim that I firmly believe was granted because of his political activities.

I am in the field plowing, minding my own business, when I see someone approaching. You can tell he is a stranger to farming and fields by the awkward way he walks, carefully high-stepping in a futile effort to prevent the turned soil from marring the shine on his tight-fitting black patent leather shoes. I pull back on the reins, say "Whoa" to my team, and watch in amusement as he nears. When I recognize that it is Wellborn, my amusement suddenly vanishes, being replaced instead by a boiling hate, hidden just beneath the surface and threatening to spring forth. He walks up and greets me as if we are bosom buddies, saying "Howdy Jim. I am up here doing a little politicking. If you're not obligated, I would appreciate your support. I'm running for representative again." I am flabbergasted, for I thought he knew how I felt about him. My face turns as red as a burning ember, and I set in to tell him, removing all doubt, about my feelings.

"Wellborn, you'll do no good here! I remember that you, in an offhand way, accused me of lying at Dad's trial. I'm on to your crooked action in getting a pardon for Frank. We stopped it the first time and would have again if you hadn't manipulated the date so that we couldn't appear. Why, the hearing was going on before we knew it was being held! My answer to you is there's no way I'd be a big enough fool to support the likes of you. I promise you I'll do everything in my power against you. I ought to whip you right now, so get out of my field while you can!"

I angrily shout, and as a parting word, in a fit of uncontrolled anger, I say, "Wellborn, the next time I see you, you're mine! Do you understand me?"

"Yes Jim, I do. I'm sorry you feel like you do. I was just doing my job."

"You're durn right you're sorry. Let me tell you now, the next job you do had better not be on me or any of my kin!" I storm. My team stomps nervously, for they can feel the tension filling the air.

My anger hasn't subsided a bit, so I unhook my mules and start to the barn, even though there are several hours of daylight left; I know in this frame of mind, more plowing is out of the question.

Jane sees me coming and rushes to the barn, thinking that something bad has happened, for I have never stopped plowing this early in the day. "Jim, what's wrong?" she asks.

"Jane, did you see who that was talking to me in the field? Would you believe it was Wellborn, asking us to vote for him?"

"I saw someone but couldn't tell who it was. Has he lost his mind?" Jane says. I am still struggling, trying to rein in my fit of anger, when Jane says, "Jim, let's go to the spring, get you a cool drink before you have a stroke." We do, and shortly the storm raging inside me begins to weaken, for Jane has a special knack, a gentle touch that always calms me down.

I can't afford to, but can't afford not to, so I take time off anyway from my farming and go all over Choestoe, campaigning against Wellborn, pointing out to the voters how I believe he has wronged me. They listen attentively, for they too haven't forgotten the good that Dad brought to this area.

The election is held, and now Rep. Wellborn is the former representative, and I might proudly add, in the Choestoe precinct he is soundly trounced. I can't brag and take too much credit for the part I play in his defeat; I know deep down it is out of respect for Dad, for his name is still much set by, and I would have it no other way.

Though the murder of my dad continues as an ever-present dark cloud hovering around me, Jane and I again try to resume a normal life of farming and raising a large family. In 1906, Homer is welcomed into the fold.

On Thursday, April 30, 1908, in the weekly editorial of the *Union County Banner,* I read this:

> The sad news reached here Sunday of the death of Judge C. J. Wellborn, which occurred Saturday at Millan, Georgia at the home of his daughter, Mrs. R. P. Jones. Judge Wellborn was born and reared in this county, and was one of the best-known men in this section of the state, numbering his friends by the score. For many years, he was judge of this judicial circuit. Later in life, he held a position at the Interior Department in Washington, D.C. Four years ago, he was appointed state librarian by Governor Terrell, which position he held until a few months back, when his health began failing and he resigned. His remains arrived here Monday night, and funeral services were conducted Tuesday afternoon by Revs. Sharp, Hughes, and Meeks, attended by a large number of friends and relatives. Interment was at the Methodist Cemetery. (1)

I sneak a slight grin, for though this news is sad to some, it isn't to me. I still harbor a lingering feeling of resentment toward the Wellborns. This notice further enhances my belief that my family wasn't treated fairly in regard to the pardoning of Frank Swaim. For doesn't the obituary notice mention that he was appointed state librarian by Governor Terrell, who just happens to be the governor who granted the pardon?

I have finally realized that in this life, nothing is permanent, and the Death Angel is constantly at work removing from this earth the good as well as the evil ones. This is further enforced upon me by news that reached us on May 17, 1910, and it is devastating to me and the other Lances in scope; we have lost a valued ally and a true friend. It was written by a committee from Allegheny Masonic Lodge #114 to honor one of their own, Brother Napoleon B. Hill, and reads thusly:

> Brother Hill was born February 14, 1832, in Rutherford County, North Carolina. His father moved to Cherokee County, North Carolina, in his young manhood. In May 1860, he married Miss Mary Evans and later moved to Union

County, Georgia, where the remainder of his life was spent, and where he and his wife reared a large, interesting, and honorable family. In the late war, he entered the service of the Confederate states, made a true and brave soldier of the lost cause, and rose to the rank of major. The war ended, and he reentered the work of a private citizen. In this role, he was an honor to his country and state, won the respect and confidence of his fellow citizens, and was honored by them in various ways. For a long number of years he was a devoted member of this Lodge and held sacredly and adhered to its obligations. He was a faithful husband and a tender, loving father, and as such, he departed this life in peace with his fellow men and his God at his home in Union County on January 17, 1910. His body now slumbers at rest in the land he loved, and his soul we hope dwells with his God he trusted. Long may his memory as a brother Mason remain fresh in the minds and hearts of the fraternity and actuate them to better and purer lives. Therefore, be it resolved that we deplore the death of our departed brother and extend our sympathy to his family and loved ones, and that as Masons we will cherish and keep green his memory and emulate his noble traits of character; that a page of the minutes of this Lodge be set apart, on which shall be inscribed this resolution; and that a copy of the same, under the Lodge seal, be furnished his widow by the secretary hereof; and that the local press be requested to print the same.

Signed W. E. Candler, F. E. Conley, and T. C. Hughes, Committee. (2)

The next six years are much quieter, as the constant turmoil that I seem to have been subjected to for the past twenty-something years has abated somewhat. I know some of this is due to the departure to Texas of some of my avowed enemies, for the mere presence or reminder of them brings on renewed anger, just as fierce as it was on that fateful day of February 17, 1890.

215

Even though things are quieter, the condition of my family health-wise is steadily declining. I am in good shape, but the two ladies who are so important in my life are experiencing some serious problems that have Dr. Erwin quite concerned. Mom is now seventy-four, and Jane is fifty-two, and is it any wonder that they are facing maladies with what they have had to endure?

The life of any mountain woman is rigorous at best, but when coupled with what Mom and Jane have gone through—the matter about Dad's death, the protection of our family, and the constant pursuit by me of righting a wrong—has aged them far beyond their years.

Dr. Erwin diagnoses Mom with heart dropsy and says it is just a matter of time. We try as best as we can to make her comfortable. She says not to worry because before long, she will again be holding hands with Dad and strolling down streets paved with gold. On the morning of April 3, she doesn't come to the breakfast table. We check on her and find she has passed on to be with her maker. Her hands are pressed together, resting underneath her chin as if she has been praying, and the most contented, gentle smile graces her face, and we know that she again is in the presence of Dad and a mighty God.

Mom is buried beside Dad in Old Salem Cemetery, and for the first time in over twenty-six years, she is totally at peace.

Jane, my beloved wife, can't seem to recover any of her strength, and she is having a lot of problems with her breathing. Her body that once was so young, vibrant, and strong seems to be wasting away, and her face has become gaunt. We are all terribly worried and try to keep our concerns hidden as best we can, but Jane has always had an intuition about matters, and she tells us that she is tired and ready to see again our three children who died as infants, her mom and dad, and my mom and dad, whom she loved so much.

We call on Dr. Erwin once more, and he treats Jane with what little medicine is available. He calls me aside and confirms our worst fears, that her malady is more serious than even we imagine. He believes she has heart trouble, and there is nothing medically that can be done. He wants us to keep her as comfortable as possible, and this we do. Jane doesn't complain, for she isn't that sort, but her difficulty in breathing belies how terrible she is feeling. Oh, it grieves me so to see the one I love, the mother of my children, my right hand, suffer like this. If only I could swap places with Jane, I'd do it in a heartbeat.

It is now mid-June, and the hard work that is a constant companion of all mountain families must go on. It becomes a necessity that I plow the fields, for the weeds are growing as rapidly as the corn. Jane seems to be feeling a bit better and insists that she is going to the fields with us. I don't want her to, because I'm afraid the oppressive, oven-like heat that settles over the plowed fields like a layer of thick blankets on a cold night will be too much for her. However, she wants to be with us continually, as if she knows something and isn't revealing it, so I relent. I hitch up my team of mules and make Jane a pallet in the wagon. We slowly and carefully weave our way down the rutted, rain-washed road toward the field, taking special caution so as not to jostle her. When we reach the field, I unhitch the wagon in the shade of a towering chestnut that is growing alongside the cooling waters of Wolf Creek, and a gentle breeze moves its leaves to and fro, providing Jane comfort compliments of Mother Nature. I gently pick her up and place her on the pallet that the children have made for her in the shade of the huge tree, where she can hear the contented, steady running of the creek and keep us in her continual sight.

I commence to plowing and the older children start hoeing, while the younger kids stay with Jane. I work for an hour or so, then suddenly I hear loud screaming coming from where Jane is resting. I turn around and see Jane lying down. I rush down the long, plowed rows and see her gasping for breath. I hurriedly raise her up, put my arms around her in a cocoon of love and say, "Jane, I love you so."

She opens her eyes momentarily and whispers "I love . . . ," draws her last breath, and passes into an eternal Heaven. I hold her in my arms for a long time. My cries of anguish and those of our children mingle to drown out the rush of Wolf Creek as it continues its trek toward the gulf.

This is June 20, three months after the death of Mom, and we know that Jane is now in the presence of those she longed to see. We bury Jane in the ancestral cemetery of the Henson's, and I know that one day my body will again lie by her side.

There is an old mountain superstition that says, "Back luck comes in three's." I didn't believe it when I first heard it, but now I do, for there was Dad, then Mom, and now Jane.

As is the mountain custom when a man is left to care for a large family, I soon am calling on a young lady who lives in Cindy Cove, a short distance for one of my trusty mules to carry me on my frequent visits.

A year later, I marry Melissa Spiva, and she moves into the Lance home. It might seem strange that I can love another as much as I did Jane, but Melissa has the same good, caring qualities as Jane, and I care for her dearly. I guess these qualities are an inborn trait of most mountain women, and I feel fortunate to fall in love with such a woman. Out of this union is born another eleven children.

For the next nine years or so, the contrary wind that fans my life and is a constant companion abates just a bit, and this enables me to function better as a father and provider, but a life lived under these conditions casts you into a mold that shackles what you could have been. I know this and accept it as a fact of life, because even now there is in me a pent-up rage that I constantly struggle with, trying to keep it hidden within myself. However, it is there, and anything remotely pertaining to Dad's murder causes it to reappear anew with as much fury as that fateful day. Because of this, I have gained an unwanted reputation as a man to be feared and not trifled with. This I did not seek, but it was thrust upon me by the evil actions of others.

Then in late November of 1925, I go to Virge Waldroup's store to procure some necessary provisions, and while I am there he says, "Jim, let me show you an article that has just appeared in the *Atlanta Constitution*, written by your nemesis, Carl J. Wellborn Jr. It reads:

"A True Story of the Georgia Mountains"
By Carl J. Wellborn (For the *Constitution*)
November 22, 1925

Just north of where Georgia's great scenic highway, so generously promoted by the *Atlanta Constitution*, crosses the Blue Ridge Mountains at Neel's Gap, there occurred a few years ago a tragedy so intermingled with romance as to be indelibly stamped upon the memory of many people yet living in that section, and was the real beginning of a sentiment in favor of law enforcement that has grown stronger with the passing years.

I refer to the murder of John H. Lance, and the incidents connected therewith, the truth of which may be easily verified by communicating with any of the older citizens in that section of the mountains.

This story verifies the old adage, "Truth is stranger than fiction."

John H. Lance was a typical Georgia mountaineer, born and reared in the section where he met his tragic death. He was a local Methodist preacher, earnest and honest. Of stalwart frame, with long hair and flowing beard, he would attract attention in any throng. He wore a homemade brown jeans suit, the cloth for which was woven by his good wife upon the old family loom that stood in a little outbuilding near his cabin home. The coat was a "Prince Albert," with two rows of brass buttons, clipped from an old army coat, running down the front. The wool from which this was made was sheared from his flock of sheep, which ran wild in the surrounding hills.

In a cove near the point where the new highway crosses Wolf Creek on the north side of the mountain, Lance had erected his little cabin home. Here, surrounded by the mountains he loved so well, he lived the quiet and happy life of the real mountaineer, until a serpent entered his Garden of Eden in the form of a "moonshine distillery." In the mouth of a mountain gulch a short distance above Lance's home, two men, known as Tom Swaim and Fed Cannup, began making whiskey with a "wildcat still" and so open and flagrant became their defiance of the law, that Lance decided it must cease. Consequently, he boldly called on them at their place of business and informed them that unless they removed their plant at once, he would report the matter to the federal authorities in Atlanta. The men became very indignant and warned Lance to interfere with them at his peril.

On a beautiful Sunday morning following this visit and interview with the two moonshiners, the Rev. Lance left his cabin to attend a little Sunday school he had organized some miles away across the hills. It was the month of May, and the mountain air was redolent with the perfume of the laurel and the ivy which were in full bloom, while the dogwood bushes gleamed like huge balls of snow against the green of the mountainsides.

After attending his Sunday school, he started his return journey to his cabin home.

At this time, there was no road across Neel's Gap, only a mountain trail running along the bluff above Wolf Gap. While walking along this trail, at a point where the road now crosses this creek, Lance was struck in the head by someone, his body being knocked from the bluff into the waters of the noisy little stream flowing below. His assailants jumped upon his defenseless body and cut his throat, entirely severing his head from the trunk. Here, after completing their dastardly work, they left the body partly submerged in the water, where it was found later in the afternoon by his devoted wife.

The county was aroused and a messenger sent to Blairsville, the county seat, for the sheriff and the coroner. At an inquest, a very strong case of circumstantial evidence was developed against young Frank Swaim, a son of one of the men involved in the moonshine distillery. Without going into particulars, suffice it to say that Frank Swaim was arrested, charged with the crime, and after a trial, was convicted and given a life sentence in the penitentiary. At this time Frank was a mere boy, only nineteen years of age. He had married a year before his conviction and was the father of a baby girl. He was passionately devoted to his wife and child. After his sentencing, he was carried from the little county jail at

Blairsville to the coal mines in Dade County to spend the remainder of his life at hard labor.

After a few heartbroken years, the girl wife immigrated to the newly opened territory of Oklahoma. This was the last Frank heard from her for many long, weary years.

It is truthfully said that "Murder will out." In a lonely cabin in the Great Smokey Mountains of east Tennessee, a man lay dying. Upon being informed of Frank's desperate plight, he begged that an officer might be sent for, and before he died he made and signed a confession in which he stated that he and not Frank Swaim was the murderer of John H. Lance, and that he killed him to prevent his betrayal of the moonshine still in which he was involved. This man was Fed Cannup.

This writer, being furnished with the facts, presented them to Governor Allen D. Candler, who immediately granted Frank a pardon, and armed with the order for his release, I at once went to the coal mines to carry him the glad tidings. Possessed of a small sum of money that he had earned by extra labor during his long confinement, he left at once for the great West in search of the wife and child he had parted with at the prison doors nineteen years before. He finally found them in Oklahoma, but how different the reality from the picture his imagination had so often painted during the long nights in his lonely prison cell. He found the girl wife now a middle-aged matron, who, after a few years struggling with poverty, had married a prosperous ranch man. His baby girl had also married and was herself the mother of a baby girl. This was the pathetic homecoming that greeted him, but not for long. The ranch man to whom his wife was now married, realizing that her heart yearned for her boy husband of the Georgia mountains, secured a divorce in order that she might return to him.

They are today respected citizens of the great state of their adoption, the grim tragedy in which they played such an important part being only a memory—a horrid nightmare that lasted for nineteen years. (3)

By the time I finish the article, my face turns ashen. I am about to lose my temper again, but I don't know in which direction to strike, for I'm puzzled by this romantic saga, which I instantly surmise is a bald-faced lie.

"Virge, what's your take on this?" I ask.

"Jim, I know that some of it is false; as an example, when Frank's pardon was signed the governor was J. M. Terrell, not Candler as Wellborn claims, and the pardon was given in actuality because of the relationship between the two Wellborns, not as a result of a deathbed confession, so in all probability the rest of the article is chock-full of lies," Virge replies.

"But why?" I ask.

"I've been thinking of that, and the only reason I can think of is that Wellborn is scared to death of you, Jim. He thinks that you will somehow or other be appeased and believe what he's written, blaming Fed Cannup as the killer instead of Frank Swaim."

"Virge, I think you're right, but Wellborn won't get off that easy, for when I find out for sure, I'll see to it that he eats his words, and I mean literally."

"Jim, it'll be hard to find out; be dead certain before you act."

"I realize this, but the truth will eventually prevail, for I know that as long as there is a Lance living in Union County, they will be searching for the real truth. Doesn't the Bible say in John 8:32, "And ye shall know the truth, and the truth shall make you free"?

"What is it, Melissa? What's wrong?"

"Wake up, Jim. Wake up. Supper is ready, and you've been having that terrible dream again!"

THE REAL TRUTH

Jim was right; however, it took more than seventy-seven years to prove unequivocally that he was, and then it was as he said, "The truth will eventually prevail, for I know that as long as there is a Lance residing in Union County, they will be searching for the real truth."

In reality, it was this fabricated, romantic saga by Carl J. Wellborn entitled, "A True Story of the Georgia Mountains" and our curiosity as to how it could possibly be true that led to this research and eventual book, proving that Wellborn's tale is filled with innuendoes and at best half-truths. In fact, never have I seen a story labeled as true that so completely misses the mark. Here is the proof:

Wellborn said: "It was the month of May, and the mountain air was redolent with the perfume of the laurel and the ivy which were in full bloom, while the dogwood bushes gleamed like huge balls of snow against the green of the mountainsides."

Truth: The murder occurred on February 17, 1890. This is still in the wintertime, and certainly there weren't any ivys, laurels, or dogwoods in bloom. In May, Frank Swaim was tried, found guilty, and sentenced to life imprisonment.

Wellborn said: His body "was found later in the afternoon by his devoted wife."

Truth: Lance's body was found by Joseph Ledford, and after he found it, he was going to the Lance home to tell the family and had gone some distance when he met Rev. Lance's wife and children coming, clapping their hands and screaming and hollering.

Wellborn said: "He [Frank Swaim] was passionately devoted to his wife and child."

Truth: If he was devoted to his wife and child, why was he out partying and drinking all over Choestoe (see Record of Trial) at all hours of the night? He was only devoted to himself and his immediate wants.

Wellborn said: "In a lonely cabin in the Great Smoky Mountains . . . a man [Fed Cannup] lay dying. Upon being informed of Frank's desperate plight, he begged that an officer might be sent for, and before he died he made and signed a confession in which he stated that he and not Frank Swaim was the murderer of John H. Lance."

Truth: Frank's pardon was granted in 1903 because of grave doubts of Judge Carlton J. Wellborn Sr., father of Carlton J. Wellborn Jr., the author of this so-called true story. Fredrick (Fed) Cannup didn't die in 1903. How can you make a deathbed confession in 1903 when you don't die until 1923? [See death certificate, Copy of Pertinent Records (1).]

Wellborn said: "This writer [Carlton J. Wellborn], being furnished with the facts, presented them to Governor Allen D. Candler, who immediately granted Frank a pardon, and armed with the order for his release, I at once went to the coal mines to carry him the glad tidings."

Truth: The governor who granted the pardon was J. M. Terrell, not Allen D. Candler, as is alleged by Wellborn. [See copy of pardon, Copy of Pertinent Records (2).] Wellborn didn't go to Dade County and tell Frank of his release; if he did, it was a useless trip, because Frank was pardoned years before and was then residing in the state of Texas.

Wellborn said: "[Frank Swaim] left at once for the great West in search of the wife and child he had parted with at the prison doors nineteen years before. He finally found them in Oklahoma."

Truth: Frank Swaim went to Tolar, Texas, where his family was living. Frank Swaim was convicted and sentenced in 1890, pardoned in 1903. 1890 subtracted from 1903 is thirteen years, not nineteen.

Wellborn said: "[Frank] found the girl wife now a middle-aged matron, who, after a few years struggling with poverty, had married a prosperous ranch man. His baby girl had also married and was herself the mother of a baby girl."

Truth: Frank Swaim's wife married George Wilson (Murphy Fortenberry Shuler Uncle), who, according to a conversation with Mrs. Shuler by Dale Elliott at Brannen Lodge, September 15, 1990, was not especially well-to-do. [See Copy of Pertinent Records (3).]

Frank and Mattie didn't have a baby girl, but a boy named Ransom Swaim, the only child born to the union of Frank and Mattie Swaim. [See document to the Historical Society of Union County, Georgia, Copy of Pertinent Records (4).]

Wellborn said: "The ranch man [George Wilson] to whom his wife was now married, realizing that her heart yearned for her boy husband of the Georgia mountains, secured a divorce in order that she might return to him [Frank Swaim]."

Truth: Mattie Swaim, Frank's former wife, remained married to George Wilson. [See grave marker, Copy of Pertinent Records.] Frank Swaim married Nora L. Collins [See grave marker, Copy of Pertinent Records.], daughter of Spear Collins, formerly of Union County. [See grave marker, Copy of Pertinent Records.]

View from Blood Mountain

Samuel Debarris Lance (3/14/1846–12/13/29)
with wife and children

James "Jim" Washington Lance
(1/31/1861–9/2/1940)

Varissa Jane Henson Lance
(11/1/1864–6/20/1916)
(Note: This is the first wife of Jim Lance)

Dr. F. J. Erwin
(9/15/1857–3/13/1924)

Samuel Debarris Lance
(3/14/1846–12/13/1929)

William E. "Buck" Candler
(2/28/1856–3/10/1927)

James Alexander Gillespie, Gunsmith
(1838–1902)

James "Jim" Johnson Collins
(5/10/1868–1/17/1967)

H. T. "Taylor" Cobb
(6/14/1846–5/31/1920)

Blairsville, Late 1920s

Thomas N. "Cussing" Henson
(1853–1942)

Rev. Thomas Coke Hughes
(6/22/1844–12/26/1932)

C. J. Wellborn, Jr.

Lafayette "Fate" Fortenberry
(6/7/1872–9/22/1952)

Major Napolean B. Hill
(2/14/1832-1/17/1910)

Virgil Marion Waldroop
(10/28/1849–10/31/1933)

William Luther Chapman
(7/17/1847–1/31/1935)

APPENDIX

In an effort to show how Jim Lance was, I have included portrayals of him as others saw him—his neighbors, family, and friends, for they were the ones who knew him best.

The book *Blood Mountain* by Edward Leander Shuler says of the Lances, "The Lances were a notable family in Choestoe, good livers, tall and handsome, always well dressed, devoted to the Methodist denomination, and especially noted for their truthfulness" (1).

In his book *Mountain Tops*, Joseph Bascom Henson states, "Jim Lance was an extraordinary man. His neighbors looked upon him as the only person who could be called upon for big favors. Joe and Nib Henson borrowed his two excellent mules for a whole month to turn land. Nothing was paid for their use. In the snow and sleet of the coldest winter night, Jim was the only person who could ride his mule to Blairsville, eight miles distant, for Dr. Erwin. When he reached Blairsville, if he found that Dr. Erwin was in some remote part of the county, Jim followed. Like the Northwest mounted, 'he always got his man.' He married Tom Henson's sister Jennie (Jane), who was considered by many the best speller in Choestoe. Of this marriage and Jim's second matrimonial venture, in all twenty-two children were born" (2).

In a classic book by Horace Kephart entitled *Our Southern Highlanders*, we find this: "When Matteo has been slain by an enemy, his friends carry his body home and swear vengeance over the corpse, while the wife soaks her handkerchief in the wounds to keep as a token, whereby she will incite her children, as they grow up, to war against their father's murderer" (3). And he also quotes from *Munsey's Magazine* of November 1903: "Captain John Bryan of the 2nd Kentucky said to the widow of the murdered Tom Baker after they returned from the funeral, 'Mrs. Baker, why don't you leave this country and escape from these terrible feuds? Move away, and teach your children to forget.'

"'Capt. Bryan,' said the widow, and she spoke evenly and quietly. 'I have twelve sons. It will be the chief aim of my life to bring them up to avenge their father's death. Each day, I shall show my boys the handkerchief stained with his blood, and tell them who murdered him'" (4).

In summation, Kephart also writes that when a feud is raging, nobody outside the warring clan is in any danger at all. A stranger in the heart of Feuddom is safer than he would be in Chicago or New York, so long as he attends strictly to his own business, asks no questions, and tells no tales. If, on the contrary, he should express horror or curiosity, he is regarded as a busybody and is likely to be run out of the country or even waylaid and silenced forever.

Miss Emma Miles, in her book *The Spirit of the Mountains*, says this: "Domestic affection is seldom expressed by the mountaineer—but it is very deep and real for all that." In fact, the ties of kinship are stronger with them than with any other Americans I know. Here again we see working the old feudal idea, an anachronism, but often a beautiful one in this age.

"God gives us our relatives," sighs the modern thinker, "but thank God, we can choose our friends!" Such words strike a mountaineer deep in horror. Rather would he go to the limit of Stevenson's St. Ives: "If it is a question of going to Hell, go to Hell like a gentleman with your ancestors"?

This, then is how we were, and still are, to a certain degree, for we are fiercely independent, closely attuned to our families' needs, stubborn—maybe to a fault—and devoted patriots ready to spill our blood so that others can enjoy the freedom that we so cherish. We make no apologies for these inborn traits, but hold them dear, for they were given to us freely by our ancestors (5).

INTERVIEWS

(1) **Late Tom Miller:** "Jim Lance was good to me. If he liked you, he would do anything to help you. I worked at Vogel State Park when it was being built, and he liked me and would loan me one of his mules to ride so I could go home on the weekends. Almost every other workhand was scared to death of him, and he was meaner than hell if he didn't like you."

(2) **Late C. R. Collins:** "Jim could never get over the tragic murder of his dad, and as a result, he seemed to carry a chip on his shoulder. He certainly was a leader of men and was a good citizen, but he was a man that no one would dare cross."

(3) **Late John Turner Sr.:** "I really liked and respected Jim, and we are distantly related. In fact, we might have drunk just a little bit together, socially, of course. Now, I'll tell you one thing: he was a good man to have on your side, for he wouldn't budge an inch, regardless of the odds."

(4) **Late James (Jay) C. Lance, Son:** "Dad was a good provider and had to be, or we would have all starved. We always had plenty to eat but very little money because Dad had to spend it fighting the pardon of his dad's killers. I'll tell you one thing for certain; under no circumstance

would Dad ever tell a lie. Now he might kill you, but he wouldn't tell you a lie."

(5) Byron Hood (April 2002): "I didn't know Jim all that good, but I knew his boys real well. I've heard tell he was high tempered. My daddy (Rev. Jim Hood) told me about a fight Jim Lance had with a feller on election day at the old law ground. Jim had him whipped to the ground and was atop of him and was looking for a rock to maul his head with."

(6) John P. Souther (April 2002): The noted author of *Between the Bald and Blood* and *War Not Forgotten* recalls being at Jim Lance's home many times playing with his son, James (Jay) C. Lance: "I ate with them often and remember Jim Lance sitting at the head of the table. I recall that he walked slowly and somewhat stiffly because of arthritis. Jim was much older than I was, but I've heard many stories about him from my dad. In particular, the fight he had with Fate Fortenberry on an election day is legendary in Choestoe."

(7) Lorene Duckworth Reece (April 2002): "Jim was a good, hard-working man; he had a high temper and never skipped a fight. He liked to fox hunt and drink corn liquor, which he often did with my daddy."

RECORD OF TRIAL

Union County Superior Court, April Adjunct Term, 1890
State v. Frank and Newt Swaim

(1) Joseph Ledford, sworn, says:

"I knew John H. Lance during his lifetime. On February 17 of this year 1890, I found his body in a creek that runs by Mr. Reece's house in this county. His hat and coat were lying in and near the path that leads up the creek and on the opposite side of the creek from his body. When I first discovered his hat and coat, I thought some drunk man had fallen in the creek and looked round for the person and discovered John H. Lance's body on the opposite side of the creek, his head kinda under and against the bank and his feet and body lying out in the creek. I did not recognize his coat and hat, but I knew the body to be that of John H. Lance. I did not see any marks of a scuffle or tracks in the path. I noticed a mark of a footprint down the bank as of someone falling in. The water was not running over his body but against his body and around his feet. I did not go over the creek to the body at that time; I thought it best to go and notify his family. After going in the direction of his house some distance, I met his wife and children coming, clapping their hands and screaming and hollering. I turned and went back with them to the body. I then went over the creek to where the body lay and pulled his body out of the creek. I noticed the water in the creek around his body was stained with blood. The body was warm. I did not take hold of his hands or his feet but his legs and his arms were limber. I know his body was warm because I put my hand on his breast. I can't say how long he had been dead. I was going home from the house of Fed Cannup's. His body was about one-half mile from Fed Cannup's. I left Fed Cannup's between two and three o'clock and found the body of John H. Lance about three o'clock. I went to Fed Cannup's in the morning, but he was not at home. Tom Swaim came to Fed Cannup's house about one o'clock that day. He had a sack on his shoulder with something in it that looked like corn in the ear. He did not come in, did not state his business as to where he was going, and went away. Frank and Newt Swaim came to Fed Cannup's house between two or three o'clock. They came in and sat down. I knew Frank Swaim but did not know Newt at the time. I remained there ten or fifteen minutes and then went away and went directly to where I found the body of John H. Lance. I had no conversation with the defendants and saw them no more that day. Frank Swaim was dressed in colored clothes. I don't think he had on his Sunday clothes; he had on his everyday clothes, and don't think they were clean clothes. I noticed one of his boots—it had a large patch on it sewed on with a whang and the patch leather was different in color from the other part of the boot."

Defense:

"I left Fed Cannup's house between two and three o'clock. I did not remain there more than a quarter-hour after the defendants came. I went the big road part of the way and then struck a trail that went up the right side of the creek. The big road crossed the creek and went up the left side. The body of John H. Lance, when I took hold of it, felt warm and limber. His hat was lying in the path, and his coat was about one step to the left towards the creek. His coat was lying as if it had just been dropped. The bank of the creek was almost perpendicular and about two feet high. The creek was about fifteen feet wide and was nigh up flush at the time. There was a foot log about seventy-five to eighty yards below where the body was found. One could not cross the creek where the body was without getting his feet wet. I suppose I was about fifteen minutes coming from Fed Cannup's to the body. I suppose it was about thirty to forty minutes from the time I first saw Frank and Newt Swaim until I found the body of John H. Lance. Tom Swaim lives about one mile from Fed Cannup's. I did not notice that the defendants were excited. I saw no water or blood on either of them. Not thinking that anything had happened, I was not looking for anything of that kind. They did not say where they were going or where they had been. I saw Frank Swaim the next day after he had been arrested and think he had on the same clothes that he had on the day before. I saw no water or blood on their boots or clothes. It looks like I might have seen it if it had been there, though I did not look for any."

(2) T. J. Butt, sworn, says:

"I was a member of the coroner's jury and was summoned on Sunday, February 17. When I was told that John H. Lance was dead, was murdered, I went up to Waldroup's, and Virge went with us. The creek in which his body was lying is one prong of Wolf Creek. I found several [people] at the place. I stripped deceased. He was stabbed in the breast and his neck was ghastly cut. It was cut almost entirely around and looked like it was done with a dull knife. The wound was rough and cut in a zigzag manner and appeared torn. I did not probe the stab. His face was bruised on the right side. There was a smooth cut in the right hand. I suppose he had grabbed the knife. His clothing was cut. I saw tracks near John Lance's body on the opposite side of the creek. I followed the tracks about one quarter of a mile. They looked to me like the parties making the tracks had jumped on their heels, the heels of the tracks being the plainest. The tracks were four or five feet apart. I saw two sets of tracks; they were close together and looked like about a number eight. The heel track of one of the parties had marks of nails as tacks in it."

Defense:
"From all appearances, I think his throat was cut after deceased was down. John Souther probed the wounds. This was Monday morning. I found the tracks about 200 yards away. I was never across the creek. I saw the tracks in the woods in a sandy place."

(3) John Souther, sworn, says:

"I am familiar with the grounds where John Lance was found dead. The hill is steep where it comes down to the creek. You can see a man coming south down the ridge some 150 to 200 yards. I followed the tracks to the top of the ridge. They were farther apart coming down than they were as they went up the ridge, and it seems to me the party was traveling faster down the ridge than they did as they went back up it. I was thirty yards from the body when I first saw the tracks. One of the tracks was a little turned over both at the heel and toe. I saw the tack prints in the heel. I saw the boot on Frank Swaim; it was about a number seven. I saw the heel of the boot, and it looked like it would make the track I saw. I examined Lance and saw the wounds on the body and breast; they were bruised. I think the wounds were made with a blunt-pointed knife or instrument. The flesh was bruised where the knife or instrument entered the body. The cut on the throat was a zigzag cut. The windpipe was cut. The head was turned back. I did not know that the cut extended to the back of the neck until I attempted to move the head and my middle finger slipped into the gash. The head was cut almost entirely off. I found one wound on the right side of the head. The cutting was done with a dull knife. I saw no knife taken from Frank Swaim. I knew from the nature of the wounds they were made with a dull or blunt-pointed knife. I saw no knife. I know where Fed Cannup lives. He lives up the ridge from where the body was found. The tracks were going in the direction of Fed Cannup's house. There were two sets of tracks; one was larger than the other. One of them made the deepest impression in the ground. I saw two tracks over where the coat was found and over where the body was found near where the head of John Lance lay. The heel of the track was the plainest. The track seemed to be made with the resting on the heel. This was the same track as the one over on the ridge. There was blood on the bushes near the body. The bank of the creek was eighteen inches high. I saw several spots of blood on the bushes near where the deceased's head lay."

Defense:

"There were two sets of tracks, one smaller than the other. I found the tracks about thirty yards from John Lance's body. I followed them

100 yards from the body. They were pointed out to me by J. M. Reece on Monday morning at daylight. I don't know from where they came nor where they went. One would have to go ninety yards down the creek to cross on a foot log. When the arteries in the neck are cut, the blood would spout, especially if in a contest or a scuffle. I have known the deceased since I can remember. He was 'bout five-foot-seven, weighed about 150 pounds, and was fifty-seven years old. John Lance had strength enough to slap Newt Swaim over if he was given equal chances. I saw no signs where people had been sitting or standing near the body of Lance. I saw such signs about sixty yards east of the body and on the same side of the creek in which the body of John Lance was found, behind a certain tree. Lance came up the creek."

State:
"John Lance's hair and head wound were full of sand, which was troublesome to get out."

(4) Joseph Lance, sworn, says:

"I saw Frank Swaim's boots; there were about a number seven. I saw them one week before Father's death; both of them were run down on the outside and had tacks in the heels. I saw them on the defendant's feet the day he was arrested. I did not examine them after he was arrested. The tacks extended below the surface of the heel. I made no comparison of the tacks in the boot heel to those made in the tracks. Frank Swaim had the boots on when he was arrested. I was with the party who tracked them up the ridge. There were two sets of tracks. When standing up on the ridge, a man could see another approach for some distance in the road. It was about 100 yards from where Father was killed to where he crossed the creek. The creek runs swift over shoals and makes a good deal of fuss. Those are the boots (boots being exhibited). I saw Frank Swaim after he was arrested. There were fester scratches both on his neck and cheek; they looked like fingernail scratches."

Defense:
"I saw the scratches before I was sworn before the coroner's jury. I can't say what done it, but they looked like fingernail scratches. I saw the

tracks where the deceased lay. I never saw any tracks on the west side of the creek. I was with Joe Ledford when the tracks were found. It was on Sunday evening. I followed them three-fourths of a mile until late in the evening when we gave up the search. The sun was two hours high when I first discovered the tracks. It is about one mile from Tom Swaim's to Fed Cannup's and about one mile and a quarter from Tom Swaim's to where the deceased was found. It was one-half of a mile from where I left the tracks to Tom Swaim's. I did not measure the tracks. I did not count the tacks in the tracks. The tracks were not made that day by any one of the party. There were two tracks, one broader than the other. We were at Tom Swaim's field when we gave up the search for tracks."

State:

"The field is about halfway between Tom Swaim's and Fed Cannup's. The path is traveled by the neighbors."

(5) J. M. Reece, sworn, says:

"I was present when Lance's body was found. I saw some tracks near where the body lay. I found them Monday morning ninety-nine steps from the body of Lance. There were tracks of two going and coming, and one was broader than the other. One made no heel impression. The other was about a number seven shoe or boot with the heel a little twisted and set forward and under the instep. There were four large square tacks or nails in the front part of the left heel, three of these tacks set square to the front. These four tacks made a distinct and plain impression in the earth. The other part of the heel was full of tacks and made plain impressions, but I took special notice of these four tacks. I followed the tracks up the ridge 100 yards, then they turned across the hollow and struck the other ridge on top of the ridge across the road leading from Tom Swaim's to Fed Cannup's. One could not see a man traveling the road that Lance traveled. The tacks led to near Tom Swaim's fence and across the path leading to Fed Cannup's. I saw Frank Swaim's boots on his feet the next morning after the killing of Lance, and when he was arrested I looked at the heel of the boot and saw the four tacks which corresponded to the impressions I saw in the earth and pointed them out to other parties who saw the tracks. I recognize this pair of boots (boots exhibited) as the ones worn by Swaim when arrested, but I do not see the four tacks; they are gone, and the heel has been cut and changed. I can see from one ridge to the other when the timber is not green, could see a man from the ridge soon after he crossed the creek. Anyone coming from Tom Swaim's could not see. The deceased walked with his head down and always walked slowly, generally carrying his coat on his arm. John Lance was considerably gray, both beard and hair. I saw a scratch on Tom Swaim's face which looked to me like it was fresh done. I can't say what made it. I saw the boots on him Monday morning, and they looked like they had been wet. I saw no other marks."

Defense:

"I did not see Frank Swaim until arrested. I never measured the track nor compared the boot with it. Frank Swaim did not object to having his boots examined. I did not count the tacks in the boots. I saw the tracks in the path in the sandy places. The sand was not deep. The tracks appeared as if the party making them was traveling fast. The hill is steep and rough, leading through laurel and over rocks. It is about one-half of a mile from Tom Swaim's fence to where Lance was killed. The tracks were in the path leading to Fed Cannup's. I hunted for tracks inside of the field. The left boot looked like it had been cut (here examining the boot). There are a good many people who live in the neighborhood near Swaim."

(6) F. L. Lance, sworn, says:

"I heard Frank Swaim say that somebody was going to be killed. I was at the time up on the ridge, and he was about to shoot me. He was saying that he thought I was reporting stills. And then he said someone would be killed over the matter. We were below Fed Cannup's when he said this. It was after night and within one-half of a mile from where John Lance was killed. This happened two or three weeks before the murder was done. He had his gun then. I was in the party who followed the tracks of the boots, the heel of which was a good deal worn but leaving a distinct mark. The shoes seemed to be worn out."

251

Defense:

"I was friendly with Frank at that time. I followed the tracks three-quarters of a mile. The gun Frank Swaim had was a Winchester rifle. I was going up to Fed Cannup's when Frank Swaim halted me. The still was destroyed a month before the murder."

(7) James Lance, sworn, says:

"I helped to guard Frank Swaim. I saw him on Monday after the killing with Fed Cannup. I saw the boots on Frank Swaim. They had something on them. I saw him go behind a big chestnut log, saw him rubbing his boots. I saw him wipe my father's blood off of his boots with frosted leaves while he was behind the log. I had a talk with Frank Swaim; still he accused me of having reported him, told me that he intended to kill me, said he knew who reported him. He said I was brave and a reporter, said he did not intend to whip anybody but would cut some damn man's throat. I had no further conversation with him. He was arrested at one o'clock. Si Reece lives nearest to where my father was killed. Fed Cannup and Frank Swaim were not present Sunday and did not come until brought by the sheriff."

Defense:

"Fed Cannup said nothing further than to ask me to take a drink, which I declined. I had the talk with Frank Swaim before Father was killed, when he accused me of reporting him; the feelings at that time were not good between us. I did not like him. It was daylight when he was behind the log. Cannup and I were guarding Frank Swaim. The sheriff was not present. Bill Curtis, John Wellborn, and Joe Lance were also guards. I don't know who saw the blood. I was sworn before the coroner's jury but did not tell about Frank Swaim's wiping the blood off of his boots; I thought there would be another trial when I could tell it. I told the circumstances to several; Waldroup said nothing to me about it. I saw the blood first at the fir. I did not tell anyone there, but told Waldroup after the inquest in the evening."

(8) Ben Nix, sworn, says:

"I was at my brother's Sunday when John Lance was killed. I went to Tom Swaim's before dinner. Frank and Newt Swaim were there drinking when John Lance passed. Frank and Newt did not mention his name but said, 'Amen and amen' to him as he passed and also laughed at him. My father-in-law, Boots Swaim, remarked, 'Yonder goes the preacher.' The boys took a drink before they saw him and afterwards. The road is thirty yards from the house of Tom Swaim. I remained ten or fifteen minutes after Lance passed. I left the boys at home. Tom Swaim was not at home, but the women and children were there. I did not see Tom Swaim that day. I left soon on account of my brother's sickness. Boots Swaim went home with me. Yes, the boys laughed at Lance and said, 'Amen and amen.' I can't say why they said it. I saw the boys next at the trial. I went there Monday morning as a witness. I left Tom Swaim's and got to Boots's about one o'clock. The boys said nothing but 'Amen and amen.'"

Defense:

"Yes, I heard the brothers say 'Amen,' I supposed referring to Lance. I left the boys at home. They had on the same clothes Monday that they wore Sunday."

(9) Lizzie Cannup, sworn, says:

"I know Frank Swaim; he was at Tom Swaim's when Lance passed. I heard him say one year before the killing that he wished he had thrown the ax at him while passing. He told me and his wife (she told him to hush). I did not see Mr. Lance myself. Frank said that he would have thrown the ax at Lance had he not been afraid that someone would see him and tell on him."

"Frank seemed to be in a good humor and was smiling when he said it. Said he did not like Lance because Lance married him without authority of law. I was at home when Lance was killed. I saw Frank and Newt Swaim the day of the killing. Frank was about as he usually was, but Newt seemed to be still and to be studying about something. They remained at Fred Cannup's one hour and then left. I was talking to my brother and Mr. Ledford. Frank and Newt had not been to see us for some time."

"Frank said to Mr. Lance that he had married him unlawful. This was at Mr. Henson's. Lance requested him to hush. Frank told me that he would have taken a chair to him, but Lance prevented it by leaving. And Frank said he would have followed him but was stopped by Charlie Henson. Frank was married twice. He did not think it legally done when Lance married him. It was the marriages that caused the talk about the ax. Frank Swaim told me that he would have cut Lance with his knife had Charlie Henson not shut him up in the house after putting Lance out."

(10) Newt Spivey, sworn, says:

"I know Frank Swaim. I heard him say once while at Charlie Henson's when talking about John H. Lance that he would have busted the damn old rascal's head with a chair but for Henson's interference. He was discussing his marriage. I never heard him say anything about cutting. It was a good while before Mr. Lance was killed that Frank was talking about Mr. Lance's marrying him."

(11) John Berry, sworn, says:

"I know Frank Swaim. I never have heard him talk about Mr. Lance. I never heard him say he was going to do anything to Lance. I was at home when Lance was killed. I live about three miles from where he was killed. I went to see his body at dark Sunday evening. My son told me of the murder. A crowd went up to see Lance. I went with the sheriff to arrest Frank Swaim. I did not see Frank Swaim on Sunday when Lance was killed. I have never heard Frank or Newt Swaim say anything about John Lance. I was talking about the still as is usual when one is reported. I heard Tom Swaim say that if John Lance did not mind his business he would get into trouble. I have never heard anything from Frank. I never heard Tom Swaim advise Frank to behave himself concerning John Lance."

(12) Sheriff John W. I. Jones, sworn, says:

"I arrested Frank Swaim about one o'clock Monday morning after the killing of John H. Lance on Sunday, February 17, 1890. He was at

Newt Swaim Sr.'s We had gone 100 to 150 yards before he asked me what I wanted with him. I told him he was charged with murder. He then asked me, 'What in the hell makes you think I done it?' Nothing up to that time had been said about who it was that was killed. I don't know whether he knew if Lance was dead or not. Frank said he could have escaped had he known I was coming. His wife was in the bed with him. Taylor Cobb told Frank after he was jailed that blood had been found on his knife. Frank said that if there was any blood on his knife it got there after it left him. He told Cobb that he had not used the knife in cutting up hogs or squirrels. 8-10 days after this, after the report had gone out over the county that blood had been found on his knife, Frank's father came to see him and asked him if he did not remember that they killed hogs on Saturday before Lance was killed on Sunday and stuck them with his knife. and he said yes. He said that he supposed that Newt remembered that he had cut his hand as he went up to Fed Cannup's. Tom Swaim told me that he had stuck hogs with Frank's knife on Saturday before the killing of John Lance. It was a week or ten days before Frank's father came to see him. When I arrested him, I saw a scratch on his cheek, oval in shape, that looked to me like a fingernail made it. And there was something like blood or matter oozing out of it. He washed his face at my house. I said nothing to him about the scratch. I did not see any scratches on his hands. I put Frank Swaim in the charge of John Wellborn, Jim Lance, and Bill Curtis while I was out after witnesses. I was absent during the coroner's trial getting up witnesses. The knife blade looked to me like it had been scoured. There was sand inside the handles and mud on the outside. I thought I saw blood on the handles (identifies the knife exhibited as the knife taken from Frank Swaim and which was a hawk-bill-bladed, iron-handled heavy knife). I turned it over to the solicitor. The blade is muddy now, but was bright. I can see the marks on it yet where it was scoured. Frank Swaim did not ask where he was to be carried, but Tom Swaim did, and I told him to the corpse."

Defense:

"Yes, a person can scour a knife blade bright. I took charge of Frank sometime Monday night but did not know what he had done during the day."

(13) Ben Collins, sworn, says:

"I was a guard over Frank Swaim. . . . I noticed a scratch on his face while washing at Sheriff Jones's. It was oval in shape. I also saw two on his neck. All appeared to me like fingernail scratches. There was blood or matter oozing out of them. This happened on Tuesday. The scratches on neck were lighter than those on the cheek, but same shape and not so deep."

Defense:

"I said nothing to Frank about the scratches. I asked him for no explanations."

(14) W. Y. Curtis, sworn, says:

"I was present with James Lance and Fed Cannup when Frank Swaim was under arrest. Frank went down the wood some fifty yards. James Lance came around, and I gave him the nod and he followed. He had a gun. I did not see anything Frank Swaim did, and I don't know what he did while absent. I heard James Lance say something about Frank killing his father."

(15) Dr. F. J. Erwin, sworn, says:

"I saw the defendant after he was brought to town. He had one mark on his left cheek about half an inch long, oval in shape. I examined the knife; I saw it on Tuesday night after the killing. Yes, I saw something like blood on it; I saw it in three places on the jaw and back spring. I also saw sand and mud on it. The knife looked like it had been scoured. The marks on the knife resembled blood. No, with the carotid artery severed a man could not live but a short time, a few minutes at furthest. I can't say how far the blood would spout. A man who dies from bleeding would not remain warm as long as if the blood was retained. It would hasten coldness to be thrown in the water, especially in February, and the body would get cold sooner in the water than out of it. A man with the carotid artery cut might remain warm one to two hours, if bled to death. I can't say how long a man would remain limber when bled to death. I did not ask Frank Swaim what made the marks and scratches on his cheek. The body of an animal would cool in about the same time as that of a man. The animal heat would remain an hour, maybe longer; a man not bled to death would remain, if in health, warm and not get stiff for three to four hours. Iron rust and dry blood look about the same color."

Defense:
"That knife would make a torn or lacerated wound and not a smooth cut. Yes, I can tell a wound made by a sharp knife from one made by a dull one. You could not stab a man with that knife."

(16) J. B. Reese, sworn, says:
"I was present at the inquest and saw Frank Swaim's boots (recognizes boots exhibited). There were tacks in the front of the left heel that are not there now. All of the tacks were there and are not here."

(17) Frank Swaim's statement:
"I was at Father's with Boots Swaim the day of the killing, stayed about an hour after Boots left. Went to Fed Cannup's, got there about two o'clock. The reason why I did not ask why they had me arrested was this: Jim Lance passed, saying his father was killed. I did not kill John H. Lance. Neither did I like him, because he married me without authority, but I soon got in a good humor with him. I did not hold enough against him to make me kill him. I stayed at Fed Cannup's about an hour as well as I can guess, then went on to where my father was. When I go back from where he was it was about sundown. This is about all I know. I don't remember how come the scratch on my cheek might have been made, maybe with a brush, or it might have been a scratch. I don't remember. I don't remember that anyone said anything about it."

(18) Newt Swaim's statement:
"I was with Frank all day from ten o'clock in the morning except about half an hour on Sunday, the day John Lance was killed, and I know he never did the killing. We stayed at Father's until Boots Swaim left. We then went to Fed Cannup's house. We never turned off the road in going from where we went to where Father was. I was home about half an hour

on Sun. when I heard from Mother of Mr. Lance's death. I never had anything against Mr. Lance in my life. If Frank did, I did not know it."

We consent and agree that the foregoing pages of manuscript include all of the testimony introduced in the trial of *State v. Frank and Newt Swaim,* charged with the offense of murder in Union County Superior Court at the May adjourn term, 1890, and we further agree that said manuscript contains all of the testimony introduced on the trial of said case and that this brief of evidence be filed in said case.

July 8, 1890
Carl J. Wellborn Jr. and M. G. Boyd, Defense Attorneys
W. E. Candler and V. M. Waldroup, Attorneys for the State

SOURCE NOTES

Page ix

"The Harvest" in *Ballad of the Bones* by Byron Herbert (Hub) Reece.*
New York: E. P. Dutton & Company, Inc.

Chapter XI

(1) "Whose Eye Is on the Sparrow" by Byron Herbert Reece, *North Georgia Review.* First published in the *Enotah Echoes,* the campus newspaper at Young Harris College.

Chapter XVII

Letter to Board of Prison Commission from Ex. Judge C. J. Wellborn Sr., December 2, 1899

Letter to Board of Prison Commission from James C. Dyer Jr., June 25, 1900

Letter to Board of Prison Commission from C. J. Wellborn Jr.

*Note: Byron Herbert Reece, noted poet and author, now considered to be one of America's greatest ballad writers, was close kin to the Lances, about whom this book is written.

Letter to Board of Prison Commission from C. Newt Swaim, July 9, 1900

Letter to Board of Prison Commission from C. J. Wellborn Jr., July 10, 1900

Letter to Board of Prison Commission from W. A. Charter, February 2, 1903

Letter to Goodloe Young from N. A. Morris, speaker of house, March 23, 1903

Letter forwarded from W. A. Charter to W. E. Candler. Received by W. E. Candler on April 4, 1903

Letter to Goodloe Young from W. E. Candler, April 4, 1903

Copy of pardon, May 11, 1903

Chapter XVIII

(1) Editorial and obituary of C. J. Wellborn Sr., *Union County Banner*, April 30, 1908

(2) Resolution honoring the life of Major Napoleon B. Hill, *Union County Banner*, May 17, 1910

(3) Article by C. J. Wellborn Jr. labeled "A True Story of the Georgia Mountains," *Atlanta Constitution*, November 22, 1925

Chapter XIV

Motion for John J. Berry to appear as a material witness for the State, taken from Union County Superior Court records for the years 1890-91. April term, 1890.

Appendix

Blood Mountain by Edward Leander Shuler
Mountain Tops by Joseph Bascom Henson
Our Southern Highlanders by Horace Kephart
Munsey's Magazine, November 1903
The Spirit of the Mountains by Emma Miles

Interviews

Personal interview with Tom Miller
Personal interview with C. R. (Roscoe) Collins
Personal interview with John Turner Sr.
Personal interview with James (Jay) C. Lance
Personal interview with Byron Hood
Personal interview with John P. Souther
Personal interview with Lorne Duckworth Reece

Record of Trial

Testimony, Joseph Ledford
Testimony, T. J. Butt
Testimony, John Souther
Testimony, Joseph (Joe) Lance
Testimony, J. M. Reece
Testimony, F. L. (Fate) Lance
Testimony, James (Jim) Lance
Testimony, Ben Nix
Testimony, Lizzie Cannup
Testimony, Newt Spivey
Testimony, John Berry
Testimony, Sheriff John W. Jones
Testimony, Ben Collins
Testimony, W. Y. Curtis
Testimony, Dr. F. J. Erwin
Testimony, J. B. Reece
Testimony, Frank Swaim
Testimony, Newt Swaim

Copy of Pertinent Records

Death certificate of Fredrick (Fed) Cannup
Copy of Pardon
Conversation (interview) with Murphy Shuler by Dale Elliott

Document to the Historical Society of Union County, Georgia
Grave marker, Mattie Wilson, Frank Swaim's first wife
Grave marker, Frank Swaim
Grave marker, Nora Collins

Copies of pertinent records are available from the Union County Historical Society, Blairsville, GA 30514.